I0675851

Books by T.J. Mindancer

Tales of Emoria

Jame and Tigh Saga
Book 1: Future Dreams
Book 2: Present Paths
Book 3: Past Echoes
Book 4: Fall Time

Hekolatis' Promise

Emoran Campfire Tales

Other Books

The Queen's Sister

Novellas

Bountiful Glen

Tales of Emoria
Book 1

Future Dreams

T.J. Mindancer

Mindancer Press
Bedazzled Ink Publishing Company • Fairfield, California

978-0-9886061-6-6 paperback

Cover Design
by

First published 2001
Renaissance Alliance Publishing
4th revised edition 2022

Mindancer Press
a division of
Bedazzled Ink Publishing, LLC
Fairfield, California
http://www.bedazzledink.com

The Saga of Jame and Tigh, Book 1

Note on Pronunciation

Jame is one syllable with a long "a." Rhymes with "fame." Tigh is pronounced "Tig." Rhymes with "twig." The spelling of her name follows the Ingoran rules of grammar where the "h" indicates the eldest daughter of the House of Tigis.

Chapter 1

JAME STOPPED TO revel in the few heartbeats of magic that happened when the sun snapped into an intense orange and set the surrounding adobe buildings aglow. She always felt an indescribable ache when the glow turned to gray, and the sun pulled away its strands of light and sank beneath the distant hills. The air was still cool from the lingering winter but the aroma of plants disturbing the desert sands told her that spring was only a week or two away.

Jame sighed and ran a hand through her short hair. Spring meant she no longer had an excuse not to visit home.

"Home," she mumbled. Where no one understood why she wanted to become a peace arbiter.

She walked across the expansive plaza that had once been the reviewing ground for the army of the Southern Territories during the Grappian Wars. That late in the day, the plaza was deserted except for students, like herself, hurrying to evening lectures in the arbiter's hall.

The crunch of wagon wheels from just outside the wall gate drew her curious gaze. She stopped walking as the wagon rumbled through the gate. The metal bars on the cage that bounced in the wagon's bed glistened in the last of the sunlight.

The wagon passed within a few paces of her, and she shaded her eyes to see the latest captured Guard and found herself staring into the palest blue eyes she had ever seen. Strong, dirt-streaked hands clutched the iron bars, and a feral woman drenched in mud and blood glared at her through ice-cold eyes.

With animal-like alertness, this once proud warrior of the Guard froze Jame in place with an overpowering presence that rolled across her like water over ice. Jame shivered as a chill that had nothing to do with the evening breeze danced along her spine.

A mad chortle erupted from the woman's throat and broke the spell she had cast. Jame blinked and caught a flash of sanity beneath the face twisted in sneering contempt.

Jame stared after the wagon, trying to sort through what she had just witnessed. She had seen hundreds of Guards brought in on wagons over the last two years since the end of the Grappian Wars. But never had her soul been gripped with the sight of such coldness or madness. Only one Guard had ever been described as having penetrating blue eyes and a compelling presence.

"Laur's waterfalls," she breathed. "That's Tigh the Terrible."

JAME SLUMPED INTO cushy pillows and stared out the window at the newly furrowed fields. She did her best to ignore the other two passengers on the coach—a pair of giggling young men from Glaus. By their own admission, they were on their first trip away from home for a cousin's joining in Rihnon.

If her aunt would stop treating her like a child, she wouldn't have to suffer the inane chatter of young men without a thought in their heads beyond clothes and gossip. In the four years she had been in Ynit, her aunt had never stopped worrying about her safety outside of Emoria. Sometimes she hated being a princess.

She pulled her pack from the floor, burrowed through her clothes, and pulled out the thick sheaf of loose papers haphazardly crammed into a leather binder. She stared at her notes for several heartbeats without reading a word. Her thoughts traveled to places she preferred not to visit. *Why did my life have to be so complicated? Because I made it complicated.*

The coach swayed and lurched. Jame and the boys grabbed the ram's horn shaped handles protruding from the gaudy panels. Rich people's transport. Jame grimaced at the opulent overdone decor.

The wide-eyed young men looked shaken during the several heartbeats of excitement and then bent their heads together in a relieved chatter. Jame didn't even hide her rolling eyes from them. She thanked Laur she'd been spared growing up around such silly young men.

She gazed at the rocky beginnings of the foothills of the Phytian Mountains. The pressure from home to come to her senses and give up the noble but impractical pursuit of peace rbiter had grown from silent entreaties to loud emotional discussions. Her aunt's strong insistence that she travel to Emoria as soon as the winter's snows had melted warned her that she was expected to make a decision about her future, and she knew that only one decision was acceptable.

She wasn't going to let four years of study be wasted on archaic ideas of what was expected of an Emoran princess. She loved her work as an assistant to the Military Tribunal. Her job could be heartbreaking and frustrating, but at the same time uplifting, and it completed her soul in ways that nothing else came close to doing. She reveled in the drama of arguing the cases of the former Guards against a society that wished these warriors who won the Grappian Wars for them would simply vanish, one way or another.

A vision of Tigh the Terrible's eyes that had haunted her dreams for the last few weeks flashed unbidden in Jame's mind. Maybe it was her kindhearted soul grappling with the realization that there was, at least, one Elite Guard who was beyond their attempts at rehabilitation. That there was a warrior who people believed deserved to just disappear. That thought gripped her in a soul-wrenching sorrow. She admonished herself for such a strong reaction to the fate of someone she had glimpsed for only a few heartbeats.

The cultivated fields on the hillsides gave way to clusters of stone and thatch roof houses. They had reached the outskirts of Rihnon—a small city nestled against the southern flank of the Phytian Mountains. Jame leaned out the window, relieved to see the market sprawled between squat stone buildings in the center of the city. She couldn't get off this snooty parlor on wheels too soon. Argis would have to be tied and gagged to travel in such a coach as this.

Argis. Jame sighed. Another problem to deal with. She lifted sad amused eyes to whatever demented deity oversaw her destiny. This visit was sure to be memorable.

The coach slowed to a cautious gait as the driver eased it around the numerous fruit and vegetable stalls. Jame pulled her head in from the window and slung her pack over her shoulder, ready to explode from the overstuffed seat the moment the coach rocked to a stop.

She jumped to the rain wet ground and put several paces between herself and the happy reunion between the young men and local family members before she stopped in the street market. The mountain air touched her senses and drenched her in an almost painful nostalgia. No matter how much she distanced herself from this part of the world, the beauty of the Phytian Mountains kept a tight hold on her heart.

"Jame."

She turned around. Argis and Tas, looking out of place in their Emoran leathers, rushed toward her. Argis caught Jame into her arms and pulled her into a joyous hug.

Jame grinned. "Hello, Argis."

Argis released Jame and held her at arms' length. "You're looking good."

Jame laughed and pulled Tas into her arms. "Tas. It's good to see you."

"You look great," Tas said. "What happened to that baggy green tunic?"

"I'm an assistant arbiter now." Jame stepped back to get a better look at her old friends. Both were clad in a patchwork of leather and armor and the hilts of their swords were visible over their shoulders. Argis's usually serious gray eyes, half hidden by short wavy hair, sparkled with happiness. Tas's impulsive, good-natured personality was reflected in her blue eyes and thick dark blonde hair that hung shaggily about her open face. "Look at the two of you. Full warriors." Jame lifted the warrior braid dangling from Tas's belt.

"We were in a skirmish with a band of Quaron raiders," Tas said. "Stopped them from taking the sheep on the upper back meadow."

"Congratulations, both of you," Jame said.

"We've made arrangements for a meal at the wayside near Epilatis," Argis said.

"Always prepared," Jame said.

Argis grinned. "Anything for my princess."

Jame managed a smile at Argis's happiness. She adjusted her pack on her back and turned to the mountains and home.

THEY FOLLOWED THE well-traveled road that switch backed up the steep ascent of the southern slopes of the Phytian Mountain range. Jame always wondered what the citizens of Rihnon would think if they knew the southern border of Emoria was just a half-day walk from their city. Of course, any traveler into the Phytian Mountains would be surprised to know they journeyed right by concealed passes into the forests and valleys of the legendary country.

Jame was grateful she kept in shape with a daily climb of every flight of steps in the rambling fortress that dominated the military compound at Ynit. In the desert flat lands, climbing steps was the only way to maintain the lungs and legs of a mountain goat the Emorans boasted they possessed. Besides, she wasn't about to give her friends one more thing to tease her about.

"Mularke won her archer braid," Tas said. "She got so drunk during the celebration she bet she could take the plume off of the queen's banner on the palace wall and turn it into an eyebrow on the painting of Hekolatis on the tavern wall with a single arrow."

Jame covered her eyes. "Oh, no."

"Mularke managed to pluck the plume off the banner, but it ended up somewhere quite a bit south of Hekolatis's eyebrow." Tas laughed.

"So where were you during this display of skill?" Jame asked.

"She was scaling the wall to retrieve the arrow and, of course, Jyac stepped onto her balcony at that moment," Argis said. "It seems the noise of part of her banner being carried off woke her."

Jame laughed. "Do any of your stories end without you and Mularke getting into trouble?"

Tas scratched her head. "Come to think of it . . ."

They came to a meadow next to a towering shear bluff. They left the road and tromped through the spring grass and patches of yellow flowers to the bluff.

"Jyac's prepared a feast in honor of your return," Argis said.

"Really?" Jame asked as they eased through a sinewy fracture in the cliff wall and into a sinkhole.

"It's been two years since your last visit." Argis frowned. "Everyone's eager to see their princess again."

"I'm also eager to see everyone," Jame said, "and a feast is always fun."

They climbed out of the hole using hand and foot holds first carved countless generations earlier and continued along a rocky stream, overflowing from the melting snows.

"We're all coming into our own now," Argis said. "We've received our braids and are having thoughts of settling down and serving Emoria."

Jame avoided Argis's gaze and nodded. "I'm coming into my own, too. I've served the Tribunal at Ynit as an assistant arbiter for the last two years."

"Working with cleansed Guards." Argis grimaced. "Jyac wasn't too pleased when you accepted that position. She feels it's too dangerous."

"I know." Jame kept from sighing.

She was now certain her fears about this trip home were a reality. The queen and Elders Council were going to pressure her to give up what she wanted to do with her life. All because she was born to be Queen of Emoria.

Chapter 2

THE FIRST SENSATION that tickled Tigh's awareness was, for the first time in weeks, she wasn't chilled from the winter cold. The warmth seduced her into bouts of deep sleep punctuated by brief spells of hazy consciousness. Foggy dreams of people bending over her and unintelligible words hitting her brain like a wet sponge became a part of her mental landscape for what felt like an endless period of time.

She opened her eyes. The room was narrow but tidy—furnished with the cot she lay on, a small desk and chair, and a stand holding a chipped ceramic basin. She could see the top of the long wooden trunk filled with her personal possessions at the foot of the cot.

The walls and ceiling were whitewashed and created an austere but not unpleasant atmosphere. A low window allowed the sun and the noises from the plaza far below to waft up on the gentle spring breeze. The window was barred.

She shifted her eyes to the door and stared for endless heartbeats at the construction of bars and wood where there had been only wood before. She was home, and, during her long absence, home had been refurbished into a prison cell.

Tigh pulled herself up and sat on the edge of the cot. Accustomed to being clothed in black leather, she gave her white leggings and tunic a puzzled look. She raised her hand to long hair and found it cropped short.

She turned at a noise and pinned a hapless assistant healer outside the door with an intense gaze. The poor man shook so hard that he rattled the bowls and plates on the tray he held. He put the tray on the floor and fled down the corridor.

Tigh frowned at this extreme reaction to her—considering she was the one behind bars—and wondered if her face was disfigured in some way.

Her legs shook as she got to her feet, and she steadied herself against the wall for several heartbeats. She half-stepped and half-lurched to the ceramic basin and squinted into the tarnished mirror. Expecting, at least, bruises and scratches, she stared at her unblemished face. Her skin had a sallow tinge, and her face was too thin.

She frowned at the hollowness in her stomach and wondered how long she'd been unconscious. Using the wall as support, she walked to the door and plopped down cross-legged in front of it. Between the amply spaced bars, she lifted the lids off of the plates and bowls. The aromas of Ingoran prepared dishes rose up with the steam and socked the pit of her stomach with an almost physical punch. She snatched up a skin of water and took a long swallow to wet her dry mouth.

Tigh heard what sounded like an assemblage of soft boots padding up the corridor. Five gray-robed healers arranged themselves in front of her door as she lifted a forkful of spiced boiled potatoes and egg to her mouth. She raked disinterested eyes over the group as they studied her with steadfast curiosity.

"So, Tigh." Loena Sihlor, a plump woman with gray-streaked red hair and the chief healer of the military compound, knelt down. "How are you feeling?"

Tigh stopped in mid-chew to stare at Leona. She then dropped her eyes and stuck the fork into a bowl of asparagus.

The group conferred together for a few heartbeats and came to an agreement that Tigh looked fine.

Pendon Larke, an elderly assistant healer, knelt next to Loena. "In case you're wondering, you've been cleansed. You've only been back in your own room for just under two days. But for the last month you've been in the cleansing wing. Don't worry that you can't remember anything about it. We've observed that none of the Guards remember the cleansing process."

Tigh put down her fork and stared at Pendon. She had been in someone else's control for a month? She had been defenseless, at their mercy? "A month," she rasped, surprised at how her voice scraped against her ears. "Cleansed."

"Yes," Pendon said. "We've also observed that most Guards don't notice their violent tendencies are gone."

Tigh looked deep within herself, felt for her very essence, and came up with a stranger.

"You are no longer Tigh the Terrible," Loena said.

Tigh pinned Loena with hard eyes. "I will always be Tigh the Terrible."

VISITORS. TIGH GRABBED the iron bar lodged well over her head between the narrow walls. She pulled up and held the position until her arms burned, and her nerves calmed.

The hard clicks of Ingoran boots against the wooden floor echoed in the corridor. She dropped off of the bar and shook her arms out as she watched the door with apprehension. Seven years and a nightmarish lifetime had passed since she had last seen any member of her family. Now her parents had traveled all the way from Ingor to see what was left of the daughter who was heir to the House of Tigis.

The gray-robed assistant healer appeared and slipped a large key into the door lock, the resulting grate of metal against metal echoed down the quiet corridor. Tigh stepped back against the window, and the door opened. Her mother and father entered the cell, and their presence seemed to suck the air out of the confined space. She could only stare at these living remnants of her shattered youth.

Paldon Tigis, dressed in a well-tailored Ingoran tunic and leggings, had the open confident face of a successful merchant. Her eyes, taking in Tigh's residence for the last seven years with a quick appraising glance, were of a darker blue than Tigh's but her black hair and fair complexion left no doubt that they were closely related. Joul Tigis, clothed in a simple, but delicately spun long tunic and leggings, cast sad encouraging green eyes at Tigh. His light brown hair had streaks of gray that weren't there the last time she had seen him.

"Paldar." Paldon stepped forward and opened her arms to Tigh. "Come give your mother a proper greeting."

Tigh had avoided human contact for the two years she had been a fugitive from the Wars and trembled at the shock of warmth from her mother's understanding embrace and soothing words of comfort. Joul stepped forward and she was passed into his caring arms.

"It's good to see you again, daughter." Joul's gentle voice lit a fire of memories in Tigh's devastated mind.

"Let's all sit and catch our breaths from the climb up those steps," Paldon said as she and Joul led Tigh to the cot and sat on either side of her. "We're not as young as we once were."

"Thank you for visiting," Tigh whispered to the floor.

"You're our eldest daughter, no matter what the state has done to you in the name of service to the Southern Territories." Paldon rubbed Tigh's muscle hardened arm. "We want to make sure you get through this rehabilitation process so you can come home where you belong."

"It's not as simple as that." Tigh couldn't keep down her anguish at the thought of being returned to society and knowing what she had been during the Wars.

"Loena Sihlor appears to be a very competent healer, and she feels you're not giving the process a chance to work for you," Paldon said.

Tigh took a deep breath and focused on a small knot in the dark wood floor. "Most of the Guards aren't known by sight. They can return to the world with only their own demons to fight against. The people know me. Not because I was the supreme commander of the last victorious campaigns but because I was Tigh the Terrible."

"But the healers say you've been cleansed of all that nastiness," Paldon said. "You're certainly the daughter I remember you to be. A little fitter perhaps, but that's not a bad thing."

"Cleansing me doesn't cleanse the people's memories of what I was and what I did." Tigh's voice cracked with intense despair at the thought of never being free again. "The cleansing didn't remove the memories of who I was from myself. I'll spend the rest of my life fighting both society's memories and my own."

"Let the healers help you. That's their job, after all," Paldon said. "You're the eldest daughter of the House of Tigis. The talent you showed for leadership in the Guards is a great attribute to our family."

"That Tigh is dead. May I forever trample on her grave."

Tigh broke away from the loose hold of her parents and bolted to the window.

"Whatever it was that made me a leader is also dead," she said to the flower-scented breeze touching her face.

"We'll be spending a few days here in Ynit," Paldon said. "We'll be back tomorrow. All we ask is you think about what we've discussed. Remember, you always have a family to come home to."

Chapter 3

JAME PAUSED AS they stepped from the tunnel that burrowed into the southern wall of Emor, the only city in Emoria, carved from a deep, wide canyon high in the Phytian Mountains. The natural caves and shelters that pocked the white rock bluffs of the canyon had been artfully fashioned into residences and shops.

A cobblestone square filled the bottom of the canyon, concealing the stream bed that flowed through the valley. Jame had always enjoyed performing the spring maintenance of the shallow wells that were used to access this water and fortifying the dammed lake further up the stream that protected the city from all but the most severe floods.

At that time of the evening, in the gray dusk, Emor was quiet. She used to know every stone of the city. *Why does it look strangely foreign now?*

"As you can see, nothing's changed." Argis sauntered into the square.

Jame frowned at Argis's back but decided not to say anything. Maybe she was just tired after traveling all day. She knew she was hungry.

They tromped across the square to the palace. A crossed sword and bow were artfully carved across the wooden double doors that stood twice the height of the tallest warrior. A smaller door was inset in each larger one for every day entering and exiting. Jame couldn't describe what she felt as she looked up at the towering walls of stone, painted with bright murals of legendary Emorans and speckled with lights flickering behind quartz windows. She was glad to see her home again and she looked forward to visiting with her family and friends, but she knew she was just visiting. Her life lay somewhere else until she had to return as queen.

"I'll go on ahead and let the queen know you're here," Tas said as they walked through a smaller door into the main hall of the palace with its cascading walls of etched stone soaring to the top of the bluff.

Jame caught the conspiratorial look that passed between Tas and Argis and realized Tas thought she and Argis wanted to spend some time alone before the evening meal. She and Argis *had* deepened their relationship during her last prolonged visit two years earlier, but she had drifted away from it as she became immersed in her new position as assistant arbiter. Now face to face with Argis again, she wasn't sure how she felt about the taciturn warrior.

"Welcome home, my princess."

"Poylin." Jame hugged a slender scout and ruffled her unruly sand-colored hair. "You have your scout braid."

"Yeah." Poylin grinned. "Now Olet can't tease me anymore."

"About not having a braid, at least." Jame ducked Poylin's playful swipe.

Several other women greeted Jame, and she laughed and talked with each of them. *Maybe coming home wasn't so bad.* She stepped on the wide curve cut into the stone and lined with torches and trudged up the steep incline to the next floor and the next curve.

She glanced at Argis, who was scowling at something. She looked down the corridor and grinned as Sark, Queen Jyac's right hand, strode to her. She looked back at Argis, who was still scowling. *What's that all about?*

"My princess," Sark said. "We're all so happy you could make it home."

"I'm happy to be here," Jame said. "You're looking better than the last time I saw you."

Sark held out her arm. "It's all healed and good as new."

"That's good to hear." Jame glanced at Argis and was surprised to see the scowl still in place.

"I'll let you get settled in," Sark said. "See you at evening meal."

Jame walked up the next curve carved out of the wall to a narrower corridor that wound through the most private living quarters. The quiet contrasted with the other floors of the palace, reminding her that the rooms around her own chamber were for her to fill with her own family. When she was ready to settle down.

Jame paused outside the door of her chamber and thought of the countless times she had crossed that threshold and had taken sweet refuge within.

Argis, seemingly oblivious to Jame's mental trips into the land of ambivalence, pushed open the door. Warm air rushed out to meet them from the chattering flame in the fireplace carved into a side wall and the warm spring fed waterfall and pool tucked in the back of the chamber.

Jame was surprised to see everything was as she had left it. A shrine to a life that felt like it had been lived by someone else.

"I bet it feels good to be home." Argis grinned as she followed Jame into the chamber. "I'm happy to see you."

Jame realized that Argis would never understand what it was like to be away from home for so long to pursue something she truly enjoyed. "I missed you, too."

Argis's odd uncertain look softened into one of happiness as she wrapped her arms around Jame and kissed her.

Jame's stomach rumbled and spared her the need to remind Argis that they were expected in the dining hall. If she had been ambivalent about her feelings, Argis's arms around her brought them into acute focus. She knew at that moment the intensity of their romance from two years before had faded. Maybe returning home hadn't been such a good idea.

"WE UNDERSTAND YOU have to adjust to having your mental enhancements cleansed," Paldon said.

Tigh sat on her cot and stared at the paper in her hand. She listened to her mother's words and knew that a sheltered merchant could never understand what she felt.

"She knows we understand." Joul turned from gazing out the window. "She's just uncertain about taking this next step. Isn't that right, Tigh?"

Tigh looked up at the use of her nickname, a sign of acceptance of her chosen identity. She was too confused and exhausted to argue anymore. "Yeah, that's it."

Paldon knelt in front of Tigh. "We know everything seems hopeless right now. Healer Sihlor said every Guard feels that way when they're first cleansed. You just have to trust us and take the next step. All you have to do is sign that paper and let the healers help you to adjust to the cleansing."

Paldon's reasonable voice had always soothed Tigh's unsettled mind when she was young. She stared at the floor. "Did they ask you to come here?"

"We received a letter explaining your situation and we offered our help," Paldon said. "You're our eldest daughter and our heir. We've long gotten past our bitterness against the state for misleading us about what it meant to be a Guard. We only saw it as an opportunity for you to gain some worldly experience."

"Besides, they wouldn't take no for an answer." Tigh raised sad eyes to Paldon. "And the compensation was hard to say no to."

"All the Guards' families were equally compensated," Paldon said. "It was only right that they paid for your services."

"They did pay us for our services," Tigh said. "Plus the spoils of our conquests."

Paldon frowned. "Spoils?"

"War is not the bright glamorous campaigns depicted in the books you like to read." Tigh gazed across the room and saw in her mind's eye bloody battlefields and ransacked cities. "We conquered, then we sacked and took whatever we wanted. We were ruthless without mercy. The Guards were used to spread fear to the next city that thought of resisting our advancing armies. We were never allowed to go near a city or army that had surrendered. We couldn't be controlled enough to act civilized. So, we fought armies in the field and were brought in to suck the life out of cities foolhardy enough to think they could beat us. We weren't treated like human beings. We were weapons tipped with poison, carefully controlled until pointed at a target.

Then we were let loose to create terror and mayhem. That's what I have to carry around up here." She tapped her head. "And it's never going to go away. The best the healers can do is help me live with the memories." She raised bleak eyes to her parents who looked shaken by her words. "Would you want to pretend to live a normal life with memories like that clawing forever against the back of your mind?"

"Even the most horrific events in one's life can be turned into something positive," Paldon said. "Concentrate on what you learned from these different cultures. You have an insight into, not only the peoples of the Northern Territories, but into many of the different cultures of the Southern Territories. You can use this knowledge to help increase the holdings of the House of Tigis. No one will care that you were Tigh the Terrible. All that matters is you were the supreme commander of the campaigns that ended the war. People will value the knowledge you hold and will respond to your natural leadership ability."

Tigh stared at her mother and knew that she truly believed what she said. The words could even be true if she had paid attention to the different cultures and cities her armies ripped through and destroyed. But her ruthlessness had blinded her to everything but her own power and vanity.

Paldon most likely envisioned the House of Tigis engaged in the ironic business of rebuilding the war-ravaged Northern Territories. If Tigh were her mother's daughter, she'd find the idea appealing, but she had never been attracted to the idea of being a merchant.

Paldon sighed. "I know it all seems hopeless now. But Healer Sihlor said the rehabilitation is a series of small steps. The first step is to sign that document. Your cleansing cannot be listed as complete until you do."

Tigh looked at the paper. A simple statement confirming that she had been successfully cleansed of the mental enhancements she had received as a member of the Elite Guard. If she signed it, the healers would start the next step in healing the gaping wounds in her psyche—a process that frightened her. But what were her alternatives? Living in this narrow cell or in equally stark quarters for the rest of her life?

She looked at the open door. Opened or closed, locked or unlocked, it didn't matter to her. She wouldn't leave because she didn't think she deserved to leave. But she couldn't stay where she was forever.

Tigh stood and helped Paldon up from her kneeling position. She stepped past Paldon and laid the paper on the small table. She picked up her quill and stared at the jar of ink. It hadn't been touched in over two years and was long dry.

"Here." Joul handed her his metal quill with a built-in reservoir of ink.

Tigh took the implement and scrawled her name at the bottom of the document.

"I HONESTLY DIDN'T know they were going to do that, Jame." Queen Jyac looked uncharacteristically nonplussed.

Jame, still in her sleep shirt, paced around her chamber as she waited for the tailor to arrive to fit her with a new set of leathers. "They had no right to challenge Argis. She has no formal claim on me."

"You've been too young for a formal claim. But you're both nineteen now. Argis is a full warrior and is ready for a commitment. The others are taking advantage of the fact that you've been away for two years, and a proper courtship hasn't taken place," Jyac said. "Argis has been a little too sure of her place in your heart and I think many of the warriors resent it."

"I don't know what her place in my heart is." Jame stopped pacing and faced Jyac. "All I know is my heart is on what I'm doing in Ynit. Argis may be ready for a commitment but I'm not. Now she's going to get her head bashed in because she's been bragging too much."

"Argis is willing to learn the consequences of a rash tongue," Jyac said. "But it's not an unreasonable assumption on her part to think that you're a couple. You were very much together the last time you visited."

"But that was two years ago," Jame said. "I've seen and done so much since then. I've changed much more than I had ever thought possible."

"I understand that you enjoy your work," Jyac said. "All I ask is for you to take the time to reacquaint yourself with Emoria and your old friends. And give Argis a chance. Your destiny is here as queen. Sometimes we have to make our decisions based on the greater good of the people."

Jame sucked in a breath. The conflict between wanting to pursue her own life and her duty to her people was forever in her mind. Sometimes she felt selfish for needing to break free of Emoria's restraining society. But the greater good extended far beyond her own people and she found tremendous satisfaction in helping the former Guards who had been treated as castoffs from the society they had saved.

She turned around at a light tap on the open door. A plumpish woman, clutching a basket of leather scraps, ambled in.

"Good morning, Trione," Jyac said.

"Good morning, my queen," Trione said. "It's so good to see you again, my princess. Added some muscle, I see. You were much too thin on your last visit."

"I now have a job where I can afford to feed myself and it's exercise just getting around the fortress at Ynit," Jame said.

"It certainly looks good on you." Trione pulled out patches of leather and rough-stitched them together. "Here, put this on and then we can get down to work."

Jame took the patchwork of leather and sighed. How many times had she been fitted for leathers? In the past, she had always looked forward to it. New leathers were a symbolic show of physical growth and new status within their society. Why did this fitting feel like the first step on a journey she wasn't ready to take?

"I DON'T ENVY you at all right now," Mularke said as she and Tas followed Argis to the sparring grounds in the meadows on top of the western bluff of the city. The cacophony of colors from the spring wildflowers made the usually plain grasslands look like a giant patchwork quilt stitched together by warriors using swords as needles—artless but breathtaking in its own way.

"I thought you enjoyed fights with impossible odds." Argis flicked an amused glance at the tall, blonde archer.

Mularke straightened. "Only when I'm too drunk to think about it."

"I can't believe you're not nervous about this." Tas doubled her steps to keep up with her taller companions. "You're going against Dinaf and Tamrin, not to mention Barbis, Beckla, Lindle, and Catelin. They're all tough fighters."

"And I'm not?" Argis spun around and pinned Tas with a menacing glare.

Tas crossed her arms. "You practice that by watching your reflection in the Temple mirror pools."

Argis glared for a few more heartbeats, then roughed up Tas's shaggy hair. "I'll win. I have a greater reason to win than they do."

"Would that be love or pride?" Mularke nimbly sidestepped Argis's lunge.

Tas stepped between them. "Save it for the sparring pit."

"Jame and I have had each other's hearts since we were children," Argis said. "It seems her absence has made everyone forget that. It's time to remind them." She turned and strode across the grass.

"I'm wondering if someone needs to remind Jame," Tas said as she and Mularke trotted after Argis.

Argis gave Tas an unamused look and then rounded the row of rough wooden barracks. She stopped, surprised to see a small crowd of warriors and scouts gathered around the neatly raked sparring pit. Younger warriors' boasts and brags resulted in regular challenges that rarely interested the citizens of Emor enough to disrupt their daily routine. Argis realized that a challenge made over her claim as Jame's suitor was anything but usual. The more witnesses the better to put away any question of her right to be at Jame's side once and for all.

She watched the six challengers lounging near the rack of wooden practice swords used by the novices. She knew that none of them really had romantic designs on Jame. They were just in the mood to put her in her place. This was their way of getting back at her a bit for rising too quickly through the warrior ranks. She was more than willing to remind them of her skill with a sword.

Argis frowned. She couldn't spot Jame in the gathering crowd. Jame had promised she would be there after she got fitted for new leathers.

Tas let out a low appraising whistle. Argis spun around. Jame and Jyac strode across the meadow toward them.

"Nice leathers," Tas squeaked then cleared her throat. "If she had worn those last night, you'd be facing three times as many challengers."

Argis stared at the Jame she thought she knew and wondered where that confident stride had come from. She was dying to get to know Jame all over again, so intriguing was this new sparkle in her eyes and huskier timbre in her voice. Her challengers didn't have a chance against what she perceived to be her destiny.

"Good morning, Argis," Jyac said.

Argis tore her eyes away from Jame, who smiled at her.

Jyac raised an amused eyebrow. "Ready to meet your challengers?"

"I'm always ready to meet those who dare challenge my heart and soul," Argis said, feeling a soaring nobility from Jame's smile.

"Well spoken words, don't you think, Jame?" Jyac said.

"Very well spoken." Jame squeezed Argis's arm. "Good luck."

Jyac laughed. "Come, we can't have people thinking there's any favoritism going on."

"I'll see you when the challenge is over and ask you to the Festival of Flowers." Argis grinned at Jame's stunned expression.

THE LENGTH OF the shadows across the courtyard told Tigh that the nervous lad with the evening meal tray would be emerging from the kitchens in another sandmark or so. She sighed and wondered what her life had come to when a tray of food was a daily highlight.

Her parents were returning to Ingor in the morning, having accomplished their mission. She knew they cared for her but after being away from the sheltered world of the merchant for so long, she no longer knew how to think like them. *I was ready to turn my back on that life before I became a Guard.* She shook away her tears. *Now there isn't anywhere I can fit in.*

Her enhanced hearing picked up the footfalls of, she guessed, a travel boot. Not the well made solid-soled boots of her parents. A more utilitarian boot . . .

Tigh spun around and blinked at a tall, thin, young woman with soulful brown eyes and long strands of wispy pale hair standing outside the door. Meah—wrapped in a plain travel cloak. A pack hung from her fragile shoulder. She had last seen Meah at the victory celebration after the campaign on the plains of Hillian ended the Grappian Wars. She'd been known for her wild hair and even wilder battle lust.

"I, uh, heard you'd been brought in. I was released a couple of days ago and thought I'd stop by before I left." Meah flicked shy, uncertain glances at Tigh.

"You've been through the process?" Tigh asked.

"Yeah." Meah nodded, not meeting Tigh's eyes.

"Do you feel cleansed?" Tigh tried not to sound desperate. "Do you feel ready to walk out of here and rejoin society?"

Meah's sad brown eyes filled with tears and her delicate features betrayed her agony. "No. But they think I am."

"I heard that they can't cleanse away the blood lust, the need to fight." Tigh knew the healers preferred to believe the superficial results of their work rather than delve into what really haunted the dreams of a cleansed Guard.

"They suggested joining a militia or a defense force to satisfy that need." Meah wiped away her tears. "They tell us we can go back to the way we were before. But that's impossible if all that's left of us is the need to fight."

Tigh's hope of attending the University of Artocia and immersing herself in scholarly study lay shattered on the wooden floor of her cell. "I thought it was too good to be true."

Meah took a breath as if she wanted to say something but shook her head instead. "I'm catching the evening coach, so I'd better be on my way." Tigh nodded and Meah turned away from the door.

"Meah." Tigh's voice cracked under the strain of her world collapsing around her. Meah looked back. "Good luck."

Meah mustered a sad smile. "You too, Tigh."

From the window, Tigh watched Meah walk across the plaza and through the city gate. Physically free but still caught in a mental prison.

The shadows across the plaza told Tigh that the nervous lad would be collecting the evening meal tray from the kitchen. She hoped he brought soup. A chill always came with the growing shadows.

Chapter 4

JAME HAD NEVER seen such inspired fighting as Argis made three touched of aggression against each of her challengers. She saw the proprietary rage in Argis's eyes. Every move Argis made shouted, "Don't go near her, she's mine."

I should be flattered. Argis's attentions used to be flattering. Jame studied her as she accepted the congratulatory thumps on the back from the other warriors.

Argis's attentions used to be important. She examined that thought a little closer. Did the fact that she wasn't flattered or that Argis's attentions made her feel closed-in mean her overall feelings for Argis had changed? Or did they simply mean she had matured beyond the simple youthful feelings of love?

"You have to admit, she's a splendid fighter," Jyac said. "Especially when she's inspired."

Jame turned and caught the mischievous glint in Jyac's eyes. "I just wish I felt as certain as she seems to feel."

"You need to take the time to get reacquainted," Jyac said. "We all feel unsettled in the ways of the heart, especially after a long separation. But the two of you have always been close and have a deep affection for each other. You just need to allow those feelings to flow again."

Jame nodded and tried not to tense when Argis broke free of her friends and strode toward her. She realized she didn't reflect Argis's happy grin. If she couldn't be happy about the reason the challenges were fought, she could at least show appreciation for Argis's warrior skills. She mustered a smile. If nothing else, Argis was her friend and friends shared in each other's victories.

Argis stopped a pace away from Jame, dropped to her knees, and pulled her sword from its sheath on her back. She pressed the flat of the blade to her lips in a salute and lowered the sword until the point touched the ground. "I dedicate the victory over these challengers to my princess. It'd be a great honor if you'd accompany me to the Festival of Flowers."

Argis's eyes glowed with such confidence, Jame knew she couldn't refuse her without both hurting and humiliating her. "It would be my honor to accompany you to the Festival of Flowers."

Having said the words, Jame thought she would feel better and wondered why her uncertainty was stronger than ever.

"OH DEAR. OH dear," Minchof muttered as she scanned the contents of the scroll in her hand.

Her small band of apprentices blinked up from their spell practice and witnessed their mentor jiggle in a little dance.

Minchof held up the scroll. "Do you know what this is?"

"A scroll?" Yana, a fifth-year apprentice, had a twinkle in her eyes.

"This, my dear apprentices, is an invitation from the Military Tribunal at Ynit." Minchof grinned at her pupils' puzzled looks. "They've invited me to create a spell that will forever erase the knowledge of how to enhance a soldier and to make it so no one can ever stumble upon the secret again."

"Is that possible?" Renar, a first-year apprentice, asked.

"Everything is possible." Minchof rewrapped an airy shawl around her ample shoulders. "But not everything is easy. I won't be able to do this alone. I'd be lucky if the research alone took less than a season. It'll also require me to go to Ynit to study these Guards firsthand and to learn how they were turned into Guards."

"Ynit?" Yana cried. "That's such a long way from here."

"As much as I want to take all of you with me," Minchof bestowed a fond look on her pack of apprentices, "I'll only be able to take a few. So, I can choose fairly, only those who get the highest marks on the next quarter exam will demonstrate to me the skills and dedication needed to create this spell."

Minchof smiled at the faces already set with the desire to work as hard as necessary to be chosen to go to Ynit.

"Excuse me, Minchof," came a quiet voice from the corner of the room. Goodemer, just fourteen, sat on a stool—her wolf head amulet clutched in her hand. "Will the apprentices with more experience have a better chance of going than us beginners?"

Minchof smiled at the tall, gangly girl with the red-brown wavy hair. "The highest scores, no matter the level, will guarantee a trip to Ynit."

TIGH STARED AT her door for several heartbeats, knowing she was supposed to go to Pendon Larke's office after her morning meal. Despite her slow and deliberate consumption of the food, the tray sat empty outside the door. Unsettling evidence that she had to be on her way.

She inspected her face in the tarnished mirror. She looked a little better than she had a few days earlier. At least she didn't look like Bal's ghost. She straightened to her full height and studied the spotless white tunic and leggings. The nervous lad had brought a clean set for her with the meal. White was not as utilitarian a color as the black she had gotten used to and the cotton weave was harder to keep clean than good leather. The clothing's lightness made her feel vulnerable and that was the last thing she wanted to feel.

She turned to the door. She had to leave soon, or they'd come and get her. In her army that would be humiliating, and Guards didn't react well to humiliation. She swallowed down the memories of that person she used to be and searched within herself for the sword-strong backbone she had once possessed.

"I can do this," she muttered. "It's just a door. I've walked through thousands of doors without a thought. It's not like I have to go outside." Her breath caught as she pushed down a panic attack. *What did they do to me that I fear walking in the sunshine and fresh air?* "You've as much backbone as a newborn lamb. Just step through the door. You can always turn back."

Soothed by that thought, she took a step and fell into a Guard trick by raising her consciousness to a state that felt as if she was floating outside her body, removing herself from her actions. She was out the door and staring down the corridor without even realizing she had moved.

The assistant healer gaping wide-eyed at her from his little table at the end of the corridor helped her relax. People staring at her in fear was as familiar as her favorite boots and the healer's stare made her forget the Elite Guard was no longer within her.

She walked down the corridor, concentrating on stretching her leg muscles. As far as she knew, she hadn't been on her feet for any length of time during the past several weeks and her legs screamed from the neglect. She glanced through the barred doors of the cells that had once belonged to her comrades and confirmed she was the only one left on that floor. She wondered if watching over this floor was considered a prime assignment or a punishment for the assistant healers.

Tigh stopped a few paces in front of the table. The assistant healer looked as if he was trying to say something, but all he could manage was a straggled noise in his throat.

"I was told I have to sign in and out," Tigh said.

The assistant healer stopped his efforts to communicate with visible relief and nodded. "Here." He pushed his chair to the wall, pointed to a ledger, and snapped his hand out of the way.

Tigh picked up the pen, scribbled her name, and, after glancing at the sand clock on the wall, the time. She straightened and captured the assistant healer's eyes with her own. His wide brown eyes brimmed with near panic. "I've been down the corridor with my door unlocked for two days. You've no reason to be frightened of me."

"That's what Pendon said," the assistant healer said in a shaky voice.

"He should know. He helped cleanse me, after all." Tigh raised an eyebrow and turned down the short corridor to the central stairs. The clatter of the chair dropping back on all four legs echoed behind her. The world was as afraid of her as she was of the world. The thought was not comforting.

She paused at the top of the large stone staircase. Her mind flashed to the last time she had walked down those steps, when she had to fight against the surging flow of black clad Guards in full battle gear. They had been on their way to the plains of Hillian for what had been the last campaign of the war. She fought back memories of that bittersweet event that had marked the end of her career as a Guard and the start of her two years as a fugitive.

The fall of her soft boots on the worn stone stairs penetrated the silence of the stairwell. She could almost see and hear the Guards huddling on the steps, jogging up and down the flights to keep in shape, testing the echo with midnight drunken vocalizations . . . the central stairwell had been a living place. Tigh couldn't remember it ever being empty or silent.

She walked numbly down two flights. The silence overwhelmed her with a profound sense of loss, and she collapsed onto the glacial step. Wave of grief the depths of which felt bottomless rolled over her. She'll never see her comrades again or raise a sword in battle alongside them. Five years of her life, filled with the heightened reality the Guard enhancements gave her, had been stolen from her. She loved being a warrior and a Guard. Nothing compared to the feeling of invincibility in battle or the elation of victory. Even if she couldn't face Tigh the Terrible's ruthlessness, her heart ached for the company of her comrades in arms.

She clenched her fists in anger. That life had been ripped away from them by the Federation Council in an act as ruthless as anything Tigh the Terrible had ever committed. Their victory had not been celebrated with parades and they never received sashes of honor. Their reward had been a relentless hunt to capture them and strip them of the life they had loyally given to the state.

Tigh snapped her head up. She wiped away her tears with her sleeve and knew she'd been there far too long. The last thing she wanted was to be found sobbing like a lost child. She concentrated on settling her thoughts and emotions and made it down the remaining flights of steps.

As she stood in the main entry hall of the fortress, she realized she didn't know which office Pendon Larke had taken over. Gray-robed healers and a few Guards in white tunics passed by, but she wasn't ready to talk to any of them yet. Her legs moved from habit, and she found herself at the threshold of her old office. She stared, puzzled at Loena Sihlor behind her old worktable.

Loena looked up and put on a welcoming smile. "Good morning, Tigh. Pendon is expecting you. He's the next door down."

Tigh stared at her, still fumbling with the idea that this was no longer her office. "Thanks." She shuffled to the next opened door.

Pendon, seated behind a table, looked up from his work. "Come in, come in. Sit." He waved a bony hand.

Tigh slipped into the office, glanced around it in search of something familiar, and sank into the visitor's chair.

"Good, very good. And on the first try, too." The wrinkles around Pendon's eyes threatened to obscure them as he grinned.

"First try," Tigh said.

"Sometimes it takes days for a cleansed Guard to make that first step outside their room," Pendon said. "You made it on the first try in only a few sandmarks. Good work."

Tigh sat back and stared dumbfounded at Pendon. The compliment did nothing to lessen the pain those few sandmarks had brought. If this was an example of the healers' blind attitude toward cleansing then it was a miracle a Guard got through rehabilitation sane, much less alive.

JAME SIGHED As she adjusted the fragile bracer clinging to her wrist—a gift from Argis. She envied the time when Emoria had been a young territory, and the Festival of Flowers had been a simple celebration of spring. Generations had added meaning to the festival, and it soon became a time when couples took the first tentative steps of courtship by attending it together. Identical bracers fashioned from flowers, leaves, and sinewy green stems showed off their togetherness.

Three days spent with her old friends had been enjoyable, and Argis had been an attentive shadow at her side. Argis was far from talkative, and Jame had never been bothered by her silence when they'd been younger. But now she felt an odd discomfort when Argis's quiet was coupled with expressions that alternated between unconcealed adoration and puzzled questioning. Argis didn't seem to have any problem that two years had passed since they had last been together and that both of them had matured and changed.

She seems to be certain about her love for me. Jame felt guilty at the joy on Argis's face when she'd delivered the bracer to her early that morning. She realized this was a dream coming true for Argis and had been her own dream just two years earlier. They had whispered about it while exchanging soft kisses in the night-shaded grottoes of the city gardens.

"Laur's waterfalls." Jame mentally kicked herself. Argis had expected her to be at last year's festival. She could only imagine the disappointment Argis had felt when she hadn't returned to Emoria. What was worse, Argis had most likely kept her feelings to herself, like a good warrior.

Jame tried to remember what she'd been doing at the time. The last two years had been an intense blur of case after case of Guards passing through the rehabilitation process. Most of the Guards had been captured in that first year and the healers and arbiter apprentices had been overworked to exhaustion and beyond.

Now she felt bad for not even sending word to Argis. But, on the other side of the sword blade, that should have told Argis she hadn't put much importance on the seriousness of their relationship. By all rights, Argis should have broken off whatever understanding they had.

Jame sighed. "But she didn't."

A gentle rap on her door startled her out of her thoughts. She tried to look cheerful and opened the door.

Argis, holding a five-petal purple flower, stood gaping at Jame.

Jame had chosen a spring green cloth tunic and leggings that matched her emerald eyes. A garland of flowers rested on her sun-bleached hair.

"You're beautiful." Argis held out the flower.

"Thank you." Jame took the flower, sniffed it, and tucked it into her garland. She smiled at Argis and took in her light brown cloth tunic and leggings that clung to her muscular body in a way that any Emoran in her right mind would find appealing. Argis's dark wavy hair was crowned with a garland, somehow adding to the nobility of her features. "You look nice yourself."

Jame waved Argis into the chamber and closed the door.

"Before we go out there," Jame carefully gathered together her words, "I just wanted to apologize for not being here last year and for not sending word that I wasn't going to show up. That was a time when hundreds of Guards were being captured and cleansed. We worked without stopping and barely paid attention to the days and moons, much less the passing seasons."

Argis's face transformed into a picture of pride and affection. "We'd heard about the heroic efforts you faced in giving up all your time and skills so you could return the Guards to society as quickly as possible. I wasn't disappointed or upset that you weren't able to make it to the festival last year. Just the opposite. I was so proud of you, I thought I was going to burst from it. I was the envy of last year's festival because I had given my heart to someone who was doing what the rest of us have only dreamed of doing. Fighting against all odds for the greater good."

Jame was speechless. Argis placed a gentle kiss on her cheek and offered her an arm.

Jame absently took the arm, and Argis escorted her into the corridor. All she could think about was how deep a mess she was in.

"SHE'D BEEN DOING so well." Pendon shook his aged head as he sat on the overstuffed chair in the small parlor off of Tigh's former office. Loena handed him a mug of tea before easing into the chair opposite him. A fire crackled in the small fireplace. "Far better than any of the others, in my humble opinion."

"So she suddenly decided she wasn't ready for the next step," Leona said.

Pendon sighed. "There hasn't been any indication that she's been resisting therapy. She's been a model patient. She's done everything we've asked without question and with diligence as far as I can tell."

"Yet she doesn't feel she's ready to continue," Loena said. "Tigh has always been a special case. I guess it was too much to expect this situation would be any different."

"I don't understand it though." Pendon paused to compose his thoughts and took a long sip of tea. "We've perfected this procedure. Every Guard has developed the proper amount of optimism to continue the process."

"Maybe more magic needs to be applied," Loena said.

Pendon rubbed his wrinkled brow. "Something seems to have happened between the time she was enhanced and now, as far as magic is concerned."

Leona gave Pendon an indulgent but patient look. "What do you mean, something?"

"Something that's affected the way she reacts to magic," Pendon said. "I got suspicious when she wasn't reacting to the spells of unconsciousness for the hypnosis sessions. As a test I wove a couple of stinging spells to her arm, and she showed no discomfort at all."

Loena frowned. "Yet she seems to have gotten through the procedure, even without hypnosis."

"There isn't anything about her to indicate she isn't ready to start interacting with other people." Pendon pushed a hand through his white hair. "She's still depressed but I think interacting with others will help pull her out of that."

"You know, there are those on the Federation Council who feel she's beyond rehabilitation and others who feel she doesn't deserve it," Leona said. "Even after commanding the decisive victory of the Wars, they'd rather she be locked away than rehabilitated."

"She knows that, and she agrees with them," Pendon said. "It's a very difficult legacy to live with."

"If we want to get her rehabilitated and out of our care, we have to make sure she continues through the process as smoothly as possible," Leona said. "If she turns out to be an explosion waiting to happen it'd be much better for us if that explosion happened somewhere else."

"You don't really think she's beyond complete rehabilitation, do you?" Pendon asked.

"I'd like to think that anyone who's been enhanced can be cleansed and returned safely to society." Loena stared into her mug and then raised solemn eyes to Pendon. "But when the Federation Council went against our better judgment and recruited individuals with traits capable of producing Patch Lachlans and Tigh the Terribles, we knew there might be problems controlling and cleansing them."

"I think she's just more depressed than the average Guard," Pendon said. "I mean, wouldn't you be if you had to live with her legacy? Fortunately, she hasn't done anything for the Council to question our decision to allow her to go onto the next step. It's just a matter of convincing her to continue."

They looked up at a gentle rap on the outer door of the adjoining chamber. Tigh, with a puzzled expression, stood in the corridor.

"Come in, Tigh," Lorna said.

Tigh entered the outer room and glanced around as if trying to figure out what had happened to her office. She hovered on the threshold of the parlor and stared at the pastel-colored decor where her black leather chairs and heavy wood furniture once stood.

"Have a seat. Would you like some tea?" Leona asked.

She blinked at Leona. "I'm, uh, looking for something."

"Something that was in your office?" Loena asked.

"In the cabinet over there." Tigh pointed to a wall occupied by shelves of books. "There used to be a cabinet."

Loena eased up from the chair and padded to a plain wooden chest below the windowsill. "Everything was put in here."

Tigh snapped her attention to the chest. She went to Loena's side and looked down at it. "Thank you," she mumbled and dropped cross-legged in front of it.

Pendon and Loena sipped their tea and watched Tigh, who stared, unmoving, at the chest for half a sandmark before venturing to open it.

Pendon was used to a number of reactions from patients faced with such tangible pieces from their lives as a Guard, but he had never witnessed the agonizing grief that shuddered through Tigh as she handled each of her treasured possessions from when she had been a Guard. He realized that Paldar Tigis actually missed Tigh the Terrible. What he didn't know was if that meant the cleansing process had succeeded or failed.

Chapter 5

JAME SMILED AS they strolled from the palace into the central square. Emor looked like a willing victim of a flower explosion. Mischievous women hefted baskets full of petals of every hue off the highest balconies overlooking the square and caused blizzards of flowers on the festive women below. She laughed as Argis stoically withstood an avalanche of petals dumped on her from a pair of masked basket handlers.

Argis didn't even have to look up to know who her assailants were. "They're in so much trouble," she said through clenched teeth.

Jame grinned. "Come on, Argis. What's a festival without Tas and Mularke playing practical jokes?"

"A festival where they don't risk being killed," Argis said, but much of the anger was already gone from her voice.

Surprised at this, Jame realized that Argis had mellowed since her last visit. A younger Argis would have been plotting immediate revenge.

Argis shook herself like a wet dog, causing the petals to fly everywhere.

Jame jumped out of the way of the colorful flurry. "Hey, if they wanted me to share, they would've dumped them on me."

"They wouldn't have dared," Argis said with a grin. "They know that would have really made me angry."

Jame grinned in return, not betraying the strange ambivalence she felt every time Argis took their relationship for granted. Of course, she couldn't blame Argis since she hadn't said anything to counter this attitude. She just wished Argis was more sensitive about it. She chuckled to herself. *Sensitive? Argis? That's what I get for spending all my time with arbiters, who are models of sensitivity. I've forgotten how Emoran warriors are. Maybe that's my problem. I need to think less like an arbiter and more like an Emoran.*

Light voices, combined in harmonious tones, reached Jame's ears from the Temple of Laur, patron deity of Emoria. Magical memories of past festivals tumbled through her mind. Not able to put two musical tones together herself, she always marveled at those who displayed the gift with such beauty and ease.

"I suppose you want to go hear the acolytes," Argis said.

Jame caught Argis's indulgent tone. As children, she knew Argis had endured the concert during every festival just to be with her.

Jame grabbed Argis's arm and dragged her around the clusters of women and girls until they joined the crowd gathered in front of a dozen lavender-robed acolytes to Laur. The acolytes sang in soft tight harmonies and accompanied themselves with the rhythmic tinkling of their delicate waterfall-shaped amulets.

As she listened, Jame felt Argis shift closer until their arms touched. Argis wiggled her fingers against her own. She gave Argis a questioning look. Argis answered by slipping her fingers through hers.

The impulse was sweet, and Jame should have felt something as she stared into Argis's tender eyes. For Argis, this small gesture was a shouted declaration of her strong feelings and would produce several rounds of good-natured ribbing from her comrades if they witnessed it. She reacted to the sweetness of it and smiled at Argis before returning her attention to the singers.

Jame had forgotten how exhausting the festival could be and by evening, was more than happy to sit at one of the long wooden tables set around the square. The bright pastel tinted festivities of the day transformed into a more sensuous atmosphere as torches sputtered to life and night draped shadows across the city. Drums and flutes painted an aural backdrop to the platters of food that were hauled out of the kitchens and delivered to the women who were ready to partake in a leisurely meal after a long day of enjoying the festival.

Argis dished out stew and hunks of bread onto plates for Jame and herself, and then filled their mugs.

Jame picked up her mug and sniffed it before drinking. Expecting the usual flower-scented punch, she was surprised to find ale instead. She caught Argis's night-darkened eyes and realized Argis had certain expectations of how the evening was to end. She also knew that, as far as everyone was concerned, she was supposed to have those expectations, too.

They'd been so wonderfully wrapped up in each other for the brief few weeks of her last visit. They had no doubt the future was theirs to share together. Why wasn't she feeling that now? It couldn't have just vanished like an illuminator's trick.

She looked into the mug and took a long drink. She opened her senses and allowed the hypnotic rhythm of the music and the muted reality of night take over and decided to let her body do the thinking for a while.

TIGH STARED AT her hands as she sat in the visitor's chair of what had been Patch Lachlan's work chamber and felt Pendon's gaze on her. She just wished she didn't have to make decisions. Why couldn't she just hide out in the mountains for the rest of her life?

"We understand you're feeling confused and lost right now," Pendon said. "That's natural. Once you start the next step, these feelings will fade."

"This is the point where the Tribunal decides if I'm fit to take the next step?" Tigh slumped and clutched her head with both hands.

"It's just a precaution." Pendon waved a dismissive hand. "The Tribunal has to appease the Federation Council. After two years of successfully returning hundreds of Guards back to society, these hearings before the Tribunal have become little more than formalities."

"I hear they're divided on whether I should be allowed back out there," Tigh said.

"One or two members of the Tribunal have a problem with everything we're doing here," Pendon said. "They can't protest too loudly because of the success of our program."

Tigh gazed at Pendon. "They have every right to be wary of me."

"You think all you have left right now are your fighting skills," Pendon said. "The next step will help you find your old skills or help you develop new ones."

"I can never go back to what I wanted to be before I became a Guard," Tigh said.

"I'd think the warrior skills and the experiences you acquired during the Wars would be invaluable for a merchant." Pendon frowned and shuffled through a stack of papers. He picked up a sheet of finely crafted paper that Tigh recognized as her mother's personal stationary. "Your parents feel you'll be an asset to the family business. It was my understanding that their discussion with you about this was what helped you decide to continue with your rehabilitation."

Not for the first time did Tigh wonder how her life had gone so wrong that she was in Patch Lachlan's former office listening to the well-intentioned but misguided words of a healer. "I continued this process because I was unhappy with the alternative."

Pendon fell back in his chair. "The alternative being?"

"Being locked away forever," Tigh said.

"If you don't want to be a merchant, what do you want to be?" Pendon asked.

Tigh studied her hands for several heartbeats. "When I was recruited into the Guards, I was preparing to enter the University of Artocia to become a scholar. My parents didn't know about it. I was ready to run away if that was the only way to become what I wanted to be."

Pendon stared with furrowed brow the now worthless document from Pandon. Tigh suspected the neat assumptions the healers made about the Guards weren't often so drastically challenged.

Pendon raised his head, his usual good humor sparkling in his eyes. "You don't have to give up that dream. As you know, many of the Guards were archivists and librarians. Several pursued quiet jobs as scribes and bards. They've all been successfully rehabilitated so they can return to what they were before."

Tigh swallowed her response. Meah's words about the healers encouraging them to join a militia or a defense group echoed through her mind. She certainly wasn't going to let Pendon know that she was on to their self-deluding games. On the other side of the sword blade, the reason that brought her to this point in her rehabilitation still loomed over her. The only thing she was sure of was she had to get out somehow, and with her memories and guilt, she couldn't do it on her own.

"Where do I sign?"

Pendon pushed a sheet of paper, an ink jar, and pen toward her.

She scrawled her name and then fell back in the chair. "What now?"

"An arbiter argues your case before the Tribunal." Pendon blotted the wet ink.

"An arbiter," Tigh said. "I pity the poor soul who gets that job."

JAME WASN'T SURE if she wanted to open her eyes or not. If the fuzz in her mouth and the rocky pitching in her stomach were any sign, opening her eyes wouldn't improve the situation. She compromised by covering her eyes with her hand and easing them open in semidarkness. As she pulled away her hand, her head joined the chorus of discomfort.

Why did I do such a stupid thing? She looked down at herself, sprawled in her festival clothes on her own bed, and sighed. *This is why. And it worked.*

Halfway through the evening, as things got hazier and Argis much more attentive, she had figured out a way to put Argis off without offending or hurting her. Frowning a little, she tried to remember how she ended up in her room. Her intention was to be inebriated enough for Argis's honor to prevent her from taking any kind of advantage. She rubbed her throbbing head as she tried to piece together the disjointed impressions.

"I guess I passed out or something," she said to the ceiling. "Now I have to figure out why I put myself into this miserable state."

The problem was, she just didn't know how she felt about Argis anymore. She valued her friendship and enjoyed her company but whatever else had been there before, was gone. *It might only be because I'm so close to getting my arbiter's medallion and I don't want any distractions until I've achieved my goal. Surely Argis can understand that.*

A wave of relief rolled through her, followed by a pounding in her head from the sound of her door opening. Moaning, she put her hand over her eyes and watched through her fingers Jyac enter and struggle to keep away an amused look.

"I've got something for that little headache . . . and stomachache and whatever else is aching," Jyac said.

"Just aim the arrow right at my forehead," Jame muttered. "And make it quick."

Chuckling, Jyac padded to the bed, sat on the edge, and held out a mug. Jame sat up and took the mug. She sniffed the vapors rising up from it and almost lost what was left in her stomach from the night before.

"Drink up." Jyac grinned as Jame grimaced and drained the mug. "Argis came to see me this morning with an apology for allowing you to drink so much. She'd forgotten you don't have a head for alcohol like some of those crazy warriors do. She admitted to keeping your mug full even when she knew you had too much."

Jame stared at Jyac. *Argis had tried to get me drunk?* "She didn't have to apologize. I'm perfectly capable of doing stupid things all on my own."

Jyac laughed and patted Jame's arm. "Don't tell her that. It's good to make a warrior repentant every once in a while."

"Yeah." Jame looked down at the mug. "I'm going back to Ynit in a few days. My last course starts soon, and I don't want to miss any of it."

"I know you have your heart set on finishing your studies," Jyac said. "We all admire your persistence in achieving such a difficult goal. One of the reasons I wanted you to visit before you began this last part of your studies was to remind you that we're all waiting for you to bring your newly acquired skills to Emoria."

"How can I ever forget my home?" Jame smiled, not having the heart to tell Jyac that she wanted to use her skills out in the world before settling back home. She didn't want to deal with any more pressure than she already felt.

"Argis is very proud of you," Jyac said. "She admires your dedication."

Jame nodded, studying the mug.

"I think I know what your problem is. You're just trying to keep from getting too attached again because you're leaving so soon. I know it was difficult for both of you when you left the last time."

"That's probably it." Jame knew that countering Jyac was futile. "I'm just so close to finishing. I can't wait until I have my arbiter's medallion."

Jyac smiled and took Jame's hand. "When you return, I think you'll find how easy it'll be to fit back into our little world. Our people are looking forward to a royal joining and I have the feeling you and Argis will be more than ready to settle down by then."

Jame tried to muster some enthusiasm but truly couldn't. "I hope so."

"GREETINGS, FIERCE WARRIOR woman." Jadic, a young man with sandy hair, whipped an invisible sword from over his shoulder and mimed a salute.

Jame grinned at the cluster of assistant arbiters gathered outside one of the dozen doors lining the round common room of their living quarters. Her friends never missed an opportunity to tease her about her Emoran background.

"You missed all the excitement," Daneran said. She was a small woman with dark hair and gentle eyes.

"Excitement?" Jame joined her colleagues and dropped her pack on the floor.

"About Tigh the Terrible," Jadic said.

"What about her?" The image of the feral young woman in the cage flashed through Jame's mind. How many of her dreams had been haunted by those eyes?

"While you were gone, she received the post-cleansing counseling from Pendon Larke," Daneran said. "I'm not afraid to admit that I was spooked by her walking around."

Jame frowned. "But she's been cleansed."

"Cleansed or not, she's still intimidating." Jadic shook his shoulders as if warding off a chill. "Those eyes alone are enough to scare the life out of me."

"Anyway, she made it through the second step." Daneran flashed Jadic an impatient look. "Her name was added to our case roster four days ago."

"Really?" Jame said. "Who took her?"

"That's the thing. None of us wants to argue her case," Daneran said. "None of us really wants to mar our records with losing a case."

"You don't think you can successfully argue her case?" Jame looked around at her friends.

Daneran shrugged. "This is Tigh the Terrible we're talking about."

"She isn't anymore." Jame picked up her pack and turned to the doorway that led to their mentor's chambers. The others assaulted her with persuasive words of reason.

"I know you always go for the underdog, but she's a lost cause," Jadic said. "She's not worth risking your career over."

"She deserves a chance to live a normal life, just like all the other Guards." Jame leveled a steady gaze at her friends. "We can't turn down a case simply because it might damage our careers. If we do that, we take justice into our own hands and become both the judge and the executioner. I'm going to take the case."

She ignored the chorus of protests and strode down the crooked corridor to their mentor.

"Ah Jame, welcome back." Ingel Renat looked up from her paper-strewn table.

"I want to take Tigh's case," Jame said. "And thank you, it's good to be back."

Ingel gazed at Jame for a heartbeat and sighed. "I appreciate your offer, Jame. But this could violate the promise to your aunt that we wouldn't allow you into potentially dangerous situations."

Laur's waterfalls. It had seemed like a harmless compromise when Jyac had insisted that she have a royal guard with her in Ynit. The last thing she wanted was something that set her apart from the other students. Besides, she didn't want her every action reported back home.

"But she's been cleansed," Jame said.

"Yes, that's true." Ingel fiddled with her pen. "But the potential for danger is there."

"But that could be said about any case involving a Guard," Jame said. "Logically, she should be less dangerous."

"The truth is, the healers aren't quite sure how effective the cleansing process is on the Elite Guards." Ingel brushed back a shock of white hair. "Their personality reversals are so extreme, residual effects from the enhancements may linger."

"Let me get this straight." Jame clasped her hands behind her back. Her friends, clustered around the door, groaned. "The healers aren't sure if the cleansing process worked, yet she's made it through the post-cleansing procedure and her name is on our case roster. Sounds to me like Tigh is being set up to give someone an excuse to find some other means of dealing with her."

"The healers are just being cautious," Ingel said.

"Then let me take her case," Jame said.

"It's a matter of how dangerous your aunt will perceive the situation." Ingel gave Jame an imploring look.

"She doesn't know which cases I take," Jame said.

"Anything involving Tigh is bound to get out."

Jame and Ingel stared at each other for several heartbeats.

"If it means that much to you, Jame, I'll take the case," Jadic said.

Jame gave Jadic a wry look. "I thought you said she was scary."

He chuckled. "It'll be a good learning experience. It'll help me develop skills at dealing with clients who scare me to death."

"Are you sure, Jadic?" Ingel asked.

"I'm sure." Jadic nodded, not looking at all sure.

AN ARBITER HAD volunteered to argue her case. Tigh envisioned a young, eager student taking the case on a dare. After four days of nervous apologies from Pendon, she figured a dare was the only way to get anyone to take her on.

She sat on the edge of her cot with her mid-day meal tray balanced on her knees and cut her asparagus into neat uniform pieces. She savored the way the sharp knife sliced through the tender shoots.

The assistant healer down the corridor was exchanging words with someone. She speared a piece of asparagus with her fork and chewed off a bit. Much to her delight, the military cooks prepared Ingoran food better than most Ingorans. She'd have to discover their secret when she finally left this place. She popped the rest of the piece into her mouth, then dissected the plate of marinated palm hearts nestled in an intriguing assortment of greens.

A throat cleared to get her attention. She almost laughed, considering she had heard this person wheezing as he climbed the final flight of stairs. The stillness on her floor acted as a magnifier for any foreign sound. She cut her vegetables into precise mouth size bits.

"Uh . . . excuse me." The voice of a young male grated her ears as it cracked from tense fear.

Tigh gathered a forkful of greens and savored the delicate flavor that saturated her mouth. She then investigated the potato dish that she had never seen before. The cooks were endlessly creative in the preparation of her food.

"I'm, uh, Jadic Pondersac." The voice quavered. "I'm here to argue your case—"

Tigh emitted a low growl and then chuckled as she stuck her fork into the mound of potatoes. The only thing left of the arbiter was the echo of rapid footfalls in the corridor.

How could she expect an arbiter to defend her if the person was frightened silly of her? She stared at the tarnished mirror across the cell and wondered if she had just scared off her last chance at freedom.

She filled her fork and tasted the new offering. No. She did the right thing. Her freedom would have been as much at risk with that trembling rabbit than if no other arbiter stepped forward and volunteered.

She had seen only one face since her return that hadn't shown any fear of her. Her enhancements gave her the ability to sense fear as keenly as a wild animal was known to do and all she had felt when she held that young woman's eyes was curiosity and sympathy.

"It'd be my luck she's the cook's assistant," she said to the wall.

Chapter 6

AFTER READING THE same sentence for the fifth time, Jame gave up trying to study. She'd been determined to stay out of the almost insane activities of her colleagues during the last two days. What began as a noble but sincere gesture from Jadic, turned into a challenge for all comers to take a try at. That in turn became a constant chatter of who had the scariest encounter with the former Tigh the Terrible.

The twelfth and last assistant arbiter, aside from Jame, had just left to meet the challenge. Her confident boasting still echoed in Jame's ears.

Jame pushed back from her little table tucked in the corner of the room she shared with Daneran and looked through the doorway into the common room. All the other assistants were clustered together trading for the umpteenth time what they would do if they had another chance to face Tigh the Terrible.

Jame knew what they had done wrong. She'd gathered from the rumors and whisperings in the corridors that Tigh, unlike the other Guards who had gone through the cleansing process, had actually enjoyed being a warrior and missed it. Whatever she had wanted to be before she was recruited, she wanted to be a warrior now.

Tigh's problem was how society would accept a Tigh the Terrible in peacetime. Her whole attitude revolved around the warrior's code of behavior and if Jame's well-meaning colleagues displayed even a bit of the fear they admitted to feeling in Tigh's presence, Tigh would think they weren't capable of defending her.

Growing up in a warrior society does have its advantages, Jame mused, as the chatter ceased, and her friends' attention turned to the outside door. *That was quick.*

A breathless Swene charged into the common room. Her long red hair was disheveled from the spring winds. "I'm not embarrassed to say that I was wrong. There's one human being in this world beyond the skills of an arbiter." The others, ravenous for the details, gathered around her.

Jame took a deep breath and stared at the wall for a few heartbeats. She stood, shook the long hours of study from her legs, and slipped down the crooked corridor to Ingel's chambers.

Ingel was watering the jungle of plants in front of the window and speaking soft words of encouragement to them. Jame wandered to the nearby wall, leaned against it, and watched this familiar daily ritual of one of the most celebrated arbiters in several generations.

"I never knew you had such an interest in the art of watering plants," Ingel said.

Jame shrugged. "If it gets me what I want, I'll learn everything there is to know about the subject."

"That's what I like about you, Jame. Always to the point." Ingel smiled and checked the soil of a small plant with large floppy leaves. "What makes you think you'll succeed where the others have failed?"

"I understand warriors," Jame said.

Ingel lifted respectful eyes to Jame. "Unfortunately, her antics with the others haven't improved the perception that she's still dangerous."

"She has a right to select her own arbiter," Jame said.

Ingel inspected a bud on a sprawling vine. "She could have chosen a less hostile method of turning down their offers."

"She's just living up to our expectations of her," Jame said. "If she were really dangerous or violent, she would have physically hurt them. From what I've gathered, she just turned on the warrior intimidation act a bit."

"Are you so sure it's an act?" Ingel put down her watering pail and pulled off her gloves.

"If she's been cleansed, it's an act," Jame said. "If she hasn't been cleansed, then the healers will be in big trouble with the Tribunal. She's been allowed to walk around here, and no one's seen any hint of aggression from her. Tigh still thinks she's a warrior. My friends aren't warriors, and they don't understand how warriors think. I was a warrior in training practically up to the day I first stepped foot inside this school."

"I still don't want to be in the position of explaining this to your aunt, if something happens," Ingel said.

"What can happen?" Jame stretched out her hands. "Her antics, as you call them, have forced them to lock her door. All I'll do is stand outside and ask if she'll let me present her case. No harm will come of it and maybe, if I get lucky, she'll let me help her."

Ingel sighed and stared out the window at the fortress across the plaza. "Tigh's on my roster and I'll eventually have to find an arbiter to argue the case. As long as she's secure behind a locked door, you should be safe enough." She turned to Jame. "All right. The case is yours."

"Thank you, thank you." Jame grabbed Ingel's hand. "And don't worry, I'll be careful."

TIGH LAY ON her cot, listening to every sound. Two sandmarks had passed since the last scared rabbit cowered at her door. Was that all that they had to offer? She wondered how the other Guards could have allowed these spineless youngsters to argue their cases for them.

Maybe the problem was with her. She blinked at the spidery patterns on the adobe ceiling and couldn't bring herself to believe she was so different from her former comrades.

She reached out her hearing at a distant sound. Just the assistant healer shifting in his chair. They may have been spineless lambs, but they had made the last two days more interesting for her. Even if her entertainment was at her own expense—a displeased Pendon Larke and a locked door.

The assistant healer was talking to someone. She concentrated on the noises. It sounded like a young woman this time. The healer seemed to be trying to dissuade her from making this visit. She frowned. All the other arbiters had been let through with little more than a sympathetic well wishing.

Two sets of footfalls echoed down the corridor instead of the usual one. Now Tigh's curiosity was afire. She wondered at how starved for diversion she was, to find a minor change in the routine so intriguing. She picked up the sound of something being placed outside her door. Probing the direction with her peripheral vision, she caught a glimpse of a chair. *Planning to be here a while?*

"Thank you." A gentle voice laced with a confident strength touched her ears.

THE ASSISTANT HEALER glanced into the cell at Tigh and then at Jame. "I'll be at my desk." He pointed down the corridor. "Don't hesitate to call for help."

Jame gave him a reassuring smile and nodded. He walked away, looking back at her several times.

Jame sat in the chair and gazed through the bars in the door. The cell was as austere and tidy as the other Guards' quarters. In shocking contrast to the last time Jame had seen her, Tigh was dressed in the simple white cotton tunic and leggings worn by the cleansed Guards. Her clean face revealed a striking fair-skinned young woman. The deep tan from years spent as a warrior had faded during her confinement. Tigh was stretched out on her back with hands behind her head and appeared unaware that anyone was outside her door.

Jame cleared her throat. No reaction from Tigh.

"I'm . . . uh . . . I'm Jame, assistant arbiter."

Tigh continued to stare at the ceiling.

"I'm going to talk a bit. I have a story I really want you to hear." Jame took in a ragged breath. This nervousness was unusual for her, and she didn't quite know how to handle it. She gazed at her hands for a few heartbeats as she centered her nerves and her thoughts. "I just want you to understand why I'm here and why I want to argue your case."

She waited in silence, trying to gauge the reaction from Tigh the Terrible. The other arbiters hadn't been given a chance to state their case before Tigh intimidated them into making a quick journey back down the corridor. Jame, having grown up around warriors, was prepared for that kind of confrontation. This lack of acknowledgment of her presence was more disconcerting than overt threatening behavior.

Jame sighed. She'd come this far, she may as well do what she was there to do. Even if Tigh didn't understand, she'd feel better for trying. She cleared her throat and spoke in an easy tone, as if she were relating the story to her friends.

"I was walking across the plaza two moons ago. It was a beautiful evening, and I stopped on my way to a lecture to revel in the last glow of the sun before nightfall. A wagon rolled in, and I thought, another Guard has been captured. I stopped to let the wagon pass and the Guard in the cage was awake and alert, taking in everything around her. She captured my attention, pulling me in with the force of her personality. I admit I probably looked pretty silly standing there with my mouth hanging open, unable to tear myself away from those intense blue eyes. Then, as the wagon rolled away, the Guard laughed, breaking the spell she'd cast over me. For half a heartbeat I caught a glimpse of the woman beneath all the grime and the blood and the cold madness. I saw sadness and regret in those eyes. I've seen hundreds of uncleansed Guards as they were brought back here. I've never witnessed even a hint of humanity in them. They were like wild animals showing nothing but rage at being captured and caged. I realized, out of all of them, that you had the best chance of being completely rehabilitated because the extremes in how the enhancements affected you came from your deep sense of humanity."

Although Tigh never moved during her narrative, Jame noticed a slight relaxing of her facial muscles and more blinking. She was listening at least.

"I was visiting back home when your name was added to our case roster but the moment I heard about it I volunteered. My mentor refused to let me take your case. I can understand about who you are always getting in the way of who you want to become." Jame paused at the minute furrow between Tigh's eyebrows. That particular arrow appeared to have hit the mark. "I was born a princess and, so I wouldn't have to put up with having a guard with me while I was away from home, the school promised it wouldn't let me get into any dangerous situations. I tried to convince my mentor I didn't think you were of danger to any of us. I mean, I grew up around warriors. My aunt would laugh at the school's idea of danger." Jame paused again, hoping for some response. But Tigh didn't even twitch a muscle. "Anyway, all my well-meaning colleagues volunteered because it meant so much to me. You didn't accept any of them, so I finally convinced my mentor to let me give it a try."

The silence lengthened until Jame was certain Tigh wasn't going to speak.

"Anyway, that's why I'm here. I want to argue your case. If you want me as your arbiter, I'll return tomorrow with a first draft of the argument."

Tigh swallowed, and her eyes seemed to be looking inward rather than at the ceiling.

"All you have to do is agree to the preparation of the case. You'll always have the choice to pursue it or not."

Another swallow rippled through Tigh's powerful throat.

"Just say yes or no."

Silence enveloped them and Jame could hear voices rising up from the plaza. She stood and took one last look at Tigh.

"Yes."

The word was so soft that Jame barely caught it. She froze and gazed through the bars, but Tigh still refused to look at her. "Thank you."

TIGH RAISED HER eyes to whatever deity oversaw her destiny and tried to let what just happened penetrate her tired, confused mind.

By the Children of Bal, that arbiter was the one.

She wound the astonishing thought through in her mind until she was convinced it hadn't been a hallucination or dream. For the first time since her cleansing, a tentative hope mingled on the fragrant breeze blowing in through the window.

STILL A LITTLE dazed from her strange encounter with the former Tigh the Terrible, Jame wandered into her room and stared in surprise at all the assistant arbiters there.

She looked at Daneran. "Are we having a party?"

"You were gone long enough. Where have you been?" Daneran asked.

"I've been with Tigh."

A dozen bodies rushed her way.

Jame took refuge in the common room. She held up her hands to fend off her colleagues. "Whoa. You're more dangerous than Tigh the Terrible."

The arbiters stopped their advance and chuckled at Jame and themselves. Ingel walked out of corridor to her chambers and leaned a shoulder against the wall.

"So, tell us what happened." Jadic looked ready to explode from curiosity.

Jame shrugged. "There really isn't much to tell. I told her why I was there and why I wanted to argue her case and she agreed to it."

"She listened?" Swene asked, astonished.

"She spoke?" Jadic's eyebrows disappeared under his bangs.

"She listened and then she said yes," Jame said. "Now if you'll excuse me, I have an argument to write."

Her friends all spoke at once and barred the way back to her room.

"Why would she accept you and not any of us?" Tanerle, the most ambitious of the group, powered her tall imposing body to Jame.

"Weren't you afraid?" Swene asked.

"She was on the other side of a locked door. Why would I be afraid?" Jame gave Swene a puzzled look before turning her attention to Tanerle. "Only Tigh knows the answer to your question."

"Don't give me that, you smooth talking Emoran," Tanerle said. "I want to know what you did to make her listen to you when she didn't let us utter more than a syllable."

Jame glanced at Ingel, who raised an eyebrow back. "I just gave the answer. To Swene. Let me ask a question in return. If you were looking for an arbiter to argue a case for you, would you choose one who was too frightened to even face you?"

Ingel stepped into the circle of stunned arbiters. "This is a valuable lesson for any arbiter to learn. Always try to see the situation through your client's eyes. Just because you're an arbiter doesn't mean people will overlook what you may consider a natural reaction, such as fear, toward a client or toward one of the two parties you have to judge."

"But how could you not be afraid of her?" Jadic asked.

"She's been cleansed." Jame wondered why, in this particular case, that meant nothing. "That should be enough of a reason, or have you suddenly stopped trusting the healers' abilities to do their job?"

"Lesson number two," Ingel said. "Always remember all the facts about a client or the defendants in a case. Don't just focus on the most sensational facts that dominate the rumors. Now Jame has work to do, and I'm still expecting an essay on Scrytians' General Laws from each of you tomorrow."

With good-natured grumbles, the arbiters went to their rooms. Jame caught a beckoning nod from Ingel and followed her.

"Now that you've gotten past the first barricade, do you have an idea of how to argue her case?" Ingel asked after she settled behind her table and Jame collapsed into the visitor's chair.

Jame gave her a sheepish look. "Not really. But I'm hoping that will come once I get to know Tigh a little better."

"Allow me to give you a few suggestions," Ingel said. "The usual arguments used for the Guards are not going to work in Tigh's case, even if they're just as valid. The Federation Council is wary of having Tigh the

Terrible out in the world, so the Tribunal is going to be a lot harder on her than the other Guards."

"But it's not fair," Jame said. "It's not her fault the enhancements made her a ruthless warrior. Besides, the Federation Council was more than happy with her when she was winning their major battles."

"Unfortunately, she was little more than a volatile weapon and the most dangerous weapons are always destroyed after a war," Ingel said. "You guessed that she misses being a warrior. That doesn't necessarily mean the cleansing wasn't successful, it just brought out some traits that had been dormant in Tigh before she was enhanced."

"Is this one of Pendon's theories?" Jame asked.

"Yes, it is," Ingel said. "But it makes sense. There's nothing of Tigh the Terrible in that confused and passive young woman I see roaming the corridors. It's now on your shoulders to find out who Tigh is today and present that to the Tribunal."

"I'll do my best," Jame said as the enormity of her task swept over her.

TIGH SAT ON the edge of the cot and stared at the neatly written and well-presented argument she held in her hand.

Jame, trying not to fidget, sat in her little chair in the corridor. Tigh proved to be a challenging client. She almost laughed at how much of an understatement that was. For one thing, Tigh never looked at her. For another thing, her method of communication was verbally spare but physically expressive. A simple shrug or lift of a hand could communicate as well as any word.

Jame spent much of their time together just deciphering the subtleties of this language of movement. She didn't think Tigh was being deliberately uncooperative. Tigh was frightened and confused and, if Jame understood her body language, not entirely trusting of the rehabilitation process.

She knew she shouldn't care about what Tigh thought of the document. Preparing arguments was, after all, a part of the job. But she was drawn to this enigmatic woman. More than she had ever been drawn to anyone. She wanted to get to know her, not say goodbye when the arbitration process was finished. She sighed and pushed down these unsettling thoughts.

Tigh laid the document on the cot, stood up, and shuffled to the window. She stared outside for several heartbeats.

"Why are you doing this?" Tigh asked without turning around.

Both surprised and delighted at the first full sentence from Tigh, Jame almost responded with what she had told her during their first meeting. But something deep inside stopped her. "Because I want to." She knew Tigh could sense she told the truth. That particular Guard enhancement seemed to resist cleansing.

Tigh turned around and for the first time gazed at Jame.

"Why?" Tigh's intense blue eyes, softened by the cleansing and haunted by the memories of what she had done as a Guard, reached straight into Jame's soul.

"Because you deserve it," Jame said.

Tigh slid down the wall and pulled her knees to her chin. "I don't deserve it."

"Yes, you do." Jame wanted to shake some sense into Tigh. "You are not Tigh the Terrible. You have the rest of your life to be the Tigh you wanted to be before you were recruited."

Tigh shook her head. "That's not possible."

"Then be the Tigh you are today."

Tigh sighed. "When people look at me, they see Tigh the Terrible." She captured Jame's eyes. "When I look at myself, I see a monster not worthy of being allowed to live a normal life again."

"When I look at you, I see a woman who has the right to a life outside these walls." Jame jumped to her feet and grabbed hold of the bars.

Tigh raised an eyebrow.

"Do you want to make up for the wrongs you did as Tigh the Terrible or do you want to spend the rest of your life in a cell, feeling sorry for yourself?"

Tigh pushed to her feet and lunged at the door. She wrapped her strong hands over Jame's smaller ones and held them against the bars. They stared at each other for several heartbeats, so close that Jame felt the warmth coming off Tigh and a strange tingle in her hands.

Tigh, confusion in her eyes, pulled her hands away from Jame's and stumbled back.

Jame took a deep breath and held onto the bars to steady her lightheadedness. She had never reacted to another person like that before.

"We'll try it your way for a while," Tigh mumbled.

Chapter 7

THE RESIDENCE FOR the assistant arbiters was unusually quiet for that time of evening. The arbiters, along with the rest of the students at the school, were out enjoying the first beautiful day of early summer.

Jame gnawed on the end of her quill and gazed out the window at her colleagues. They were dashing around the green and kicking a leather ball in a loose game of Glak. The preparation of Tigh's argument had taken longer than she usually spent on a case, and her regular course work had suffered. So, while her friends showed off creative techniques at playing Glak, she had to catch up on writing assigned essays. Anyway, she mused as she smiled, Tigh was well worth missing a game of Glak over.

Jame enjoyed the time she spent with the quiet warrior. They had developed a kind of rapport and found they could comfortably work together. Everyone else looked at her as if she had sprung wings when she told them she wasn't having any problems with Tigh. But the others refused to see beyond Tigh the Terrible. Jame found it sad because she discovered in Tigh a sweet, almost shy woman with a wry sense of humor that seeped into their interactions.

A hard click of boots against the wood floor of the common room captured Jame's attention. Many of the arbiters wore soft-soled boots so they wouldn't disturb the studious quiet of the school. She took in the fine cut of clothing worn by the approaching pair before she noticed the woman had startling familiar features.

"Jamelin Ketlas?" an older version of Tigh asked, as the pair stopped on the threshold of the chamber.

"Yes." Jame put down her quill and stood to greet her visitors.

This was a surprise. One of the sad tragedies of the rehabilitation process was that too many of the Guards' parents had turned their backs on their children once the true nature of the enhancements had been revealed. Tigh was probably the last Guard anyone would suspect of having a supportive family.

"I'm Paldon Tigis and this is my life companion, Joul," Paldon said. "We're here for Paldar's hearing tomorrow and were so looking forward to meeting you that we sought you out right away. We hope we're not disturbing you."

"Oh, no." Jame waved a hand at her desk strewn with books and paper. "Just catching up on some schoolwork. There's a small parlor where we can go and talk, if you'd like."

"As long as we're not keeping you from your work, we'd very much like to chat with you for a while," Paldon said.

Jame didn't have much personal experience with Ingorans but still recognized the almost legendary politeness and ability to put others at ease that made them the best merchants in the Southern Territories. It also put her on her guard because they were notorious for striking bargains that made the other person feel they were the ones getting the better deal. She couldn't imagine why they would want anything other than the full rehabilitation of their daughter.

"Tigh is also my work." Jame smiled as she led them to a small chamber furnished with several hide chairs and a low table. She lit a fire and hung the always full pot of water over the flame.

"First off," Paldon began as they settled into the chairs, "we both want to thank you for taking Paldar's case. We know there's been some doubts from all parties involved, including our daughter, about a positive outcome to this endeavor. But we have no doubt that she not only can rejoin society but will be a welcome asset to it."

"That's very refreshing to hear, Merchant Tigis," Jame said. "So many parents have turned their backs on their children during the cleansing process."

Paldon gave Jame the perfect self-confident smile of a merchant. "They just don't understand that once the enhancements are removed, their children are back to who they were before with one very important difference. They now have new skills and experiences that can only strengthen whoever they were before they were recruited into the Guards."

Jame politely nodded and turned to the fireplace, pulled three mugs off a shelf, and pinched some herbs into each of them. A flowery fragrance tickled her nostrils as she poured the boiling water over the herbs.

She knew that everyone, from the healers to the Tribunal to the parents of the Guards, had set ideas on what the cleansing process was supposed to accomplish. None of these ideas reflected the reality but it didn't seem to matter as long as their self-delusions weren't contradicted.

"It does take the cleansed Guard time to adjust to being the way they used to be." Jame decided the best strategy was to remain noncommittal until she understood Paldon's reasoning.

"That's why we're pleased with the rehabilitation program," Paldon said as she and Joul accepted the mugs of tea. "It's very thorough and well regulated. Unfortunately, our concern is not with the efforts all of you are making in returning the Guards to society. We're concerned about Paldar's reluctance to go through the process."

"It's a natural reaction," Jame said. "Some Guards have a harder time adjusting than others."

Paldon frowned. "That's what we don't understand. She was such a well-adjusted child, well on her way to becoming an excellent merchant, with the combination of her striking looks and a wonderful presence that is the greatest gift a merchant can possess. Even as a youngster, she could smooth talk her way through a bargain as well as many of the established merchants. She truly had the gift."

"We were very proud of her." Joul's gentle eyes creased in fond memory.

"You can imagine our concern that she seems to have lost this gift," Paldon said. "We barely recognize our daughter in that withdrawn, uncommunicative young woman hiding in that tiny room."

Jame composed her demeanor and words, understanding both the flaws in the rehabilitation process and that Tigh was not the person her parents seemed to think she was. According to Pendon, her behavior had been an act until she escaped to pursue what she really wanted to do. Jame could relate to Tigh's motivation, having done the same thing herself at the same age. The difference was, Tigh never had the opportunity to pursue her dream and now the faulty cleansing created a new Tigh needing new paths to follow.

"She's only been through the first two steps in the process." Jame realized Tigh now had two battles to face—gaining her freedom from the Military Tribunal and her parents' expectations. "I'm sure you'll see a difference once she's around people again." Jame was certain there'd be a difference, just not what Tigh's parents expected.

Paldon smiled. "That puts our minds at ease. We know the healers mean well, but sometimes their evaluations can be a little too clinical and optimistic. But arbiters are trained to look at situations from all sides and form fair judgments. We know you'll do everything you can to help Paldar so she can return to her place in the House of Tigis."

Jame took the compliment with a gracious smile but wondered how much easier life would be if people weren't continually pressured to meet someone else's expectations.

PALDON TIGIS'S WORDS came back to Jame as she paused before Tigh's door. A miserable looking Tigh was slumped forward with her elbows on her knees and hands buried in her hair. This certainly wasn't the lively, smooth-talking young woman Paldon had described.

Jame slipped the key into the lock and opened the door. She hoped they could stop this nonsense of locking Tigh's door after the hearing. She hoped her argument was strong enough to allow Tigh to go on to the next step in her rehabilitation.

"We still have a sandmark before the hearing," Jame said.

Tigh nodded, not raising her head.

Jame sat at the little desk. "Your parents stopped by last night."

"My parents," Tigh said to the floor.

"They're here for the hearing." Jame watched with fascination Tigh's body language.

"For the hearing," Tigh repeated as if trying to figure out a riddle.

"They're concerned for your well-being." Jame noted the rigidity in Tigh's shoulders.

"Concerned," Tigh muttered through a ragged breath.

"They seem to think you should be as you were before you were recruited." Tigh remained silent.

Jame opened her mouth then paused, then made the decision of trust. "You know, I'm here against my aunt's wishes. I begged her for years to allow me to attend this school and to train to be an arbiter. My aunt still thinks I'll go quietly home after my training is complete. I didn't have the heart to tell her I wanted to pursue this profession until I have to return home."

"I was going to run away," Tigh mumbled to the floor.

Jame stayed still, not wanting to spook her.

"To Artocia. I studied on the sly to gain the knowledge requirements to enter the University." Tigh looked up at Jame. "You're destined to become Queen of Emoria."

Jame sucked in a startled breath.

"I've been asking around." Tigh gave her a sheepish look. "I'm the first-born daughter of the House of Tigis. That means I'm destined to inherit the family business."

"And you were going to run away from that?" Jame asked.

"Gladly," Tigh said. "Unlike you, I don't have to return at some point in my life to become this person everyone expects me to be. I have two younger sisters who can do the job just as well."

"I'm resigned to the fact that I'll rule Emoria someday," Jame said. "But I feel my life is so much more than waiting for that day."

"How do you plan to do what you want?" Tigh asked.

"The only way is to stay away from home." Jame shrugged, fighting the conflicting emotions the idea invoked.

"Away." Tigh nodded. "But you don't want to be forced to do that."

Jame sighed. "No. I love my aunt and Emoria, but I'll stay away if that's what it takes."

Tigh studied her hands. "Maybe your aunt will eventually come around."

Jame grinned at the warmth that seeped through her from Tigh's sincere words and at the knowledge that she had found some cracks in Tigh's reserve.

NEVER IN HER two years as an assistant arbiter had Jame seen more than a score of people in the spectator seats of the hearing chamber. All of the available five score seats were filled and the walls of the airy chamber were lined three people deep.

From her seat in the defendants' box to one side of the Tribunal's bench, Jame recognized her own peers, younger students from the school, and quite a few healers. Tigh's parents, sporting supportive expressions, sat in the front row, which was reserved for close family and friends of the Guard and any person of importance who attended the hearing.

Next to the Tigis clan were several representatives from the Federation Council, each wearing the colors of their territory. Jame, feeling a touch of nervousness, studied the quiet group. She had not expected the Federation Council to take such a visible interest in this hearing. After all, it was just the first in a series of hearings a Guard had to go through before the rehabilitation process was complete.

"What's wrong?" Tigh whispered.

"The Council has sent some observers," Jame said.

"That's not normal?" Tigh rubbed her palms on her spotless white leggings.

"I've never seen them attend a hearing before." Jame put a hand on one of Tigh's restless hands.

Tigh stared at the hand on her own. "If, uh . . . If it doesn't work out today, it won't be your fault."

Jame whipped her head around and stared at Tigh. "But—"

"Listen to me," Tigh whispered as her power to command attention seeped through. "You have the best strategy for my case. If the Tribunal doesn't rule in our favor, that means they're not interested in being fair or in setting me free."

Jame shook her head, not wanting to believe it. "What's the use if they treat these hearings as a farce?"

Tigh's eyes softened into admiration. "I take back what I just said. I don't think the Tribunal stands a chance against you."

Jame opened her mouth but the spectators quieted. The Tribunal was ready to enter. She realized she had to win for the simple reason that Tigh had that much faith in her, and she didn't want to let her down.

The small door on the opposite side of the Tribunal's bench scraped open. The seven brown-robed Tribunes swept in and settled onto their cushioned seats behind a deep stone table. Jame was pleased to observe they were also surprised to see the Federation Council representatives. At least there wasn't a concerted conspiracy against Tigh.

Sitas Largrun occupied the middle seat of the Tribunal's bench, a distinction, Jame noted, Sitas didn't look happy about. The Tribune occupying the middle seat had to keep order and the presence of Tigh the Terrible was too volatile to hope this overflow of curious onlookers would remain passive throughout the hearing. The whispers were already in the air after the respectful silence at the Tribunal's entrance.

"Keeper of the Bench, bring the chamber to order." Sitas nodded at the uniformed soldier who stood by the Tribunal bench.

The Keeper of the Bench raised a hollowed metal tube dangling on a short chain and struck it three times with a metal stick.

With the chamber silent, Sitas studied the top sheet of a neat pile of paper. "Our first case today is the hearing for Paldar Tigis to pass on to step three of the Guard rehabilitation program. She'll be represented by assistant arbiter, Jamelin Ketlas." She glanced up at the spectators. "We don't expect this hearing to be any different from the others that have been presented here. If any of you are here because you think something interesting is going to happen, I suggest you find a better way to spend your time." The spectators remained still. "Very well. You may take the floor, Jamelin."

Arguing cases before the Tribunal and a handful of concerned relatives and friends gave Jame little preparation for facing close to two hundred people who, she knew, were going to soak up her every word and movement. The only thing that gave her confidence as she stood up was that Tigh thought she was capable of arguing her case.

Jame grounded herself by clasping her hands behind her back. "First off, we'd like to thank the Tribunal for allowing us to present this case before them. Second, we'd like to thank all those who have taken time from their busy day to come witness this case."

That wasn't a part of the formalities and more than one puzzled look flashed across the spectators' faces.

"And last, I'd like to thank Tigh for allowing me to present her case. It has been a profound honor to work with her."

Jame hid a smile at the spectators' surprised expressions.

"I'm here to help Paldar Tigis of Ingor pass to the next level in her rehabilitation." Jame turned to the Tribunal. "She's been successfully cleansed, and the Board of Healers has determined she's mentally ready to interact with other people. In most cases I've both defended and witnessed, these two factors have been enough to allow a former Guard to pass through to the next step. But Tigh was not an ordinary Guard, nor has she been an ordinary patient through the rehabilitation process. Because of this, there's been concern that the cleansing hasn't worked as well on her as with the other Guards."

The Tribunal shifted and exchanged quick glances.

"Since the concerns that have reached my ears have been vague, I haven't been able to form specific arguments to address them." Jame noted the odd combination of curiosity and unsettlement in the Tribunes' faces. "So, if the Tribunal will permit, I wish to conduct this hearing according to Bailikon's procedure."

Sharp gasps followed by low stunned twitters filled the chamber. The words "foolhardy" and "crazy" rose above the others.

"Your boldness is refreshing, Jamelin," Sitas said. "But let me take this opportunity to remind you that only Bailikon, herself, has ever been successful in presenting a case according to her own procedures."

"Thank you for the reminder, Tribune Sitas." Jame bowed her head. "I'm well aware of the odds of making a successful case following this procedure. Bailikon possessed an exceptional gift. But I also know it's the only means I have to present Paldar Tigis's case with any chance of a successful argument. So, I stand by my request."

"Do all the Tribunes accept Bailikon's procedures?" Sitas looked to either side of her.

Her colleagues' expressions ranged from intrigue to outrage. Onderal, a small, compact man with a tight grim face, let the anger smolder in his eyes but he nodded a terse agreement.

"You may continue, Jamelin."

"Thank you, Tribune Sitas," Jame said. "According to Bailikon's rules the argument for the defense is built from a series of agreements between the arbiter and the Tribunal. Each agreement is accepted as inarguable truth upon which the case can grow. In other words, it's my job to figure out what you will accept as a successful defense of Paldar Tigis."

The rumble from the chamber grew so loud that Sitas signaled the Keeper of the Bench, twice, to sound the chime for silence.

"Some members of the Tribunal have not been shy in voicing their doubts that Tigh the Terrible's cleansing has been less than successful," Jame said. "Two days ago, outside this chamber, I overheard Tribune Onderal state that Tigh was pretending to be cleansed. Certainly, a member of the Tribunal would never make such a statement unless there was evidence to back it up. So, my first question is, what evidence has Tribune Onderal uncovered to come to such a conclusion?"

"Why didn't you ask me when I allegedly made that statement?" Onderal leveled an intense gaze at Jame. "Or is it easier just to make things up and turn a hearing into a street corner carnival?"

"I think Tribune Ewan will recall that I tried to ask but you interrupted my question, telling me not to bother you and then you entered your private chamber," Jame said.

Onderal sneered. "So, you're now implying that Tribune Ewan heard me make this statement?"

"You made the statement to Tribune Ewan," Jame said.

Ewan, a thin, fidgety woman of advanced age, darted uncertain glances at Onderal. "I believe Tribune Onderal was simply making an offhand observation."

"Excuse me for being a little confused. But aren't we supposed to maintain discretion about voicing opinions that concern pending hearings, especially in a public place?" Jame knew that Onderal was notorious for making offhand judgments and statements, but most people were too afraid of the power of the Tribunal to challenge him on it. Given the choice between fear of the Tribunal and defending Tigh, there was no choice as far as she was concerned.

"We're only human," Sitas said.

"So does that mean you don't think Tigh is pretending to be cleansed?" Jame asked.

Onderal glared at Jame. "I haven't given it much thought, one way or the other."

"You haven't given it much thought, yet you state an opinion on it in public." Jame gazed at Onderal with sincere confusion. "Let me approach this from another direction. What would it take to prove Tigh is not pretending to be cleansed?"

Sitas stared at Jame. "What would it take?"

"Yes. What do I have to do to prove that Tigh has been cleansed and is ready to take the next step in her rehabilitation?"

Tribune Acran rubbed her ample chin in thought. "We'd have to think of a way to prove she isn't violent anymore."

"We're all violent under certain circumstances, Tribune Acran," Jame said. "How do you propose to distinguish between our thresholds of violence and Tigh's?"

Onderal stood up. Incredulous anger radiated from him. "Threshold? There is no threshold. There's a gaping hole that she could leap through at the least provocation."

Jame struggled to keep from grinning as her insides whooped with hopeful joy. Tigh's strategy worked. Irritate the weakest point of the enemy and they'll defeat themselves.

"Define least provocation," Jame said.

Onderal gazed at Jame. "Any provocation."

"So if someone came at her with a knife, what would happen?" Jame asked.

Onderal crossed his arms. "She'd kill that person without thought."

"What if she wasn't taken by surprise? What if she knew someone was going to come at her with a knife such as in practice?"

"She'd kill that person," Onderal said. "That's why Guards weren't allowed to practice their skills on living things. It was the one flaw in the enhancements."

Jame was sure Tigh had a thing or two to say about that.

"Does the Tribunal agree, if the cleansing was not successful, Tigh would kill anyone who raised a hand to her?" Jame cast steady eyes over the seven Tribunes.

Sitas looked at each of her colleagues and received hesitant affirmative nods.

"If that's the case," a rough voice roared from the standees along the wall behind the defendants' box, "I have a fifty-fifty chance of ridding the world of Tigh the Terrible."

A tall, battle-hardened woman in leather-armor sprang from the spectators along the side wall with a knife flashing in the filtered light. She reached a hand over the low back of the defendants' box, pulled Tigh up off the bench, and pressed the blade against her neck.

Shock cascaded over the hall as a handful of soldiers approached the assailant who let go of Tigh and handed the knife to Jame.

"She was just helping me with my demonstration," Jame said to the soldiers. "Thank you for your help, Tanley."

The warrior, eyes filled with respect, nodded and returned to the back of the chamber.

Tigh sank onto the bench.

Jame turned to the Tribunal. "Do we need to continue?"

"Give us a sandmark to deliberate," Sitas said.

The Tribunal stood and swept through the little door near the bench.

Jame's knees gave out, and she sat down hard on the bench. A tentative hand took hers and gave it a squeeze. She turned her head and all her nervousness and apprehension faded at the pride in Tigh's eyes.

Chapter 8

JAME WATCHED THE restless audience as they spun out opinions and speculations on the brief but dramatic proceedings. She sighed at the heated discussions amongst students and assistant arbiters. This was going to be the only subject worthy of discussion for weeks to come. She wondered if she could move into the wagon house until her well-meaning peers found something new to talk about.

She shifted her eyes to Tigh. She knew that Tigh was in a meditative state, and she'd give anything to learn how to shut everything out and weave a contented inner world to inhabit for a while.

Tigh seemed to be confident that Jame had waged a victorious battle, and the Tribunal's or her peers' opinion of her bold attempt to follow Bailikon's procedure weren't as important to her as Tigh's praise. To have the former Supreme Commander of the forces that led the Southern Territories to victory compliment her on her courtroom strategy cleared away any doubts that she was destined to be a good arbiter.

Jame slid her gaze to a corner of the chamber where the Federation Council representatives were clustered. She prayed the Tribunes weren't being pressured into making a less than fair decision.

The small door leading to the Tribunal's chamber creaked open and the spectators quickly retook their seats.

The seven Tribunes shuffled in and settled behind the bench. Sitas didn't have to ask the Keeper of the Bench to bring the house to order. The quiet was so deep Jame swore she heard the sand filtering through the sandmark clock.

"Will the defendant rise," Sitas said.

All eyes went to the defendants' box.

Jame and Tigh stood and exchanged brief glances.

"Every once in a while someone comes along who displays a special talent for arguing a case," Sitas said. "Jamelin Ketlas, possessing the legendary daring of her Emoran ancestry, has fashioned a new approach to Bailikon's procedure. Having heard many cases from Jamelin over the past two years, we know she most likely has several more equally compelling arguments prepared for this case."

Jame tried not to grin at Sitis's inquiring gaze.

Sitas nodded. "Since it's been proven that Paldar Tigis no longer possesses the impulse to kill when provoked and given the signed certificates that she has successfully passed through the first two steps of rehabilitation, there isn't a sound reason to keep her from taking the next step."

A murmur rose up from the spectators. Sitas lifted her hand for silence.

"Like any other Guard going through rehabilitation, this decision will be reversed if the Guard displays any behavior that is considered dangerous to others. We now place Paldar Tigis in the care of the counselors." Sitas looked at the Keeper of the Bench. "Next case."

Jame didn't realize she'd been holding her breath until Sitas finished speaking and she swayed from lack of air. A hand on her shoulder snapped her back to reality, and she took a long breath of relief. She turned to Tigh and witnessed a joyful glint in her eyes and a grin tugging at her mouth. *I did that. By the waterfalls of Laur, she has a wonderful smile.*

Jadic and a slender, light-haired woman in a white tunic and leggings approached the defendants' box. Jame and Tigh stepped through the knee-high door, finally free from the ordeal.

"It'd be my luck to follow your brilliance," Jadic said. He backed up and side-stepped around Tigh into the box.

Jame smiled at Jadic. "You'll do great."

"Good luck," Tigh said softly to the young Guard.

"Thank you," the Guard murmured as she raised sad, knowing eyes to her former commander.

"They say it gets better after this," Tigh said.

"Thank you, Commander." The young Guard straightened and stepped into the box.

"That was a nice thing to do," Jame said as they walked to the door that led to the defendants' chamber.

Tigh gave her a surprised look. "I hope she believes it because it won't happen unless she does."

A straight-backed woman, dressed in the deep greens and pale yellows that were the colors of Ingor, stepped in front of them.

"I'd like a word with you," the woman said in a voice that told Jame she was used to getting her way. "I'm Rantigar Wentis, the Federation Council representative for Ingor."

"Jamelin Ketlas," Jame said.

"Did I hear the Tribune say that you're from Emoria?" Rantigar studied Jame as if she were a piece of merchandise.

Jame nodded. "Yes."

Rantigar frowned. "There weren't any Ingoran arbiters available?"

"The choice of arbiter is up to the defendant." Jame held back a rising anger at this arrogant woman.

Rantigar turned to Tigh. "You didn't ask for an Ingoran?"

Tigh shrugged. "I rejected the Ingoran arbiter. I accepted the Emoran arbiter. No further discussion or explanation is necessary."

Rantigar opened her mouth, then shut it. Jame thought it interesting that she hadn't been prepared for an argument.

"Will Jamelin continue as your arbiter?" Rantigar asked. "There are several more hearings to go and perhaps the Ingoran would be better suited for those."

"Jame will continue as my arbiter as long as she consents to represent me." Tigh sounded confident but Jame caught her questioning glance and, barely able to keep away a grin, nodded in agreement.

"Don't make too hasty a decision," Rantigar said. "And don't hesitate to let me know if there's anything I can do to help. We're all anxious for you to return to Ingor where you belong. Good day to both of you." Not surprising, she went to Tigh's parents who waited in the doorway.

"Did you really mean that? About letting me represent you?" Jame asked as they ducked through the door to the defendants' chamber where a pile of papers awaited their signatures.

"Of course." Tigh looked surprised. "As long as you want to represent me." Her voice held a hint of uncertainty.

"I want to continue to represent you," Jame said as the happy realization she was going to spend more time with this intriguing woman washed over her.

GOODEMER'S ENTHUSIASM WANED as the open top coach they sat in left the foothills behind and rumbled through a scruffy arid land. Although they were north of Maymi, the midday heat was sharper, and the ground was not the rich black soil she was used to but dull tan sand that looked as if it had never been touched by rain.

"What interesting looking plants." Yana gazed at the oddly shaped low-lying vegetation covered with delicate brown needles. "I thought sand was only found on beaches."

"This is a desert," Minchof said.

"And people actually live in such a place?" Goodemer asked.

"Ynit is on the southern edge of the desert." Minchof rubbed her chin. "The dry climate makes it ideal for year around training of soldiers. The military compound was built first, and then the city grew up around it through the centuries. You'll find the architecture much different than what we're used to in Maymi. They've learned to fashion bricks from this sand. In fact, we should be seeing the outer walls very soon." Minchof held onto the top edge of the coach and lifted her stocky frame to see over the back of the vehicle. "Just as I thought. You can all look but don't jostle the carriage too much."

Goodemer, Yana, and a rangy young man named Tret, twisted on the hard bench and watched as the tall sand wall of Ynit rose from the desert floor.

"It's huge," Yana said.

Minchof smiled at their wide-eyed enthusiasm. "It's not as large as Artocia or Ingor, but it's a good size city."

The coach veered away from the gaping main gate of the city, and the apprentices flashed inquisitive glances at Minchof.

"Where are we going?" Tret asked, nervously eyeing the coach driver.

"To the military compound." Minchof grinned. "It's on the south side of the city and has its own gate."

The architecture shifted from the ornamental display of the city buildings they had glimpsed over the wall to an austere uniform facade. The coach slowed and stopped next to the gatehouse. A sleepy-eyed soldier, squinting against the intense sunlight, stepped from the building. Minchof handed her a scroll with the seal of the Federation Council stamped onto it.

"Quarters have been prepared for you," the soldier said and gave the instructions to the driver.

The adobe brick plaza that extended before them took Goodemer's breath away. She had read the immense brooding buildings bordering the square had been built to accommodate both the armies and the military headquarters for the Southern Territories. It was eerily deserted, reminding her that the army was gone except for the small peacetime regiment.

A disconcerting feeling clung to Goodemer as the coach, the only disturbance in the quiet, rattled toward a small lane between what looked like barracks.

The doors of a larger building flung open and noisy, excited people surged onto the plaza where the coach passed close by. The jarring contrast to the previous emptiness and silence rocked Goodemer's apprehension about this much too foreign place. The coach squeaked to a stop as the crowd clustered unheeding around it.

Goodemer could feel the people's excitement vibrating in the air. Something extraordinary had just happened. She gently probed the random magic around them and determined that no spells had been cast. The atmosphere shifted and focused back to the building. She twisted around but saw nothing out of the ordinary in the trickle of people walking through the doorway. Except . . . everyone stepped away from a tall woman in white who kept her eyes on the ground. Another smaller young woman with shaggy light hair led the taller woman around the crowd.

Minchof leaned forward and said, "It looks like a hearing has taken place. Hearings before the Tribunal are a part of the rehabilitation of the former

Guards. That one must have been a member of the Elite Guard to be receiving this kind of reception."

A shiver ran through Goodemer despite the midday heat.

"I didn't know they were still rehabilitating them." Tret eyed the passive looking dark-haired woman.

"I don't think all the Guards have been captured yet." Minchof studied the white clad woman with interest. "But that isn't our concern. We're here to make sure something like this never happens again."

The coach lurched forward, and Goodemer turned to watch the progress of the odd-looking pair to the massive fortress-like building that dominated one side of the plaza. She didn't need to open up her newly discovered skills at detecting changes in atmosphere to feel the flow of energy between them.

Interesting, she mused. The desire to know their story washed over her and she latched onto it with the single-minded focus of a fourteen-year-old.

TIGH STARED AT the enthusiastic counselor, wondering if she realized how crazy her words sounded.

"I know you don't believe me now, but we've discovered that this is the best starting point for reintroducing Guards back into society," Renat Yinga said.

Tigh leveled a pained look at Renat. "By scaring the injury or illness out of the patient?"

Renat blinked at Tigh then emitted an uncertain laugh. "A sense of humor is good. You'll spend the first few weeks observing and assisting the healers. This'll allow you time to get used to the infirmary and for the patients to get used to seeing you around. We'll meet every other day and discuss how you're doing."

Tigh found herself wishing Jame was next to her murmuring reassuring words in her ear. Jame had a way of soothing away her uncertainties. Jame had a way of almost reading what she was feeling. The idea was both frightening and comforting.

Renat scribbled a few lines on a piece of paper. "Give this to Bede Komlic. He's in charge of the injury ward in the infirmary."

Tigh took the paper and stared at the strong handwriting. "Are you sure this is a good idea?"

She had avoided people for two years and since her capture never had to deal with more than a handful in a single day. To be surrounded all day by people whose initial reaction was fear was enough to fray her nerves to the point where she could fulfill their fears of violence. Remembering the blind uncontrolled rage that had supposedly been cleansed away, she was more afraid of herself than they were of her.

"Every Guard begins their journey back to society by working in the infirmary," Renat said. "There have never been any problems."

"You know my cleansing wasn't like the others," Tigh said. "How can you be so sure I won't snap and do harm instead of healing?"

"You've always been a unique case," Renat said. "But I trust Pendon's judgment on this. If the cleansing hadn't been successful, your behavior would have reflected it by now. Go to the infirmary and give it a chance. If you need to talk between our scheduled meetings, my door is always open."

Tigh knew she'd rather talk to Jame. She was the only person who understood her fears and her ambitions. For that matter, Jame was the only person she had learned to trust. Maybe if things got too rough for her, she could seek out Jame's advice. The idea of approaching someone for help because she was a friend left her lightheaded. She had a friend.

Bolstered by this wondrous thought, Tigh nodded. "I'll give it a try."

"JAME."

Jame turned at the sound of quick light steps echoing in the main corridor of the fortress and saw Pendon Larke hurrying after her.

"Good morning, Pendon," Jame said.

"Good morning to you, Jame," Pendon said. "I've been wanting to talk to you about the fine work you did in handling Tigh's case."

"Thank you, but I was just doing my job." Jame studied the floor to hide the rise of warmth to her cheeks.

The last couple of days had been embarrassing for her, to say the least. She had to endure endless compliments, and everyone seemed to want to get to know her better. Some of the more ambitious student arbiters were only interested in her abrupt notoriety, while others in the compound recognized that being friends with the skillful future Queen of Emoria was a sound political move. What surprised her was the shy worship she saw in the eyes of the young student arbiters who took to following her around, not to mention the numerous invitations to dinner or for an evening in Ynit.

"That was more than just doing your job and you know it," Pendon said. "I observed Tigh during the hearing, and she responds to you differently than she does to everyone else. She trusts you and likes you. Consider these things a gift and handle them appropriately."

"I consider her a friend," Jame said. "And thank you for not warning me to be wary of her and to not get too close."

"There's a better chance of you hurting her than the other way around," Pendon said, laying a thin hand on Jame's arm.

"I know," Jame said. "I want to be her friend, and I'll do everything I can to help her through this ordeal. I would never hurt her."

Pendon studied Jame for several heartbeats. "I'm pleased she's found a trusted friend."

Jame glanced at the sandmark clock at the end of the corridor. "Oh no. I'm almost late for class."

Pendon laughed and waved her on her way. "Get going. Can't do for the defender of Tigh the Terrible to be late for class."

Jame grinned. "Thank you for having faith in Tigh."

She hurried down the corridor, rounded the sharp corner to a back wing of the building, and stopped as if an invisible wall blocked her way.

Tigh was walking toward her—slumped shouldered with hands hooked under a loose low-riding belt. She was oblivious to people passing her, off in another world as far as Jame could tell.

"Tigh," Jame said.

Tigh looked up, startled. She straightened and shuffled to the wall, as if being out in the middle of the corridor was too conspicuous for her.

"Hey," she said.

Jame was unexplainably happy to see Tigh again although it had only been two days since the hearing. "Have you met with the counselor yet?"

Tigh nodded. "I have to report to the infirmary tomorrow."

"All the Guards start out in the infirmary." Jame wondered why she felt tongue-tied.

"That's what the counselor told me." Tigh scuffed the toe of her boot against the worn floorboards.

"I'd like to hear about what you learn there." Jame just wanted to spend time with Tigh and get to know her better. "Would you, uh, be interested in joining me for the evening meal tomorrow night? You can tell me all about your first day."

Tigh looked so astonished that Jame was afraid she'd say no.

"All right," Tigh said.

"Great. I'm late for class. I'll pick you up at the infirmary." Jame trotted down the corridor. She glanced back several times at Tigh and smiled at the stunned gaze following after her.

"I'M LOOKING FOR Bede Komlic," Tigh mumbled to the assistant healer seated at a small table in the foyer of the infirmary.

"Ah, we've been expecting you. I'm Pakar, assistant healer." The young woman with the black hair and the healthy bronzed skin of the people of Ynit smiled at Tigh. "Bede will be here when the sand hits the quarter mark."

Tigh raised an eyebrow. "Can you foresee the future?"

Pakar laughed. "Bede always walks through the door when the sand hits the quarter mark. He says, 'good morning,' then he walks into the ward and checks the overnight reports. Then he comes back in here and asks if there's anything that needs his attention. It never varies. Ular, who has worked here for thirty years, says she's never known him to deviate from this routine."

Tigh pondered this for a heartbeat as a long absent hint of mischief lurked around the corners of her mind. She wandered to the opened double doors of the long ward and peeked in. She saw the overnight reports and slipped them under a pile of papers next to them.

"Please, have a seat," Pakar called.

Tigh wandered back into the foyer with a nonchalant expression. "I think I'll wait outside." She sauntered out the door before Pakar could respond.

She knew she was acting like a mischievous child, but it helped take away her apprehension. Besides, she'd have something amusing to tell Jame.

She wanted to hear Jame's laughter again. It rang so sweetly in her ears. She still couldn't believe Jame had invited her to share the evening meal in a public place, even if was only a mess hall within the compound. But it also meant being with Jame for no other reason than two friends sharing a meal. The thought took her breath away.

She snapped back to her current challenge and looked around, putting her solid problem-solving skills to use. She wasn't interested in the easiest solution to the challenge she set up for herself. That defeated the purpose of making the exercise as absurd as possible.

Delicate vines that weren't indigenous to the arid climate of Ynit clung to the adobe wall of the infirmary. Tigh noticed that all of the plants on either side of the doorway looked as out of place as a mountain cat in Maymi. Their neat arrangement and meticulous care told her that these were someone's serious hobby. Her ability to absorb and retain much of what she read allowed her to make the connection between Bede's name and the upper coast of the Nirlion Sea where these plants grew.

"Let's see what it takes to get healer Bede to forget about his daily ritual." Tigh pulled several tendrils of the vine away from the wall. Much to her delight they were long and pliable. She found a few more vines on the other side the door and laid them on the ground so it looked as if the tendrils coming from opposite directions were reaching out to each other with the ends not quite touching.

Satisfied with her handiwork, Tigh strolled to a small bench in front of the nearby visitors' quarters and sat as if enjoying the clear morning air. She didn't have long to wait before the object of her experiment strode out of a tiny lane that led to the cluster of houses where many of the people who worked within the compound lived. As Tigh had hoped, the thin, rather intense man of middle age, kept his eyes riveted on the ground as if concentrating on not letting anything distract him from his morning ritual.

Tigh wished Jame was there to witness the comical expression on Bede's face when he stopped in mid-stride and stared at the vegetation strewn across his path.

"That's impossible." Tigh's keen hearing picked up Bede's mutterings. "Wizards. That's it. Those young wizards are practicing their mischief."

Bede returned the vines to their proper places.

Tigh ghosted to the door in time to see Pakar's relief as Bede strode into the foyer. Instead of "good morning," he muttered "wizards" as he walked through the doorway into the ward.

Tigh sauntered in and grinned at Pakar's astonished expression. Without pausing she followed Bede.

The poor man stared at the small table where the overnight reports were supposed to be.

"My reports. They're always right there." He looked up and down the ward as if he didn't know what to do.

Tigh felt a little guilty about upsetting Bede's daily ritual. Something, she realized, Tigh the Terrible would never have felt. She pulled the bundle of paper from beneath a stack of ledgers next to the door.

"Is this what you're looking for?"

Bede spun around. His astonished brown eyes first took in Tigh and then focused on what she held in her hands.

"My reports." He looked as if his world had turned right side up. "Thank you. You have no idea what kind of day it's been. Bede Komlic. You must be the new intern. Tigh, isn't it? Come this way. We'll get you settled in."

Tigh arched an eyebrow at the lack of reaction to her name and trailed after him.

Chapter 9

JAME TRIED TO ignore the flutter in her stomach as she approached the infirmary. She shouldn't feel nervous about meeting a friend for an evening meal. A friend she had spent the day thinking about in anticipation of this simple sharing of a meal. Argis never made her stomach flutter like this. She resolutely pushed Argis out of her mind. She entered the calm quiet of the infirmary foyer and her nervousness eased a bit.

Pakar looked up. "Ah, Jame. May I help you?"

Jame smiled. "I'm just waiting for Tigh."

Pakar nodded. "Our new intern." Her expression was both pleased and puzzled. "She certainly made quite a first impression on healer Bede."

"I bet she did," Jame murmured.

"I've never seen him take to someone as quickly as he took to her," Pakar said. "He went on and on about her tidy and efficient mind and how she seemed to understand his idea of order."

Jame realized she was staring at Pakar and searched around for a response. "She's a very tidy person."

"Ah, there she is now." Pakar smiled at the doorway to the ward.

Tigh, with an inscrutable expression, was trying to concentrate on what Bede was telling her as he walked her into the foyer.

"Don't worry about the reactions of some of the patients," Bede said as Tigh's eyes met Jame's. "They're always a little nervous around new interns."

Tigh gave him a confused look. "Uh, yes. Thank you."

"We'll see you back here after the morning meal tomorrow," Bede said. "Have a nice evening."

"You, too," Tigh said as she grinned at Jame.

"You look none the worse for wear," Jame said.

"Uh, it wasn't as bad as I thought it would be." Tigh glanced at Pakar, who smiled at her.

"That's good." Jame had been worried about how Tigh would react to this strange new environment.

They stepped out into a still warm evening as the sun splashed the thin clouds on the horizon with intense oranges and reds. Jame knew the desert air would be chilled after dark.

"The sunset is beautiful tonight." She stopped to watch the hues intensify on the clouds.

"Yes. Beautiful," Tigh said.

"Where do you want to eat?" Jame turned to Tigh, who snapped her eyes to the ground.

"Your choice." Tigh's voice was husky. She cleared her throat.

"Do you have a favorite place?" Jame asked, fascinated by Tigh's behavior. She'd witnessed similar reactions many times in Emor when tough warriors were smitten by that infamous invisible foe they had no defense against.

"I take my meals in my room," Tigh said.

"Where did you have your midday meal today?" Jame took in Tigh's sheepish expression. "You didn't eat?"

"I, uh." Tigh scuffed her boot on the adobe brick ground. "I'm not very comfortable eating by myself. Surrounded by people, I mean."

"What about eating with someone else? Surrounded by people?" Jame asked.

Tigh lifted her eyes. "That depends on who the someone else is."

"I hope I qualify, since that's what we're about to do," Jame said.

Tigh looked back at the ground. "You qualify."

Jame couldn't believe Tigh was actually blushing. She touched Tigh's arm. "Let's go somewhere special."

JAME LED TIGH into a lane that spiked off the massive plaza. On either side of them were narrow mismatched buildings that looked as if they would all fall if one of them collapsed. Tigh remembered the blacksmith and tanner, amongst other crafts people, worked out of these buildings.

The wall surrounding Ynit proper stood in their way. Tigh gave Jame a questioning look.

"This way." Jame walked down a narrow alley that fronted the wall to a small door with a sword and bow etched on it tucked behind an outbuilding that partially blocked their way.

Jame grinned at Tigh's surprised expression and rapped on the door. A small panel slid open then closed.

The door opened, and Jame and Tigh entered a corridor where the smells and the dull clank of utensils against metal pots told them the kitchen was nearby.

"Well met, my princess." The small white-haired woman acknowledged Jame with a slight bow of her head.

"Well met, Otlar," Jame said. "This is my friend, Tigh. We're here for the evening meal."

Otlar flicked her eyes over Tigh. "Well met, Tigh."

"Well met, Otlar." Tigh wondered a bit about the ritual greeting. Like just about everyone in the Southern Territories, she knew very little about Emoran culture.

"Please, come this way." Otlar led them past the open door of the sprawling kitchen and through the back entryway into the common room.

After two years of avoiding all human contact and then the months of limited interaction within the compound, a bittersweet nostalgia flooded through Tigh. The sounds and smells hit her senses, bringing back the more pleasant experiences of being a Guard. She had spent long nights in establishments such as this as they celebrated victories and wore down their overabundant energy after battle.

Tigh had heard of Emoran safe houses but had never been inside one. She took in the fireplaces on three walls, lit more for light than for heat at that time of year. Oil lamps made up for most of the deep amber glow of the room. Tables of uneven sizes sat in the middle of the room and benches, padded with Emoran weave coverings lined parts of the walls. Tapestries depicting Emoran victories hung next to heroic displays of swords, bows, and staffs. Only a handful of tables were occupied by—as far as she could tell—merchants, travelers, and a few soldiers.

Otlar led them to a corner of the room that had small tables separated from each other by artfully engraved and painted panels of wood. They slipped onto the short benches and faced each other by the light of a single oil lamp. Tigh felt the tight intimacy as the space enveloped them.

"Ale or tea?" Otlar asked.

"Tea for me." Jame looked at Tigh.

"Tea also." Just sitting across from Jame and being able to look at her all evening was intoxicating enough for Tigh.

"Tigh's an Ingoran," Jame said.

Otlar nodded and flashed a hand signal to a server. "Enjoy your meal."

Jame grinned, and Tigh wondered what she'd been so nervous about.

ARGIS GROWLED AS an enemy stronger than any warrior or even a member of the Elite Guard stood in her way as she desperately tried to reach her goal. The insurmountable mental barrier confounded her senses as they came back to the same building for the third time.

"How do these Bal forsaken people live in this maze?"

Tas pulled her horse up next to Argis's. "There must be some kind of trick to it. I don't think we went that way." She pointed down a street lined with closed shops.

"We've been that way." Argis scowled as she studied the four routes out of the crossroads they were in.

"The one that goes the way the soldier at the gate told us to go, came back on itself." The only way they hadn't tried was the one that went in the opposite direction of the Emoran safe house. "We haven't gone that way." She nodded toward a street splashed with torch light and too many people for comfort. The citizens of Ynit clearly favored the street for their nightly entertainment.

Tas scratched her head. "But—"

"We've been the other ways." Not wanting to get into another discussion about it, Argis guided her horse into the-daughter-of-a-Yitsian-snow-creature street. Her muttered curses and frustrated glowering were enough that she didn't have to worry about the good people of Ynit getting too close.

JAME WATCHED WITH curiosity as the young serving girl placed several food-filled dishes and an empty plate in front of Tigh. She looked down at her own fare of rabbit stew and rice, and was surprised by how different Ingoran cuisine looked.

"What's in this dish?" She pointed to a small ceramic bowl containing some kind of vegetable covered with a pale-yellow sauce.

"That's cucumber in mustard sauce," Tigh said. She took Jame's fork from the table, stabbed a bit of cucumber, and held it up as an offering.

Jame eyed the delicate white slice and then sniffed it. She took the fork and ventured into a new culinary world.

"Interesting." Jame allowed the subtle sensations of the delicate flavors tickle her imagination. "It's so light. How can it possibly fill you up?"

"It fills one up without being stuffed," Tigh said.

Jame pondered this while chewing on a mouthful of the rabbit stew. The taste was certainly different from the cucumber. "I admit, all I want to do sometimes is take a nap after a big feast."

Tigh dribbled a spoonful of milk sauce onto her plate and placed several dumplings filled with spiced potatoes and spinach on top of it. She then smothered one of the small dumplings in the sauce and popped it into her mouth.

"Next time, I think I'll try Ingoran," Jame said.

Tigh looked up. Shyness, hope, and wonderment flickered across her face before she molded it into a passive mask. "Next time?"

"Someone has to make sure you eat," Jame said. "So, I predict there will be plenty of next times."

Tigh's cheeks reddened and she looked too stunned to speak.

Jame gazed down at her stew and gathered another mouthful onto her fork. She kept making the mighty Tigh the Terrible blush. What an interesting skill. Then she remembered what Ingel had told her when she first started defending Guards. Their emotional development remained where it had been when they were recruited. Tigh may have seen twenty-two years and led a victorious army, but emotionally she was a fourteen- or fifteen-year-old who had, most likely, lived under the sheltering fold of her family. She knew Guards only emotional need had been to fight and their only lust had been for blood in battle.

"Tell me about your day." Jame placed a hand on Tigh's arm, stopping her from pushing the greens around her plate.

"IT STARTED OUT kind of interesting." Tigh became more confident as Jame laughed and appeared to be enjoying her story, convincing her that she could live on Jame's smiles and laughter.

By the time Tigh finished her account, the plates had been long taken away. They sipped spiced tea and shared a bowl of sliced fruit.

"You know, the healer's assistant said you made quite an impression on Bede." Jame's eyes sparkled with mischief. "He told her he had never met anyone so tidy and efficient and who actually understood his need for order."

Tigh almost sputtered her tea and laughed with Jame until they wiped away the tears. She lifted the quilted cozy off the teapot and poured more tea into Jame's mug. Jame's smile seized her and held her as a willing hostage.

"Jame!"

Tigh caught the startled and stricken look on Jame's face before they turned to the source of the interruption.

"Argis." Jame's voice cracked.

Tigh's mind tumbled out of control at Jame's reaction to this tall warrior. The stranger grabbed Tigh by the shoulders, pulled her away from the table, and dragged her across the room, past tables of patrons who seemed to know better than to get in the way of a vengeful Emoran warrior. Tigh twisted around to make sure Jame was unharmed. A smaller Emoran held Jame back.

An older Emoran held the door open as Argis shoved Tigh onto the quiet abode brick street.

"Argis! Stop this," Jame shouted as she cleared the threshold.

Tigh staggered from the impact of Argis's fist to her face and collapsed in stunned shock to the ground.

"Tigh." Jame rushed to Tigh. She helped her sit up and examined where Argis had hit her.

"Jame! Get away from her." Argis's voice was filled with frustration.

Jame glared at Argis. "Why did you do this? What are you doing here?"

"We need to talk. Alone," Argis said.

Tigh frowned through the throbbing ache on her cheek as she tried to make sense of this Emoran warrior. Why was she talking to Jame like that?

Like she . . . A pain that had nothing to do with her cheek slammed through her. She pulled her knees to her chin and put her head in her hands, unable to cope with the only thing that could threaten these newfound emotions surging through her.

"I'll talk to you," Jame said. "Go inside with Tas. Give me time to make sure Tigh is all right. Otlar will tell me where to find you."

Argis watched Jame for several heartbeats, fists clenching in tense indecision. Finally, she nodded, turned on her heel, and strode through the still gaping doorway.

Tas studied Tigh and Jame for a puzzled moment and followed Argis into the safe house.

"Are you all right?" Jame asked, pulling Tigh's arm away from her cheek.

"Go talk to your friend," Tigh mumbled, filled with lonely resignation.

Jame squeezed Tigh's arm. "I'm not going to leave this spot until you promise me something." Tigh buried her head further behind her knees. "Whatever Argis has to say to me will not change anything between us. I had a choice whether to be in Emoria with Argis and all my other friends and family, or to be here in Ynit. My choice was to be here. I had a choice whether to spend the evening meal with you tonight or spend it with my colleagues. My choice was to be with you."

"She didn't give you a choice," Tigh said.

"Yes, she did," Jame said. "She just doesn't realize it. That's why I have to go talk to her. I can't go through my life with the expectations of others hitting me at the most inconvenient times."

Tigh lifted her eyes from behind her white-covered kneecaps. "Is that what this is about? Expectations?"

"Mostly." Jame sighed. "But it's only because of what she holds in her own mind, not what's in mine. I want to tell you my story after I see Argis. I only ask one thing in return."

Struggling with the need to trust Jame, Tigh nodded.

"Have Otlar take care of that cut. And wait for me."

Tigh lowered her eyes. A part of her wanted to run as fast as she could away from everything that led to the hurt that burned through her at the thought that another may have already claimed Jame's heart. But she'd never seen any lie in Jame's attitude toward her as she had seen in so many others. Nothing could hurt more than what she was feeling, except hurting Jame by not giving in to such a small request.

"I'll wait."

"Promise me," Jame said.

Tigh looked up at the raw emotion in Jame's voice and saw the desperate pleading in her night darkened eyes. At that moment, huddled on cold bricks in the middle of the night, surrounded by the brooding adobe of Ynit, she realized her life had meaning again. That meaning was called Jame.

"I promise," she whispered.

JAME TOPPED THE steps and saw Tas pacing the length of the short corridor. Smart of Otlar to put them in a little used part of the establishment, in case any loud discussions disrupted the other guests.

Tas stilled her agitated feet and hung her head in embarrassment. "She heard about you defending Tigh the Terrible and went crazy. She thinks you're being forced into helping her. I came along to keep her out of trouble."

Jame took a deep breath to get her anger under control and put a hand on Tas's shoulder. "Thank you for being a good friend. Do you think I'm being forced into anything?"

Tas shook her head. "It doesn't look like it to me."

"I was just doing my job and tonight, I was giving my friend a chance to relax a bit after her recent ordeals," Jame said.

"She heard the two of you laughing . . ." Tas ran a hand through her shaggy hair. "You know how Argis can get."

"Yeah, I know. Wish me luck." Jame rapped on the door and pushed it open.

"Tigh's the lucky one," Tas mumbled as she slumped against the far wall.

Jame gave Tas a curious look then closed the door behind her and let the silence spark for several heartbeats while she waited for Argis to turn away from the window. The muscles in Argis's back tensed with anger and confusion.

"Why are you here?" Jame finally asked.

"We heard that you were defending Tigh the Terrible," Argis said to the window. "The school had pledged to keep you out of danger."

"I wasn't in any danger," Jame said.

Argis spun around. "How can you say that? She's Tigh the Terrible."

"Was Tigh the Terrible," Jame said. "Besides, if she were still dangerous, you'd be dead."

"Why didn't she fight back?" Argis asked. "The impulse to fight can't be cleansed from them."

"That's true. But the impulse to fight when provoked is gone," Jame said. "She has no idea why you assaulted her. You walked into a public establishment and dragged a stranger into the street and flattened her with your fist."

Argis stared uncomprehending at Jame. "You're an Emoran princess. That should have been enough to tell her that I was just trying to protect you."

"From what? Eating too much?" Jame shook her head and raised beseeching eyes to Laur. "We were sharing a meal."

"Why?" Argis asked.

"We were hungry." Jame fought to keep her anger down. Argis's jealous possessiveness may have been endearing when they had been young but now it grated on every nerve in her body.

"Do you share a meal with all your clients? In a safe house? In an intimate corner?" Argis crossed her arms in a smug challenge.

"No. Tigh's the first," Jame said. "I consider her a friend."

"A friend?" Argis's incredulous bark echoed off the white-washed walls. "Now I know I have to get you away from here. How could you be so naive to think Tigh the Terrible sees you as anything other than a conquest?"

"How can you be so naive to think you know everything about someone you've never even seen before, much less spoken to?" Jame worked to control her anger. "If you're questioning my ability to recognize suitable friends, I'm questioning my choice of you as a friend. It's always been about you and what you want me to be in relation to you."

Argis looked dumbstruck. "Everything I've done has been for you."

"I have a choice on how to live my life before I become queen." Jame kept her words steady, but her voice quavered from too many conflicting emotions. "I told you before I left Emor that I may decide to be an arbiter for a while. You wouldn't even listen to me. You just patted me on the head and told me how proud you were and then went on about your plans for when I returned to Emor for good."

"You really want to do that rather than come home and start a life with me?"

The desperate look in Argis's gray eyes wrenched at Jame's soft heart. She wished Argis would just understand instead of reacting to her words as if they were mortal blows.

The image of another emotionally wounded warrior colored Jame's thoughts. She'd caused the pain of two warriors that night. *How did I get myself into this mess?* She admitted it was her softheartedness that had stopped her from breaking off with Argis when she first realized she wasn't sure of her feelings anymore. Except the only rival for Argis's affections at that time had been her desire to become an arbiter.

Now it was different. She couldn't deny she enjoyed Tigh's company in a way she had never experienced with Argis.

"At this time, yes." Jame held up a hand before Argis could respond. "What if you were told you had to give up being a warrior because it wasn't what everyone wanted you to be?"

"This is different," Argis said.

"In what way?"

"You're our princess. You need to be where we can protect you." Argis ran a hand through her short-cropped hair.

"That's not true and you know it," Jame said. "I do have a choice as to how to live my life. Many Emoran princesses have gone out to experience the world before settling in Emoria. It's just the recent idea of isolationism has made this tradition less common. Jyac didn't send you here. You took it upon yourself to come here and try to control how I'm living my life."

"Control?" Argis choked on the word. "We're to be joined. I think I have some say in your decisions for the future."

"Would you be willing to come with me while I pursue being an arbiter?" Jame asked.

Argis looked as if she'd been slammed in the face with the flat of a sword.

Jame sighed. "Go home, Argis. I appreciate your concern for my safety but I'm in no danger. I'll visit Emor when I've finished my schooling. We'll see how I feel after I've received my arbiter's medallion."

"I'll return home under one condition." Argis straightened in an attempt to restore her dignity. "Be careful around that woman."

"I'll be careful around her," Jame said.

Argis captured Jame's eyes. "And you'll return to Emor before you take any arbiter positions. So we can talk."

"I'll return to Emor, and we'll talk." Jame nodded, feeling relief they had come to some kind of agreement. Maybe by that time she'll have thought of a way to make everyone happy.

Chapter 10

"YOUR FRIEND IS out back," Otlar said before Jame had a chance to open her mouth.

"Thank you." Jame gave Otlar a grateful look. "Did she let you take care of her cut?"

"She did." Otlar nodded.

"This is for the meal and for the disruption." Jame held out several pieces of silver.

Otlar shook her head at the money. "She took care of it."

Jame frowned. "Tigh?"

"She paid for the meal and apologized for the commotion," Otlar said.

Jame chuckled. "I didn't know she had any money."

"Have a good night, my princess," Otlar said.

"You too, Otlar," Jame said.

She negotiated the back corridor into the cool dark air. As her eyes adjusted to the gloomy alley, she focused on Tigh slumped against the opposite wall, knees pulled tightly to her chin.

Jame crossed the small alleyway and sank cross-legged next to Tigh, who looked as if she was bracing herself for another blow. The tension from her confrontation with Argis flowed out of her. Something about the passive Tigh, even in her tense state, had a calming effect on her.

"I'm sorry we were interrupted like that." Jame studied Tigh's tight features, half hidden in shadow, and knew she had to work hard to bring Tigh back to her. "I haven't enjoyed myself like that in years." Tigh blinked but kept her eyes focused on the scuff on her knee. "I have to tell you, I don't know if I'm angrier at Argis for ruining the good time I was having with you or for punching a stranger in the mouth."

Tigh swallowed and glanced at Jame. "I'm sorry I acted like I had some kind of . . . You know what I mean." She cast an agonized gaze at the safe house door.

Jame stared at Tigh for several heartbeats before she understood the strange apology. Instead of being angry about having to sport a ripened bruise and cut lip for the next several days, Tigh was preoccupied by what she thought was an inappropriate reaction to the woman who hit her. Tigh was mortified she was jealous of Argis.

Jame knew she was about to step into the same territory she thought she had inhabited with Argis, except this one had more vivid and realistic landscapes. She let that thought seep through her consciousness.

"I didn't feel you were out of bounds with your reaction. And you do have some kind of hold on me."

Tigh stared at her, stunned. Jame was certainly getting a lot of practice in hitting warriors on their blind side that night.

"Come on, let's take a walk." Jame stood up and held a hand out to Tigh, who still looked as if the evening was going to leave her miserable, in spite of Jame's words. "I promise my story will have a happy ending."

"For you or for me?" Tigh asked.

Jame took Tigh's hand. "For both of us."

TIGH WAS AMAZED at how the events of a single evening could go from wonderful to miserable to utterly magical. Sauntering through the quiet back streets of Ynit hand in hand because Jame refused to release her hand once she had a firm grasp of it. Listening to Jame's soothing voice as she told her life's story. Understanding it more than Jame probably realized. At least understanding the essence of it as far as family expectations and how narrow the sheltered worlds where they were raised could be. Standing in awkward shyness outside the arbiters' residence and covering the disappointment that the long evening was ending too soon with the promise of sharing the next midday meal. The quick kiss to her cheek that set fire to her senses . . .

"Tigh?"

Tigh cast a sheepish look at Bede. "Sorry."

"Are you sure you're all right?" Bede asked. "Maybe you hit your head when you fell—"

"I'm fine. I didn't hit my head," Tigh said. "I'm just tired."

Bede studied her for a heartbeat then nodded and turned back to the young boy on a cot. "Now once the wound has been stitched, we put this salve on it to ease the pain and prevent infection."

Tigh wrinkled her nose at the bitter odor of the herbs in the salve. Guards, being nearly invincible in battle, never spent much time in infirmaries during the Wars.

A familiar voice reached her keen hearing and she turned to see Jame enter the ward. She looked at the sand clock. Too early for the midday meal.

"Excuse me," she mumbled and met Jame halfway down the ward.

"Hey," Jame said. "I know, I'm early. Pendon wants to see both of us about the little incident last night."

"Pendon," Tigh said.

"He just wants a full report. For the records," Jame said.

Tigh shook her head. "They're going to make a fuss over it."

"It wasn't your fault, and you weren't the one who exhibited violent behavior," Jame said.

Jame's indignation soothed Tigh's fears. "I'm glad you're my arbiter. I have to tell Bede." She trotted past nearly empty beds to Bede.

"Pendon wants to see me. About last night," Tigh said.

"If you need a few good words, just let me know." Bede placed a fatherly hand on her arm.

Tigh was stunned. She never expected anyone to volunteer to say kind words about her. "Thank you."

Still a bit dumbfounded, she joined Jame and they walked out of the infirmary.

"Why do you think they're going to make a fuss about this?" Jame asked as they strode across the plaza to the fortress.

Tigh shrugged. "Because he wants to see us both."

"I'm a witness to the incident," Jame said.

"You're also my arbiter," Tigh said. "As a witness, you would have been asked to submit your statement in writing."

"They can make as much fuss as they want," Jame said. "They can't do anything because you didn't react with violence."

Tigh could almost see Jame's keen mind working out the arguments in her defense. The idea that someone would stand up for her took her breath away. The fact that it was Jame filled her with a disbelieving wonder.

They entered the fortress and strode down the wide main corridor to Pendon's office.

An assistant healer met them at the door. "Please come this way."

Tigh exchanged glances with Jame, and they followed the healer to a consulting chamber. As they stepped across the threshold, Tigh no longer needed to speculate on the nature of the meeting. Pendon, looking apologetic, sat at an oval-shaped table. Leona and Tribune Sitas flanked him, neither a surprise to Tigh. But the presence of Rantigar, raking cool eyes over Jame, put Tigh on her guard.

The irony that she was going through the same pressures from home as Jame wasn't lost on her. But for the first time she was possessed with the urge to fight for both their rights to lives of their own choosing. Besides, she didn't like the disdain in Rantigar's eyes when she looked at Jame.

"Thank you for coming." A subdued Pendon motioned them in. Tigh and Jame sat in the chairs closest to the door. "I'll turn it over to you, Tribune."

"We're here at the request of Representative Rantigar, to reevaluate Tigh's choice of arbiter," Sitas said.

Tigh and Jame looked at each other, stunned.

Sitas turned to Rantigar. "Please state your case."

"Thank you, Tribune Sitas." Rantigar nodded. "I'm here at the request of the parents of Paldar Tigis. They feel an Ingoran arbiter would be more suitable in handling their daughter's case through the rest of the rehabilitation process. An Ingoran arbiter has the knowledge of how merchant families protect and nurture their members and can use this insight to ultimately convince the Tribunal that Paldar Tigis can be safely released into Ingoran society."

"I'm perfectly happy with my choice of arbiter. Can we go now?" Tigh placed her hands on the table and half rose out of her chair.

"You don't understand." Rantigar kept her voice even. "The Federation Council has agreed to accept these conditions for your rehabilitation."

"For the House of Tigis to shelter me? Keep me hidden behind the scenes, doing inventory and balancing the books? Slinking in the shadows as the family's embarrassing little secret?" Tigh asked. "I'll take my chances with Jame."

"And put yourself at further risk of violence from your arbiter's people?" Rantigar asked, incredulous. "The Emorans are a tribe of warriors and, unlike Ingorans, their way of dealing with displeasure is with violent confrontation. We agree on one thing, though. They're as against having their princess represent you as we are."

"That's not true," Jame said. "My aunt, the queen, has not expressed an opinion, one way or another, on any of my cases."

"But the incident last night," Rantigar said.

"Was the reaction of an old, misguided friend," Jame said. "It was just an unfortunate coincidence that my friend arrived in Ynit on the same evening Tigh and I were sharing a meal in the Emoran safe house."

"Where she shouldn't have been in the first place," Rantigar said.

"Why not? The Ingoran cuisine is excellent." Tigh leveled a passive gaze at Rantigar.

"It's not the proper environment for you right now," Rantigar said.

"Isn't that for me to decide?" Tigh still pinned Rantigar with her gaze.

"Right now, your parents know what's best for you and you should honor that," Rantigar said.

"My parents seem to have forgotten that I've passed my twenty-second birthday," Tigh said.

"What?" Sitas turned to Rantigar. "You gave the impression her parents still have a legal hold on her."

Rantigar's smug expression faltered. "They feel that they do, given the fact she's still the legal ward of the state until she's considered safe for society and if this can't be done, they're ready to take over the legal responsibility for her." Rantigar recovered her confident smile. "It wasn't lost on them that, after two years of alluding capture, you were caught within a week of your birthday. They accepted it as a coincidence, and you had lost track of time."

The words were laced with a strong cadence of warning to Tigh that her parents were willing to forgive her if this was a minor act of rebellion.

"It was no coincidence." Tigh allowed the shocked silence to settle over the chamber. "Before I was recruited into the Guards, I was secretly studying what I needed to know to pass the entrance exams to get into the University of Artocia. I was going to run away on my sixteenth birthday—the youngest age they let students into the University—if my parents didn't grant my wish to go there. I was still under the legal age when the Wars were over and the last thing I wanted was to be cleansed and sent home to a life I didn't want in the first place. I hid where no one would think to look for me and counted off the days until I was legally my own person."

"That's not possible," Leona said. "You were still Tigh the Terrible."

Tigh clasped her hands together on the table. "I also had a brain. That's why you recruited us. Remember? If Paldar Tigis didn't want to become a merchant, what makes you think Tigh the Terrible wanted to return to that? I may have been ruthless and cruel, but I wasn't crazy and irrational."

"Your parents aren't going to let you go that easily." Rantigar's mouth hardened, and her tense straight body trembled as the rage she tried to control fought to be released. She glanced at Jame.

"They have two other daughters who will make excellent merchants." Tigh shrugged, not missing the speculative look Rantigar cast at Jame. "As for making it successfully through the rehabilitation process, I'm confident Jame will be able to present a convincing case to the Tribunal when the time comes. But if not, I'll choose to remain a legal ward of the state."

Before Rantigar could respond, Sitas held up a warning hand. "Tigh is within her legal rights to make whatever choices she wants." She stood. "I want to thank the representative from Ingor for wasting our time this morning. I apologize for taking you away from your studies, Jame. And Tigh, I'm sorry for this misunderstanding."

Tigh bowed her head. "Apology accepted. If I'd known Rantigar was being retained by my parents to intervene in my rehabilitation process, I would have warned you about it."

Rantigar stood up and looked as if she was ready to fly over the table at Tigh.

Tigh stood, allowing the full power of her physical strength to saturate her body, and crossed her arms. "Give my parents my regards, Rantigar." She turned to Sitas. "I'd like to put in a request to have bodyguards assigned to Jame until my rehabilitation is completed. I wouldn't want any harm to come to her because she's my arbiter."

Jame put a hand on Tigh's arm. "Now wait—"

Tigh silenced her with a serious glance.

"A most prudent precaution, Tigh," Sitas said.

"Queen Jyac will appreciate your concern," Tigh said. She turned and strode out of the chamber, followed by Jame.

Tigh paused outside the door in the corridor filled with people going for their midday meal and raised an eyebrow at Jame. "Hungry?"

Jame's expression was a jumble of indignation and confusion, until it relaxed into resignation. "There's one thing you're going to have to learn about me. I'm always hungry enough to eat."

Tigh laughed and led the way to the nearest mess hall.

WITH RELIEF, JAME scratched out the last sentence of her essay. Finishing it meant she could spend more time with Tigh after the evening meal.

"Done already?" Daneran looked up from her desk across the room. "I can't come up with a third argument for Pilor's Contradiction."

Jame stood and stretched out the long sandmarks of sitting. "It's a contradiction. That means any argument can fit into it. You just have to follow Pilor's formula for presenting the case."

"But it won't make sense."

"It may not make sense, but it'll still be logical." Jame grinned.

Daneran laughed. "That made no sense."

"But it was a perfect example of Pilor's Contradiction," Jame said. "I think the purpose of this exercise is to teach us to extend our minds beyond the predictable so we can tackle the more complicated cases."

Daneran crossed her arms in mock challenge. "This coming from the woman who won a case using Bailikon's procedure."

"It was a gamble," Jame said.

Daneran snorted. "Now that's an understatement. If she had struck back at your hired assailant that would have been it."

"There was never any doubt about that," Jame said. "The gamble was whether the Tribunal was under pressure from the Federation Council to keep Tigh from advancing through her rehabilitation."

"I can't believe you weren't a little apprehensive about the attack," Daneran said.

"I had more confidence in Tigh's ability to control her violence than Tigh did herself," Jame said. "In the end, I had to prove it to her."

Daneran frowned. "Prove it?"

"We tested it."

"You tried to attack her?" Daneran's shocked expression was almost comical.

"Several times until she realized she'd been truly cured of the impulse to strike back," Jame said. "The moment of realization had been a wonderful sight to witness. She finally started to believe the cleansing was successful."

Daneran gave Jame a knowing look. "You mean Tigh isn't trying hard to be successful for you?"

Jame stared at Daneran. "What do you mean?"

"You know what I mean," Daneran said. "You've suddenly found something more interesting than studying all the time, and she acts like a bashful puppy when she's with you. Then our studious little Jame is in the middle of a confrontation between a jealous Emoran warrior and a former Guard. And all this time we thought that your whole life was going to class and doing homework."

"Argis is an old friend." Jame sighed at Daneran's raised eyebrow. "All right. She's more than an old friend but that's over now." She caught her breath at the words that had tumbled out. *It really was over*, she marveled, and her mind felt lighter and freer. "We entered into an understanding when we were both very young. Long before I came here. During my last visit home, I didn't have the heart to tell her my feelings had changed. I thought it was just the pressure from being so close to finishing my studies. Then I met Tigh. Argis had found out I was arguing Tigh's case and thought I was in some kind of danger from her."

Jadic poked his head through the open doorway. "Ingel wants to see you, Jame."

Jame rolled her eyes. "All right. Thanks, Jadic."

"What about your story?" Daneran asked.

"I'll tell you the rest later," Jame said.

She smoothed down her tunic and stepped past Jadic into the common room.

She entered Ingel's chambers and knew this meeting had nothing to do with her studies. The furrow between Ingel's brows as she studied a sheet of paper on her desk had Jame wondering what kind of trouble she could possibly be in.

"This is a letter from the Tribunal informing me a soldier has been assigned to you for as long as you represent Tigh." Ingel held up the sheet. "If this case has put you in some kind of danger, you know I have to remove you from it."

Jame sank into the visitor's chair. She had forgotten about Tigh's request and how it would impact the school's agreement with her aunt. *Why did things have to be so complicated?* Fortunately, Tigh had explained the true situation over the midday meal.

"Are you familiar with the Ingoran code of honor?" Jame asked.

"If an Ingoran catches another Ingoran engaged in embarrassing or illegal trade practices, then the Ingoran is honor bound not to report this lapse of judgment if the other Ingoran ceases the activity," Ingel said.

"Tigh caught Rantigar," Jame said. "It seems that Tigh's parents retained Rantigar to get Tigh legally turned over to them. And it may have worked if they had been forthcoming about Tigh's true age."

Ingel frowned. "That information was collected when Tigh was recruited."

"When I reminded Tigh of that, we stopped in the records chamber and discovered she had been listed as being only fourteen when she was recruited instead of fifteen. Her parents had signed the document," Jame said. "Tigh can't understand how such a mistake could have happened because merchants never sign anything without thoroughly reading it."

"But what does that have to do with you being in danger?" Ingel asked.

"Ingorans don't take on a less than desirable commission unless they're certain about it," Jame said. "Rantigar wouldn't have risked her standing as a representative of the Federation Council if she thought she couldn't deliver a rehabilitated Tigh to her parents. Being the firstborn daughter, Tigh is the heir to the House of Tigis, and Rantigar, thinking like any other Ingoran, was sure she wouldn't jeopardize that by antagonizing her parents. Under any other circumstances this would be true. But before Tigh was recruited, she was secretly studying for the entrance exams to the University of Artocia and was planning on running away on her sixteenth birthday if her parents didn't agree to her wishes."

Ingel fell back in her chair. "That explains what has baffled everyone since she was enhanced. No one could figure out how an apprentice merchant could turn into such a ruthless monster."

"She was a gentle and studious person. Her parents had lamented she was too softhearted for the merchant business," Jame said. "So Rantigar's argument that her parents wanted her back into the family fold didn't have the intended impact on Tigh. Not even when Rantigar said the Federation Council had already accepted a return to Ingor and to the family business as a condition for Tigh's rehabilitation."

"By Bal's Children," Ingel said.

"But they wanted Tigh to have an Ingoran arbiter," Jame said. "Tigh wants me to continue as her arbiter. When Rantigar cited the incident last night, saying Tigh shouldn't have been in an Emoran safe house, she reminded her that she was twenty-two and could do what she wanted. Rantigar was not expecting this little fact to come out and scrambled to cover her argument up to that point. But Tigh told her she had waited until her twenty-second birthday to be captured so she wouldn't be legally bound to her parents."

"What?"

"Tigh then apologized to Sitas, saying if she had known Rantigar had been retained by her parents, she would have warned the Tribunal," Jame said. "Then she requested to have a soldier assigned to me for as long as I represented her because I stood in the way of allowing Rantigar to fulfill her contract with Tigh's parents. But it'll really be until Tigh can get a message to her parents, instructing them to settle their business with Rantigar, and she's free of the contractual obligations."

"Ingorans have always thrived on intrigue," Ingel said.

"I'll be honest with you," Jame said. "Tigh thinks I was in danger as long as Rantigar thought she could deliver Tigh and collect her commission. But that changed when Tigh caught her. Rantigar is honor bound to end the agreement she has with Tigh's parents."

"That's true," Ingel said, "but I don't want to have to explain Ingoran honor codes to your aunt if anything happens to you."

"Let me put it another way." Jame sat up and scooted to the edge of the seat. "What would happen if you took me off Tigh's case?"

Ingel gazed at Jame for several heartbeats. "Two words. Be careful."

"Thank you." Jame grinned. "And I'll be careful."

Chapter 11

JAME LEANED AGAINST the door jamb of the children's ward and watched in fascination as Tigh stitched a gash on a small girl's arm. As Tigh sewed tiny even stitches, the girl cheerfully chatted about her family, her pet goat, and her pesky brother.

Jame bit her lip to keep from laughing at Tigh's patient look of resignation. She couldn't have asked for a better argument for her case than the fact the children not only loved her but insisted she be the one to take care of them.

"Children see others much clearer than adults do," Bede said from behind her. "They have the gift to see the beauty of the soul beneath even the passive detachment of your friend."

"I wish others had that gift," Jame said.

"You've been a good friend to her." Bede laid a fatherly hand on Jame's shoulder. "Most of the Guards put in my care are truly lost souls who have to go through their rehabilitation alone. All the healers and counselors in the world can't equal a good friend."

"She's been a good friend to me, too," Jame said. "We help each other."

Bede smiled. "We'll miss her, but we know she has to move on."

Jame gave Bede a conspiratorial nudge. "I bet she'll come back if a child requests it."

"I know she will, without hesitation," Bede said. "Find something she can do where she'll be of service to others. I know she wanted to be a scholar, but I don't think that will ease her restless soul."

Jame nodded. "She knows that. She's a complicated composite of who she was before she was recruited and who she was as a Guard."

"You know, Loena and Pendon are going to spend the rest of their lives trying to figure out what went wrong during her cleansing process," Bede said. "From their point of view, Tigh's their only failure. From my point of view, having worked with the other cleansed Guards, Tigh's their only success."

"You're right," Jame said. "They've been going backward to find the foundation for a Guard's future, when they should have been going forward. And the only way to do this is to work with the whole person up to the point of cleansing."

Bede looked impressed. "We could have used some of your insight when we began this process. Tigh is in good hands."

"Thank you." Jame bowed her head in embarrassment. She returned her attention to Tigh who was helping the little girl off the stool.

"REMEMBER. ON THE central square, we'll be the ones with the yellow sashes." The little girl put her hands on her hips and looked up at Tigh.

"I'll remember," Tigh said.

The girl grinned and skipped happily past Jame and Bede.

"What was that all about?" Jame asked.

"Uh," Tigh scratched her head, "she's going to be in a procession at the Summer Solstice festival."

"Then we'll be sure to be there to see her."

Tigh lifted startled eyes to Jame. "I didn't think, I mean, I wasn't sure . . ."

Bede put an understanding hand on Jame's arm and went back to the main ward.

Jame followed Tigh to her tidy workspace. "We have a similar festival in Emoria. It's called the Festival of Flowers. Besides celebrating the coming of spring, it's when couples make a public acknowledgment of their togetherness by wearing bracers of the same design and with the same kinds of flowers. In Ynit they wear an identical token, but it's the same idea. What I'm trying to say is, I'd be honored to go to the Solstice Festival with you, if you want to go."

"You would?" Tigh asked with wonderment. "As just a friend?" She looked down at the ball of stitching thread in her hands.

"That's up to you." Jame gently lifted Tigh's chin. "I'm ready to take the next step, if you are."

The ball of stitching thread fell to the smooth stone floor as Tigh attempted to restart her heart. She managed to find enough air to push through her vocal chords and whispered, "Yes."

She almost landed on the floor next to the ball of thread at Jame's joyful smile. She had no idea how she survived such a miraculous blow to her senses.

"Come on. You look like you need some air." Jame grabbed Tigh's arm and led her away from her tidy workspace. Tidy, except for the forgotten ball of thread on the floor as silent evidence that Tigh's world had just changed forever.

A PART OF Tigh's mystique as a Guard was, she possessed nerves as strong as the sword she wielded. She had commanded an army and had made impossible wagers and never showed a hint of fear or nervousness. She was fearless. So why were her hands trembling and her stomach fluttering too much to eat?

Tigh pulled on the soft fawn-colored leather tunic that Jame had picked out for her. After several months being encased in white cloth, the leather felt strange and familiar at the same time and the matching leggings hugged her muscular legs in a way that Jame was sure to approve of.

She peered into the tarnished mirror and ran a hand through her shaggy hair. It had grown quickly since being shaven off during the cleansing process. The eyes that gazed back at her were clearer and the haunted expression was gone.

Her sharp hearing picked up footfalls on the stairs. The assistant healer no longer kept vigil over the floor, and she wasn't expecting any visitors that morning.

As the footfalls sounded closer, Tigh closed her eyes and muttered a string of colorful oaths. Her parents paused outside the open door. She cast a passive glance at them, then grabbed a belt of twisted strands of leather and tied it around her waist.

"We're lucky there are guest rooms in the compound, because all the rooms in town are filled." Paldon strode into the cell followed by Joul. "The Tribunal should have had more sense than to schedule your hearing the day after the Summer Solstice."

"You didn't have to come." Tigh flashed another look at them as she fetched her boots from the corner of the room.

"Of course, we did," Paldon said. "We care about what happens to you. When we saw the state you were in after your cleansing, we were desperate to do anything to make sure you made it through the rehabilitation process and be brought home where we could take care of you."

"So, you retained Rantigar to make a deal with the Federation Council," Tigh said.

"We really thought you weren't capable of thinking for yourself," Paldon said. "And to be honest, we're still worried about your emotional state."

Tigh captured Paldon's eyes. "What do you mean?"

"Your frustration and anger at Rantigar made you say some foolish things." Paldon's compassion softened her pale blue eyes. "We know it was just your instinct to lash out at her, and we forgive you for it. But we're worried about this irrational behavior."

Tigh shifted her gaze between her parents before deciding she didn't want to ruin her day with Jame. Her parents would eventually understand that everything she said during the confrontation with Rantigar was true. Maybe, by that time, they'll be able to accept it. In the meantime, there was only one answer she wanted from them.

"Why did you lie about my age when I was recruited?" She was surprised to see embarrassment and guilt on her parents' faces.

"It was a foolish decision that we immediately regretted," Paldon said. "As you know, they were looking for girls with the right combination of intelligence and strong physical characteristics. The younger the better because they found a young mind took to the enhancements better than someone who was older."

"They offered more money," Tigh said.

"You were only a couple moons past your fifteenth birthday and so it wasn't that far from the truth," Paldon said. "They paid one hundred and twenty silver pieces more for a girl under fifteen. We thought it was fair, considering they were taking our heir away from us."

"You succeeded in embarrassing the healers in charge of rehabilitation, the Tribunal, and, let's not forget, the Federation Council," Tigh said. "And Rantigar lost her seat on the Council. All this for one hundred and twenty silver pieces. Why did you continue to pretend I was under legal age?"

"Because we wanted to protect you," Paldon said in a voice that pleaded for forgiveness. "You have to believe that. As long as they thought you were underage, they were willing to let you be rehabilitated because they knew you'd be returned to our care."

Tigh took a deep breath. "Let me think it through." She needed Jame's insight to lift the confusion she felt toward anything that had to do with her family and Ingor.

Paldon let out a relieved sigh and put a hand on Tigh's arm. "That's all we ask for." She fingered the supple leather. "This is nice."

"I'm going to the festival." Tigh tried to sound matter of fact, but she knew a soft blush colored her face.

Her parents exchanged surprised looks.

"Alone?" Paldon asked.

"I'm going with Jame." Tigh sat down on the cot and pulled on her boots.

"Your arbiter," Paldon said.

"Yes." Tigh leaned over to her trunk at the end of the cot and picked up a leather braid with purple strands of thread running through it. Jame's sense of humor took over when she had searched for the token for them to wear. Finally, with a mischievous glint in her eyes, she gave Tigh one of her Emoran princess braids. Just so there wasn't any misunderstanding, she had explained.

"That's an interesting accessory," Paldon said as Tigh tied the braid to her belt.

Tigh raised a challenging brow. "It's the braid of an Emoran princess."

Paldon raised her own eyebrow. "You're wearing her braid to a festival?"

"Yes." Tigh stood and smoothed down the tunic.

Before Paldon could respond, Joul put a cautioning hand on her arm. She nodded to him and relaxed.

Tigh knew they were already thinking of several young women from Ingor's highest society who would make a good match for her. Once she came to her senses and forgot about arbiters and everything from this world and returned to Ingor.

"You're not worried about your hearing tomorrow?" Paldon asked.

"No." Tigh let a glimmer of a smile touch her eyes as her parents realized their intervention hadn't been necessary. She was making it through the rehabilitation process on her own, with the help of a wily assistant arbiter.

Paldon studied Tigh. "I hope you're right."

"I wouldn't worry, Mother," Tigh said. "Healer Bede thinks I'm the most successfully cleansed Guard they've ever had."

Not giving her parents a chance to respond, she slid past them and sauntered down the corridor, humming a tune the breeze had carried through her window that morning.

"WHOA. THERE'S AN Emoran warrior in my room."

Daneran paused in the doorway and watched Jame tie an Emoran braid onto her belt. Jame had traded the brown leathers worn by the assistant arbiters for her new set of Emoran leathers. Since a lot of the people attending the festival dressed up in whimsical clothing and costumes, she knew she could get away with wearing her Emoran clothes.

"So, is this just getting into the spirit of the festival or are you sending a subtle message to the Tribunal about tomorrow?" Daneran asked.

Jame laughed. "I never even thought about that. But I can't help what the Tribunal thinks of it."

"Or what they'll think about you going to the festival with your client," Daneran said.

"They can think what they want about that, too," Jame said.

"It's too late now at any rate." Daneran grinned. "I know we've been teasing you about it, but it's only because we're all envious. Solstice is a lot more fun with a special someone than attending it with a pack of friends."

"I know. I've always been a part of that pack." Jame looked at herself one more time in the long mirror and straightened the braid so it wouldn't be hidden in the patchwork of leather.

Jadic came up behind Daneran and stared dumbfounded at Jame. "By the Children of Bal."

Daneran looked over her shoulder and laughed. "Pick your jaw up off the floor, Jadic. I have the feeling she's taken."

Jame studied the floorboards, praying the statement was true.

"The lucky warrior is headed this way," Jadic said. "She's not looking too bad herself."

Jame smiled at her friends. It had taken weeks, but her colleagues had finally overcome their fear of Tigh and had even gotten used to her quiet shadow.

"I'd better get out there," Jame said. "She's still shy about coming in here."

"Have fun." Daneran waved as Jame stepped into the common room.

"I plan to." Jame glanced back with an impish grin.

She skipped down the few steps of her quarters and waited for Tigh to approach, admiring the way the light-colored leathers clung to her sleek muscular body.

Tigh strode with a graceful strength and seemed oblivious to the startled stares from the clusters of people gathered to go to the festival. Jame couldn't keep away a silly grin and it was answered by a shy smile from Tigh.

"Those leathers look really nice on you," Jame said when Tigh stopped in front of her. The strong confidence that was apparent when Tigh walked turned into a bashful slump.

Tigh cast furtive admiring glances at Jame. "You're beautiful." She blushed and studied the adobe bricks beneath her feet.

Jame forgot to breathe. Those were bold words from the reticent Tigh, and they went straight to her heart. She grasped Tigh's hand and waited for her to lift her eyes. "Let's go enjoy the festival."

Jame led Tigh to the city gate into the already surging brightly dressed crowds. Street corner magicians summoned multicolored displays of lights. Wandering jugglers kept balls and odd shaped trinkets in the air. Children with long rainbow ribbons fluttering out behind them darted around clusters of adults.

"Singing." As if pulled by the music itself, Jame tugged Tigh in the direction of the melodious voices.

The listeners surrounding the choir were so packed together that Jame couldn't see any way to winnow through them to get a clearer view. She stared forlornly at the backs of the listeners and sighed.

Tigh leaned into Jame's ear. "Do you want to see the choir?"

"I'd like to but . . ." She waved her hand.

Tigh backed Jame up several paces while glancing at a second-floor balcony. Before Jame had a chance to ask, Tigh scooped her up, took two long steps, and launched them into the air. They made a tidy flip and landed on the balcony. A splattering of delighted laughs erupted from the bystanders who witnessed the ingenious trick.

Jame could only laugh at the outrageous feat. Her body felt the imprint of where hard muscles had held her close, and she experienced an immediate ache to feel those arms around her again. Then she remembered they had to get down from the balcony.

"Thank you." Jame squeezed Tigh's hand. "You're pretty handy to have around."

Tigh delighted her with a pleased smile.

As she listened to the voices soar with ancient desert inflections, Jame couldn't help but be reminded of the last time she stood with a warrior enjoying a choir. Unlike Argis, Tigh was not afraid to hold her hand in public, and she actually paid attention to the music.

AS THE LAST musical tones faded into the adobe walls around them, they waited for the audience to wander on to other venues before they attempted their descent. Tigh remembered how Jame felt cradled in her arms and shyly picked her up again. Much to her discomfort, Jame slid her arms even tighter around her neck. The herbal fragrance from Jame's hair and the closeness of her face to her own, weakened her knees.

Concentrating on making the leap without breaking both of their necks, Tigh launched upward, cleared the balcony with a flip, and landed on the unforgiving adobe bricks. Jame was agonizingly slow in slipping out of her grasp. She was sure the assault to her mind and body would kill her on the spot.

"Let's go this way." Jame pulled a bemused Tigh down a lane lined with vendors selling everything from exotic food to festival ribbons.

GOODEMER FELT THEIR energy before she saw them. She turned from her study of friendship tokens and took in the sight of Tigh and Jame sauntering hand in hand from vendor to vendor. Finding them more intriguing than any friendship token, she shadowed them when they wandered out of the lane and into a quiet sculpture garden.

"It's just nice to get away from the crowds every once in a while," Jame said.

They roamed past a winding avenue of giant statues of the Children of Bal into the garden of guardian beasts.

Goodemer subtly probed their psyches and was surprised to discover they were still hesitant about expressing their full feelings for each other.

How could they not see how the other feels? Their bodies are practically shouting at each other. She sorted through her newly acquired spells and found one that could nudge them to the place they obviously wanted to be in their relationship. She could give them just a harmless boost.

Jame ran ahead of Tigh into a field of clipped grass with what appeared to be a partially buried statue of a woman scattered about. The only parts that showed were hands as tall as Tigh and even larger feet, and further down the field, a head crowned with a garland of stone flowers.

Tigh climbed into the palm of one of the hands.

Jame laughed in delight. "Clever."

Tigh jumped off the statue and trailed Jame to a huge foot. Both laughed at the big toe arching over them.

Tigh gave her head a quick shake as if bothered by a flying insect. As she watched Jame's climbing skills, she whipped her hand next to her ear and looked around perplexed.

"Why doesn't the spell work?" Goodemer muttered. The second attempt had been strong enough to penetrate the most stubborn brains. Not one to concede defeat, she spun an even stronger spell and aimed it right at Tigh's heart.

Tigh slapped her chest and glanced all around, looking a little frantic.

"Are you all right?" Jame jumped off of the stone foot and approached a frowning Tigh.

"A bee or something is bothering me," Tigh said.

Maybe she wasn't weaving the spell right. Goodemer flung the same spell at Jame.

A shocked Tigh saw the sudden predatory look of desire on Jame's face, took a step backwards, and tripped over the little toe of the statue. She landed with a grunt on her back and could only stare as Jame deftly cleared the toe, fell on top of her, and captured her lips with her own.

Goodemer stood frozen with her hands to her mouth. She would never cast another spell again if she had ruined this magical relationship.

She watched as Tigh relaxed and wrapped her arms around Jame. They seemed to be quite content to explore each other's lips.

They finally broke apart. Jame sheepishly climbed off of Tigh. They grinned and laughed from relief and happiness.

Goodemer let out a long-held breath and raised her eyes in thanks to Bal.

Chapter 12

JAME WAS RELIEVED to see only a handful of curious spectators in the audience for Tigh's second hearing. That alone should let the Tribunal know everyone thought this was just another routine case.

Tigh's parents sat in the front row. Jame didn't quite know what to make of them. The idea that they lied about their daughter's age for an extra one hundred and twenty silver pieces appalled her. Although the amount was a fortune to her, Tigh had said it was a trifling sum to her parents. But merchants were compelled to work for the best deal no matter how small the increase in profit. Tigh had insisted her parents were truly concerned about her, they just didn't understand she wasn't interested in inheriting the family business.

No. Tigh had shyly admitted she was interested in pursuing a life with Jame, wherever that happened to take them. Tigh had a quiver full of skills that could bring in extra silver if need be. She had been further surprised by Tigh's admission that she would have offered to be her companion, if Jame had wanted only friendship.

Now Jame was about to go before the Tribunal and once again persuade them to allow Tigh to go on to the next step in her rehabilitation. Only this time the outcome impacted on both their futures.

"There's Bede," Tigh said in Jame's ear, sending a shiver of memories of the night before when she had relaxed in Tigh's arms as they watched the fireworks fill the sky with magic.

Jame gave Tigh an amused look. "Did you ever tell him about the practical joke you played on him?"

"Uh, no," Tigh said. "I thought I'd wait until after this hearing."

Jame nodded. "Good thinking."

The small door to the Tribunal chambers opened and the seven Tribunes filed in and sat at the bench. Jame was relieved to see that the presiding Tribune was Ewan and not Onderal. At least, Ewan gave the impression of being fair.

The thin Tribune fidgeted with a pile of papers and then cleared her throat and turned to the defendants' box. "Our first case today is the hearing for Paldar Tigis to pass on to step four of the Guard rehabilitation program. Assistant arbiter, Jamelin Ketlas, will present her case. You may take the floor, Jamelin."

Jame stood. "Thank you, Tribune Ewan." She noted the curious interest on the Tribunes' faces. So, they thought she was going to pull another trick on them. Interesting. "Since the last time I presented Tigh's case before you, she has proven all the fears and doubts concerning her cleansing are unfounded. She has excelled in her training as a healer. So much so that she was given an assignment in the children's ward. Yes. In the children's ward where her young patients ask for her to take care of them because their friends liked her. No other Guard has been assigned to work with children, but healer Bede recognized Tigh's gentle nature and knew that children would respond to it." She paused to take in the surprise that flashed across the Tribunes' faces. "But if you want to make the proceedings more interesting, I could try to present it according to Pilor's Contradiction this time."

The reactions from the Tribunal ranged from Sitis's amusement to Onderal's outrage.

Ewan cleared her throat. "As much as that would be an intriguing exercise, I don't think it'll be necessary. For the record, we require Healer Bede to speak on the defendant's behalf."

Bede Komlic presented the Tribunal with a pile of papers in a neatly tied folio. He then took his place before the bench.

"I have only one thing to add about Paldar Tigis," Bede said. "I've never seen a more successful cleansing. I commend Loena and Pendon for their fine effort at restoring to us this gentle, beautiful soul. It's been a pleasure working with her these last few weeks and all of us in the infirmary will miss her."

Jame glanced at Tigh's parents, enjoying their astonished and confused expressions. She knew the last thing they wanted to hear was their too softhearted daughter would not be returned to them a hardened fighter.

"Thank you, Bede," Ewan said, and the Tribunes engaged in a conversation of murmurs. By simple body language it appeared that Onderal still had strong reservations about Tigh and held his ground on what looked like a small point.

Ewan returned her attention to Jame. "Onderal is concerned about the incident at the Emoran safe house."

"What kind of concerns does he have?" Jame was fully prepared for a discussion on the subject.

"Concerns that she's broken her pledge not to engage in behavior that is dangerous to others," Onderal said.

"Actually, the behavior in question was only dangerous to Tigh," Jame said. "The reason she was in that position in the first place had to do with me rather than her. An old friend from Emoria took offense to us sharing a meal together. She struck Tigh, but Tigh made no violent move toward my friend. I gave my friend an angry lecture and sent her back home. I'm sorry, Tribune, I don't understand your concern."

Onderal straightened with a challenge in his eyes. "She invites violence and that makes her just as dangerous to others."

"Can you prove that?" Jame asked. "Or are you basing this assumption on what you think may happen when Tigh is back in society? My friend didn't strike Tigh because she used to be Tigh the Terrible. She attacked Tigh because she was sharing a meal with me. So actually, your argument is more suited to me than to Tigh. I'm the one who invited the violence. In the weeks that Tigh has been free to wander this compound and to visit Ynit, no one has ever been compelled to do violence against her."

Onderal stared at Jame for several heartbeats and then sank onto the bench. The Tribunes muttered a fast exchange.

Ewan turned to Jame and Tigh. "Will the defendant rise?" Tigh stood. "Paldar Tigis has successfully passed the third step in her rehabilitation. We now place her back into the care of her counselor so she can begin step four." Ewan turned to the Keeper of the Bench. "Next case."

Jame and Tigh grinned and just stopped from hugging. Jame felt as if they could conquer the world together. One more step and one more hearing and Tigh the Terrible would be put to rest forever.

THE MILITARY ARCHIVES was probably the best maintained archives in the Southern Territories outside the University of Artocia. Many of the cleansed Guards had been archivists and librarians and the military archives was a monument to their skills.

Enjoying the musty silence, Tigh returned armloads of books, folios, and scrolls to their proper places on the narrow ranges of shelves. The mindless activity allowed her thoughts to roam into a future that had looked bleak just a few moons earlier and was now filled with delightful possibilities. All it took was a single person to bring hope back into her life. She just had to find a way of contributing to their keep. Maybe she could be a healer . . .

"Tigh?" Jame's soft searching voice drifted over the tall ranges of shelves.

"Here." Tigh stepped into a narrow aisle that divided the ranges.

She watched as Jame picked her way around the piles of books and scrolls waiting to be reshelved. She could tell that something was bothering her. Why else would she be seeking her out in the middle of the afternoon?

"Hey," Tigh said as she put down her folios.

The sweet smile Jame gifted her with was enough to brush away the lingering insecurity about their relationship that occasionally needled her.

"I got my assignment for my field case." Jame sighed and plopped down on a low stool used for reaching the higher shelves. "I wish I'd just let a pair of Emoran guards follow me around. There were plenty of cases in Ynit and in some of the villages around here, but the school thought they presented too much of a danger for me. So, they assigned me to a case in Glaus."

"Glaus?" Tigh already felt the sting of separation. "But that's a day's journey by coach."

"I tried to convince Ingel it was too far away, but she felt it was a simple enough case and shouldn't take more than a few days." Jame slumped against the end of a range of books. "A sandmark is too long to be away from you." She looked up into Tigh's eyes.

Tigh knelt in front of Jame. "If they're worried about danger, they shouldn't be sending you so far away."

Jame shrugged. "They're sending a peace warrior with me. It's the last thing I have to do before I get my arbiter's medallion. Although I hate the idea of being away from you, it'll only be a few days."

"Peace warrior." Tigh settled her thoughts on these soldiers of the legal system. "I thought it wasn't a dangerous case."

"It's just a precaution. A concession to the school's agreement with my aunt." Jame pushed stray strands of hair away from Tigh's face. Tigh closed her eyes at the tender touch. "I'll be leaving in the morning."

Tigh opened her eyes. "There's a place in town that serves the best Ingoran food outside of Ingor. It also has intimate balconies that overlook the Rih River."

"Are you asking me out for a romantic evening meal?" Jame wrapped her arm around Tigh's neck.

Tigh stole a kiss. "It's more of a meal in a romantic setting."

"You've been spending too much time with these books." Jame laughed and stole the kiss back.

"Is that a yes or a no?" Tigh breathed in her ear.

"Yes."

A throat cleared. Tigh and Jame pulled away from each other and looked up.

An amused Pendon Larke, with arms crossed, looked down at them. "I really hate to interrupt but you're between me and the book I'm after."

Tigh stood, dragging Jame up with her. "Sorry."

Pendon strolled past them then turned around. "You can continue your discussion. I'll be a while."

JAME PEERED OUT of the coach window with relief as they finally broke free of a thick humid forest with trees that reached as high as the cliffs of Emoria. Glaus, fashioned from these extraordinary trees, looked as if a rainbow exploded over the patch of cleared land clinging to the western edge of Glaus Harbor. A typical seaport city, Glaus sprawled away from the Cerasus

Ocean in a patchwork of painted wooden buildings leaning against each other with all the grace of the drunken sailors that roamed the waterfront.

"Have you ever been to Glaus?" Jame asked her quiet companion.

Indot, a lean and muscular woman, closer to Jyac's age than Jame's, pulled away from own thoughts to focus on Jame.

"Once or twice," she said with the economy of words that was as much a characteristic of warriors as their weapons skills.

Jame settled back into her seat and studied the peace warrior assigned to her. A chaperone more like it, she scowled to herself. She wished Tigh sat across from her.

The clatter of the coach's wheels against cobblestones alerted Jame that they had entered the city. A jumble of colors passed by as the buildings closed in around them. After a long day of travel, the coach finally lurched to a halt in front of a dirty white building.

Jame shouldered her pack and jumped from the vehicle. Never had she spent so long sitting in one place, much less a place that constantly rocked and bumped.

Indot shouldered her own pack and spoke a few words to their driver. She then led Jame through the aged double doors of the building. After the late afternoon sun, the large entry chamber was as dim as a cavern.

When her eyes adjusted, Jame could discern the dark wood that cast the chamber into an invariable gloom. A half-moon service table with a pair of bored-looking clerks behind it occupied the middle of the chamber.

Indot strode to the table as Jame lagged behind, taking in the benches filled with bleak-faced families and friends of defendants. She observed the well-dressed arbiters exchanging high-toned postures and attitudes and felt better about her position as a volunteer arbiter for a defendant who was unable to afford the fees that fed those arbiters' egos.

By the time Jame reached the half-moon table, Indot had retrieved the documents for her case. She held out a quill to her.

Jame signed in, and the bored clerk nodded at the double arching staircase that dominated the back section of the chamber.

"Right stairs, next floor. Tell the attendant you want to see Aft Lindigan," the clerk mumbled.

With each step upward, Jame felt a shiver of anticipation. She was about to tackle her first case outside the sheltered domain of the military compound. This was what she thought she wanted to do with her life. Now came the test of whether reality fit her dreams.

TIGH WAS MISERABLE. Not feeling like eating, she roamed the compound as the summer sun stretched the day into night. She decided she just didn't dislike being separated from Jame, she hated it. The uncertainty of whether Jame was all right or not devoured her thoughts.

She knew her reaction was extreme. After all, Jame was only to be gone a few days, and the school went out of its way to get her a case that wasn't dangerous. She ran a hand through her hair. Reasonable logic had nothing to do with how she felt about her.

Her feet seemed to know what was best for her, even if her mind didn't. She stared at the infirmary door for several heartbeats. Bede would still be there despite the late hour. The infirmary was his life, and he was as reluctant to be away from it as she was to be separated from Jame.

She pushed the door open and nodded to the assistant healer who oversaw the injury ward at night. At the threshold of the ward, she scanned the half empty cots and focused on a side door. Her keen hearing picked up Bede's soothing whispers over the tearful whimpers of a child. Tigh followed the sounds like metal to a magnet.

SIMPLE STRAIGHTFORWARD CASE, indeed. Jame soaked up the insincerity in the bright innocent gaze of Aft Lindigan. The young man was charged with going against a joining contract with the owner of a popular tavern. Aft insisted he'd been lured into the contract with promises that Hendigard, the tavern owner, would hire Aft's older sisters. According to Hendigard, the contract made no reference to the hiring of these siblings, and she was not obligated to honor any offhand statements she had made concerning their employment, especially before she met them.

Hendigard had made one mistake, and that was what made it a simple straightforward case, especially for someone with Jame's abilities. Because Aft was illiterate, Hendigard gave in to his request to enter into a verbal contract before witnesses rather than a written contract. The agreed upon witnesses seemed reputable enough for Hendigard but they later swore in written documents that she had promised to hire Aft's sisters as a part of the joining contract.

Hendigard had been too busy with her business to bother with minor details such as checking out the witnesses. After all, she had no reason to suspect any ulterior motives from the young man she wanted to spend the rest of her life with.

Ulterior motives. They hit Jame in the face from the first moment Aft opened his mouth. The sweet tongued young man was sorry for the misunderstanding and although he dearly loved Hendigard, he had an obligation to his only living family, who for reasons he couldn't understand had problems finding work. He was willing to let Hendigard out of the contract for only the silver that she had offered as the traditional joining gift, symbolizing a prosperous start for the joined couple.

After listening to three sandmarks of deliberately worded testimony from the witnesses and from Aft's equally smooth-tongued sisters, Jame knew she was being used in a ruse to relieve Hendigard of her hard-earned silver.

She also knew she had to withdraw from the case.

An arbiter's job was twofold within the judicial system of the Southern Territories. They could either serve as a judge for cases, or they could choose to argue a case before a judge. Jame excelled at judging but couldn't bring herself to present a case when she knew her client was guilty.

And in this case, not only was her client guilty of breaking the contract but guilty of conspiring to enter into the contract for the purpose of getting silver out of Hendigard.

She wished Ingel was there to counsel her on what to do. After enduring the hard glares from Aft's sisters, who were veterans of the Grappian Wars, she wished Tigh stood behind her rather than Indot.

She hoped she could remove herself from the case before her aunt heard about it. Jyac would know she had been in Glaus because she was staying in an Emoran safe house. If she got lucky, details of the case wouldn't reach Emoria.

She thanked Laur and all her sisters when the judging arbiter called a recess for the day before she had to opportunity to present her argument. That gave her one night to find a way out of this mess.

TIGH RAISED HER head and stared at the paper-strewn desk in confusion. She had fallen asleep while indexing the new folios for the archives. She squinted at assistant archivist Treyar who was watching her and gave her a sheepish shrug. Treyar replied with an understanding smile.

Surprised that it was almost time for the evening meal, she stood from the hard wooden bench and stretched out her long muscles.

"Try to get some sleep tonight," Treyar said.

Tigh shrugged. "I'll try."

A PAIR OF city guards blocked Jame's and Indot's path within sight of the door engraved with a sword and bow.

One of the guards pointed at Indot. "You're to be taken into custody for disturbing the peace last night."

"She's a peace warrior," Jame said. "How could she have been disturbing the peace?"

"She was involved in a drunken brawl with some sailors outside the Ship and Sail," the guard said.

"Were the sailors injured in this brawl?" Jame crossed her arms, ready to challenge every word the guard uttered.

The guard straightened. "According to the report, one has a bad gash on the back of the head, and another has a broken jaw."

Jame lifted Indot's hands. "Are these hands swollen or bruised from hitting someone in the jaw?"

"If she's innocent, she'll be set free," the guard said.

"I have to go with them, Jame," Indot said. "It's probably a case of mistaken identity. Send word back to Ynit and tell them what has happened."

"I will." Jame nodded as the guards flanked Indot, and they walked down the street. "We'll get you out."

Jame approached the Sword and Bow and was not pleased to see Aft's sisters lounging in front of the door. She straightened and continued walking, determined to brush past them but they blocked her way.

"Too bad about your warrior." The one called Sed flipped a small knife.

"The lies you told will be disproved." Jame put her warrior training to use and leveled cold steady eyes at the pair.

"That's true." Sed shrugged with a sneering grin. "But by that time, you'll have won our brother's case for us."

Jame looked the burly sisters up and down. "Or you'll do what to her?"

"So. The little arbiter is a sharp one," Sed said, flipping the knife between her hands. "We'll kill her."

Her sister, Gerd, joined her in a mean chuckle.

"Have a nice evening. Arbiter."

The sisters laughed even harder and stepped out of her way. Jame walked past them and rapped on the door. Balwen, the proprietor, let her in.

Jame stepped into the narrow corridor and took a few heartbeats to calm down. She was in trouble, and she had only one slim trick to play.

"Are you all right?" Balwen put a hand on Jame's arm. "Where's your shadow?"

Jame took a few deep breaths and then launched her brain into action. "She's been arrested on false charges." She ignored Balwen's shocked expression. "I need two things. I need to get a message back to Ynit to let them know what's going on here. Is there anyone here who can do that as quickly as possible?"

Balwen nodded. "My sister's daughter is a scout. She'll do it."

"The second thing is, get a message to the judging arbiter saying I won't be able to argue the case until my peace warrior has been replaced." That would, at least, give her more time to work out a strategy.

Balwen frowned. "Will the arbiter go for that?"

"Fortunately for me, it's a part of the arbiter bylaws," Jame said. "If it's been deemed necessary that an arbiter needs a peace warrior, then the hearing must be postponed until a peace warrior has been provided."

In the meantime, all she had to do was keep both Indot and herself away from the wrath of the Lindigan sisters. She'd have given anything to hear Tigh's reassuring voice at that moment.

Chapter 13

AFTER ANOTHER LONG night in the children's ward, Tigh wandered into the mess hall frequented by the soldiers in the compound. The tables were full as soldiers coming off night duty mixed with those about to start their day.

Tigh, too exhausted to care, propped up against the wall next to the door and waited for a vacant spot on a bench.

She heard Jame's name and realized she'd dozed off. She opened her eyes and saw a young woman in Emoran leathers and Kartlin, the peace warrior coordinator, at the door.

"What do you mean, Indot was arrested?" Kartlin asked. "A drunken brawl? Indot has never touched anything stronger than spiced tea."

"That's all I know." The young Emoran was clearly intimidated by the roomful of noisy soldiers.

Kartlin read something on a piece of paper. "We have to get Jame out of there." She turned and strode out the door followed by the bewildered Emoran.

Tigh took all of two heartbeats to clear the haze from her brain, rush out the door, and trot down the corridor to the central stairs. Her determined footfalls, as she ran up the steps, echoed through the deserted upper floors of the fortress.

Once in her cell, she turned around several times, trying to focus on what she had to do to get to Glaus. "Come on. You can do this."

First things first. She couldn't go anywhere in her white rehabilitation uniform. She dropped to her knees, opened her trunk with shaking hands, and removed the fawn-colored tunic and leggings.

Just the feel of the leather hugging her body boosted her confidence enough to overcome the nervous flutters in her empty stomach. She hadn't had any normal interactions with the real world since she became a Guard and before that, her outside experiences had been limited.

Jame was in trouble, and she had to get to Glaus. That's all that mattered.

"How do I get there?" Tigh's exhausted mind stalled on the idea of impenetrable distance. "How did Jame get there?"

She thanked Bal for the generous pension granted the former Guards and dug deeper into her trunk for a heavy leather bag. She stared into the bag at the pile of silver. How much did it cost to hire a coach to Glaus? Frustrated at her lack of everyday knowledge, she grabbed a handful of pieces and stuffed them into her belt pouch.

She looked at herself in the tarnished mirror and was shocked to see a pale face with unkempt hair and swollen, red eyes blinking back at her.

She turned to leave, but a nagging void kept her feet in place. Something was missing. She pulled from her trunk a small sheath holding a delicate knife. It would do, she nodded as she tied the sheath to her belt.

She rushed out the door and ran down the corridor. They could do whatever they wanted to her for leaving the compound without permission. Nothing, even her rehabilitation, was more important than saving Jame.

THE PROBLEM WITH Emorans who were several generations removed from the home territory, was they had an exaggerated idea of proper Emoran behavior in certain situations. The pocket of Emorans who maintained the safe house and the blades shop next door had a great desire to help their princess. Unfortunately, they could only think of two actions that were true to what they thought was the Emoran way.

Jame spent most of the day convincing them not to kidnap the Lindigan sisters or attempt to liberate Indot from the city jail. The last thing she wanted was to be in the middle of an incident between Emoria and the city of Glaus. Despite the sisters' threats, Jame knew the jail was the safest place for Indot. The city would have to answer to the Federation Council if anything happened to a peace warrior or peace arbiter in its custody.

"We can't just sit here and do nothing." Naderol, a compact young woman with short brown hair and matching eyes, plopped both elbows on the table and scowled. She reminded Jame of Tas.

"We are doing something," Jame said. "We're waiting for Ynit to respond to my message."

"But you're our princess," Naderol said. "We can't allow you to be treated like this."

"No one here knows I'm a princess. They probably don't even know I'm Emoran because I'm an arbiter." Jame took a sip of spiced tea. "After this fiasco, I'm not sure if I'll even receive my medallion."

"It's not your fault your client turned out to be guilty," Regar said. She was a tall levelheaded woman seated next to Naderol.

"But they know, even if all this mess hadn't happened, I would've asked to be taken off the case," Jame said. "I can't bring myself to defend the guilty, although they have the right to a fair hearing."

"Sometimes guilt is not always obvious," Regar said.

"I know, and that bothers me a lot," Jame said.

Naderol gave Jame a puzzled look. "But you're not really going to be an arbiter. You're going back to Emoria when you finish your studies. Right?"

Jame's thoughts filled with the images of a dark-haired warrior traveling by her side as she worked as an arbiter at large. Jyac wasn't going to be happy with her choice of companion. Argis was going to be livid. No. Going back to Emoria was not a wise choice at the moment. "I plan to be an arbiter for a while. I need to explore the world before I settle in Emoria."

"But you're going to be joined," Naderol said.

Jame took a deep breath while she found the proper response. "Any rumors you've heard concerning that are false."

Regar and Naderol exchanged astonished glances.

"You haven't entered into an understanding with Argis?" Regar asked.

"No formal understanding." Jame knew that whatever she said would get back to Emoria. The speed of an Emoran rumor was quicker than the wind, so the saying went.

"Formal or informal," Regar shrugged and relaxed, "you do have an understanding."

"There may have been an understanding once." Jame was tired of resisting the truth in her heart. She was in love with Tigh. "But that understanding no longer exists."

"You and Argis are no longer a couple?" Naderol asked.

"We're no longer a couple." Not wanting to endure any more questions, Jame pushed up from the table. "It's getting late, and I need to do some work before I turn in."

"Good night, my princess," Regar said as she and Naderol stood. "Sleep well."

Jame smiled. "Thanks."

She trudged up the steps to the guest rooms, trying not to picture the reactions back home when her words reached there. On one side of the sword blade, her life was clearer than it had ever been. On the other side, it had degenerated into a hopeless mess that got more confusing by the heartbeat.

An astonishing thought came to her, and she paused at the top of the steps. Her life was now intertwined with Tigh's, whether she received her medallion or not. If Emoria wanted her to come back they'd have to accept Tigh, and Tigh would have to want to live in Emoria.

Caught up in this amazing revelation, Jame navigated the short corridors to her room. Being a princess, she had the best chamber in the establishment, removed from the small common rooms on the other floors.

She pushed her door open, strolled across the threshold, and sensed another presence in the room behind her. The door slammed shut and a large strong hand covered her mouth, while another hand grabbed her arm and pinned it to her back.

Casually flipping a knife and sporting a smirk, Sed sauntered out of the shadows. She made a show of looking Jame over and lifted a few strands of Jame's hair. Jame tried not to grimace at the touch.

Sed sneered and her eyes turned cold. "What's this about needing a peace warrior to argue a case?"

Peace warrior? Jame's frightened mind reacted. *What I need is a miracle.*

IT FELT AN eternity since the coach wheels clattered onto the cobblestones of the city street, but it was scarcely a quarter sandmark before it jolted to a halt in front of a door illuminated by a single sheltered light. Tigh had spent the day too tense with worry to give in to her overwhelming exhaustion and emerged from the vehicle onto unstable legs. The driver had delivered her to Glaus without delay, and she gave him the agreed upon amount of silver.

The door etched with a sword and a bow opened. A coach with the colors of Ynit could only mean one thing, and an older woman beckoned Tigh into the safe house. "Are you the new peace warrior from Ynit?"

Tigh blinked at her and wondered why she hadn't thought of using that ruse. "Yes. Paldar Tigis." She was surprised at how raw her voice sounded. Now she felt foolish for not taking advantage of the long journey to catch up on her sleep. She couldn't help Jame if she wasn't alert.

"I'm Balwen, the proprietor," the woman said. "The princess's room is on the second level, toward the back. A rabbit is on the door. Tigis? We serve Ingoran food. I'll prepare a room for you."

Tigh almost told her to not bother but stopped. "Thank you."

As soon as they entered the common room, Tigh hurried to the back stairs and only her heavy exhaustion kept her from running up the steps.

"Rabbit on the door," she muttered as she wandered the narrow corridors leading to the back of the building.

She stopped and listened. She didn't need to see an animal on the door to know which chamber Jame was in. Her enhanced hearing picked up an arrogant voice behind the door at the end of a short hallway. An all too familiar voice, filled with defiance and fear, answered.

Safe house, indeed, Tigh reacted in rage. She took long strides and exploded into the room.

A tall muscular woman held Jame. An equally large woman hovered nearby. All three sets of eyes shot to the opened door. Before Tigh had a chance to do anything, the women's arrogance faltered into fear.

The woman released Jame and, with the other, backed away from the doorway. Tigh's sleepy mind was mired with confusion.

"Did I forget to mention my best friend is Tigh the Terrible?" Jame asked as she backed away from the women.

Finally catching on, Tigh straightened and leveled her most intimidating glare at them.

"Please," one woman whimpered as she huddled on the floor with the other woman.

"What's going on here?" Balwen asked from behind Tigh.

A group of Emorans crowded the corridor.

"The Lindigan sisters were trying to coerce me into arguing their brother's case," Jame said. "Would some of you mind securing them and making sure they are safely escorted to the city jail?"

Naderol grinned. "With pleasure."

Tigh stepped away from the door and several Emorans entered and dragged the terrified sisters away. They cast curious glances at her.

Tigh almost tumbled to the floor by the impact of Jame's body against hers. Jame buried her head onto Tigh's shoulder as they wrapped their arms around each other. Tigh was so relieved and happy she couldn't stop a few tears from sliding down her cheeks.

Balwen shut the door on her way out.

Tigh's world was right again. Jame was safe and in her arms. The lack of sleep and food caught up to her all at once and her mind tumbled.

Jame braced Tigh up and led her to the bed. She then knelt in front of her. "You look awful." She brushed strands of hair out of Tigh's eyes.

"I guess I haven't gotten much sleep," Tigh mumbled.

"I missed you, too." Jame gave her a gentle kiss. "I was praying for a miracle and then you burst through the door. How'd you do that?"

Tigh managed a weary smile. "I overheard Kartlin about you being in trouble. I got here as fast as I could."

Jame gazed at Tigh with affection-filled eyes. "Does anyone know you're here?"

Tigh looked at the floor. "They've probably figured it out by now."

Jame pulled Tigh into her arms. "We'll worry about that later. You need sleep, and I need to write out a formal complaint against the Lindigan sisters."

"Don't go out alone," Tigh said.

"I'll send the complaint by courier," Jame said. "Don't worry. I'm not going anywhere without my warrior."

Those words sent a wistful pang through Tigh's heart. "I want to be your warrior."

"You are my warrior. And I'll do everything I can to make you my peace warrior." Jame pressed her lips against Tigh's in a gentle reaffirming kiss.

"Peace warrior," Tigh mumbled. "I like the sound of that."

"Now I want you to get some sleep."

Tigh was barely aware of Jame's efforts to get her boots and leathers off and being tucked into bed. Her heart felt safely at home, and she fell asleep, knowing what fate had prepared for her life.

TIGH GLANCED AROUND the chamber. The quick moment of panic was replaced by the memory of where she was. She was in Glaus. In the Emoran safe house . . . She wasn't alone. She rolled over and gazed at the vision of Jame's face relaxed in peaceful sleep. The intimacy of their positions made her lightheaded, and she sat up to clear her roiling brain.

Jame stirred from the movement. "Good morning."

Tigh took some settling breaths. "Morning."

Jame sat up and studied Tigh. "I'm surprised at how well I slept. I've never shared a bed with anyone before."

Tigh turned to her. "What about—?"

"A patch of meadow, a shadow behind the warriors' barracks, a hidden crevice in the palace, never a bed," Jame said. "Emoria's rather strict about some things."

"I've never shared a bed with anyone before either." Tigh pushed down memories of finding release with other Guards in any place that was convenient. Sex was just something to do to keep them from giving in to what they really lusted for—engaging an enemy in battle.

"I'm sure we'll get used to it," Jame said. "If you still want to be my warrior that is."

Unable to speak, Tigh needed to reassure Jame she most definitely wanted to be her warrior. She twisted around, pulled Jame into her arms, and gave her a heartfelt kiss.

Jame smiled. "I'll take that as a yes."

Tigh took Jame's hand into both of hers. "I have a lot of memories, things I have to work through. You'll have to be patient."

"We both have things we have to work through," Jame said. "We can do it together."

"I think I like that." Tigh glanced around the room. "Is this one of the things you're going to have to work through?"

"Let's just say Balwen, the proprietor, gave me a motherly lecture last night when I took my message concerning the Lindigan sisters to her," Jame said. "They think Argis and I had some kind of spat, and we'll get back together again. They'll understand in time, but this is what I'll have to go through until they're convinced, I'm not interested in Argis anymore."

"What would completely convince them?" Tigh asked.

Jame sighed. "Emorans can be so stubborn with their ideas. It doesn't help that I'm a princess, and they've been hearing stories about me since I was born. Nothing less than a joining will convince them that Argis and I aren't just quarreling." Jame caught her breath. "I mean—"

Tigh studied the smaller hand in her strong large hands. "If that's what it takes."

"But I wouldn't want that to be the only reason." Jame wrapped her free arm around Tigh's neck and pulled her close. "There's only one reason I want to be joined with you." She gazed into Tigh's eyes. "I love you."

The impact of the words was such a blow to Tigh reeled from the impact of the words to her senses. She felt close to blacking out. How could words create such a physical reaction? She labored to pull air into her lungs and gently squeezed Jame's hand. "I love you, too."

Jame grinned and collapsed against Tigh.

A rap on the door interrupted their peace.

"A delegation has arrived from Ynit," Balwen said through the door.

"Delegation?" Tigh asked.

Jame sighed. "Why can't anything be easy?"

JAME KEPT GLANCING back at the pair of soldiers trailing them as they walked down the crowded street. She thought it was insane for the Tribunal to think Tigh was a danger to anyone. She turned to Tigh and frowned at the carefully controlled grimace on her face. "Are you all right?"

Tigh's startled expression turned sheepish. "The morning meal."

"Wasn't it good?" Jame said. "It tasted all right to me."

"Cooks who aren't Ingoran tend to make the food too spicy," Tigh said. "They think they're making up for the lack of meat or something."

"I never thought of that," Jame said. "So, your stomach's upset."

Tigh sighed. "Yeah."

Jame watched Tigh's stoic attempt to ignore her discomfort. This was the woman the Tribunal thought was a danger to society? She almost laughed at the irony. They approached a narrow shop, and she turned to the soldiers. "I need to step in here for a moment." Before they had a chance to respond, she ducked through the doorway.

Jame smiled at the shopkeeper. "A small bag of those." She pointed to one of the dozen small wooden barrels on a slab of wood.

The shopkeeper darted a glance outside the door. "Two coppers."

Jame paid and wondered what rumors were already stirring about certain visitors from Ynit.

She strode out of the shop and held up a parchment bag. "This ought to help." She opened the bag and revealed molded balls of mint leaves and sugar.

"Thank you." Tigh selected a ball and popped it into her mouth, then took the parchment and tucked it into her belt pouch.

"Let me know the next time food bothers you," Jame said.

They paused in front of the Glaus Inn, and Jame wrinkled her nose at the sprawling building that seemed to have expanded more from necessity than design. The gilded carvings and deep blue paint shouted its self-importance to the surrounding somber government buildings.

Her opinion of the building didn't change as they crossed the threshold. Unlike common inns, the interior was a hushed study in superior attitude. A young man clothed in the blue-and-white livery of the establishment intercepted them before they could take another step into the foyer.

"This way," he murmured and rushed them across the elegant main chamber before any of the guests had reason to complain about the presence of people who clearly did not belong. Jame wondered what the surreptitiously watching guests would think if they knew she was a princess or Tigh was from a prosperous merchant family.

The young man opened a delicately engraved and painted door and motioned his unwanted charges through it. He then shut the door behind them.

Jame and Tigh paused in front of the door to observe who thought it necessary to make the quick journey from Ynit. Ewan and Sitas represented the Tribunal. Pendon Larke and the counselor, Renat Yinga, were there to assess Tigh's present state of wellbeing. Ingel watched Jame with a troubled frown.

"Come in. Sit down," Ewan said.

Jame and Tigh sat in the elegant chairs opposite the delegation from Ynit.

"The coach business between Ynit and Glaus has been brisk of late. We're here because we need to deflect any possible strain on our relationship with Glaus. We talked with the city leaders late last night. They had been willing to do anything to make up for the false arrest of a peace warrior and for submitting an inexperienced assistant arbiter to a case that turned out to be a part of a dangerous conspiracy."

"But I ruined that." Tigh's whole body was a study in misery.

Jame was torn between consoling Tigh and giving the others a sharp opinion on their agreement with Glaus. She put a hand on Tigh's arm and leveled her gaze at Ewan. "Is that what they think?"

"Yes. They're alarmed Tigh is in their city," Ewan said.

"It doesn't matter that she saved me from being bullied by the Lindigan sisters and that her presence was enough to get them to confess to everything?"

"Like the Lindigan sisters, they see only Tigh the Terrible," Ewan said.

"So, you're going to continue this false assumption rather than stand up to the truth?" Jame straightened. "You give in, and Tigh will never have a chance to go out into society."

"We've presented it as a slight setback in her rehabilitation," Ewan said.

"A slight setback?" Jame centered her rage on her argument. "What did you promise them? That you'd send Tigh back to Ynit in the care of soldiers? Then what? You eventually decide she's been rehabilitated and is free to go into society? The damage will have already been done. She's in the last step of the rehabilitation process. To suddenly treat her as if she'd never been cleansed not only sends a false message about her, it puts the entire cleansing process into doubt. Now I ask you. Are you interested in doing a quick washing over of the situation here or are you willing to take advantage of this opportunity to stand by your rehabilitation program?"

Jame sat back and watched as her words impacted each person across the table. Her argument had, at least, taken a ready response away from them.

A large hand slipped into hers, and she looked into Tigh's eyes, which were filled with pride and affection. She squeezed Tigh's hand, and they shared a private smile.

Ewan took a deep breath and nodded. "You present a very compelling argument, Arbiter. Are you willing to argue for Tigh's right to be treated as a free citizen in Glaus?"

Jame sucked in a shocked breath. "In a heartbeat."

Chapter 14

TIGH SAT CROSS-LEGGED on the hearth of the small fireplace in Jame's room in the Sword and Bow. Although the officials of Glaus would have been happier if she was in a nice cold cell in the city jail, she hadn't done anything criminal to merit a stay in that facility. A compromise had been made that she had to remain in the Emoran safe house until the time of her hearing. She had thought this was a good idea until the constant glares and offhand remarks from the resident Emorans forced her to take refuge in Jame's chamber.

They all thought they knew how Jame should be living her life and who she should be spending it with. *Sounds familiar*, Tigh sighed.

They had so many battles to fight before they could be together. This latest battle was a brave move by Jame, and if she didn't win, their hopes would be as good as lost. But victory would make everything else so much easier to attain.

Tigh picked up light footfalls outside the door and detected the aroma of food. The door opened, and Jame walked in followed by a young girl from the kitchen.

"Just put it there." Jame pointed to the small table in the middle of the chamber and then smiled at Tigh.

The young girl glanced at Tigh as she put the wooden platter filled with covered dishes on the table.

"Thank you," Jame said.

"Have a good evening, my princess," the girl said shyly before skipping out of the chamber.

"Hungry?" Jame asked, waggling her brows. "I had a talk with the cook, and they didn't add any extra ingredients this time."

"Except maybe poison," Tigh mumbled as she stood and approached the table.

Jame sat down. "My country people giving you a hard time?"

Tigh dolefully nodded as she took the other chair and moved it so she could sit next to Jame rather than across from her. Jame smiled at the action.

"Thank you for the food. Thank you for everything." Tigh lowered her eyes.

"Hey." Jame lifted Tigh's chin with a caressing hand. "I'm being selfish, you know. I don't want anything to stand in the way of us being together."

"You're a miracle to me, and I won't ever do anything that would force us apart." Tigh clasped Jame's cheek in the palm of her hand.

"The only thing that can force us apart is the ignorance of others." Jame leaned into the warm hand. "This hearing will be an important step in educating everyone on who the new Tigh is."

Tigh shook her head. "But it's only one city. Your career could be harmed by my presence."

Jame gave her an impish grin. "You can only enhance my career and reputation. After all, I'm the one who has successfully argued your cases and had the good sense to choose you to be my peace warrior. Any defendant can feel safe there isn't going to be any trouble from dissenting parties."

Tigh held Jame's confident eyes for several heartbeats. "Do you think it'll really work?"

"I really do." Jame turned her head and brushed her lips against Tigh's hand.

Warmth spread through Tigh from that simple touch, and she captured Jame's tantalizing lips with her own. "I put myself into your capable hands."

"Completely?" Jame mumbled as she playfully nipped at Tigh's nose.

"Completely," Tigh said.

"All right." Jame grinned. "Let's eat."

Tigh laughed as she released Jame.

Jame put out the plates and pulled the lids off of several dishes. "What do we start with first?"

Tigh blinked at the food and then raised astonished eyes to Jame. "You're trying Ingoran food?"

"Yes," Jame said. "I want to learn all the ritual that goes with it, too."

A delighted Tigh pointed to a dish filled with thin slices of celery in a clear sauce. "We start with the watery vegetables."

Jame grinned. "Watery vegetables."

"YOU'RE A GOOD teacher," Jame said.

Between the almost mystical quality of the Ingoran ritual, the delicate flavors of the food, and the tantalizing warmth flowing between them, she was certain it had been the most wonderful meal she had ever eaten.

"I'm only as good as my pupil," Tigh said.

Jame sighed at the rap on the door. She gave Tigh a mock look of exasperation, went to the door, and pulled it open.

Balwen, glancing past Jame at Tigh, sighed and held a small scroll out to Jame.

"This is from the queen," Balwen said.

"Thank you, Balwen." Jame took the scroll and kept down the swell of apprehension in her full stomach.

Balwen gave Tigh one more look, nodded to Jame, and then trudged back down the corridor.

Jame closed the door, walked to her chair, and sank down onto it. She put the scroll on the table and stared at it for several heartbeats.

Tigh put her hand on Jame's arm, capturing her attention.

"You said the age of consent in Emoria is eighteen," Tigh said. "She can't make you do anything you don't want to do."

"I know." Jame looked down at the scroll. "But she's so certain about what she thinks is going on in my mind and how I'll feel once I'm an arbiter that she won't listen to anything else."

Tigh picked up the scroll and held it out to Jame. "May as well get it over with."

As Jame took the scroll, their fingers touched and the shock from just that casual contact was enough for Jame to stare into Tigh's eyes for several heartbeats.

Jame snapped away from Tigh's intriguing gaze with a quick shake of her head, took possession of the scroll, and broke the seal. She read the strained formal words and heard in her mind all the unwritten words and emotions.

Jyac was concerned that Jame's peace warrior had been arrested and that Jame had been threatened. She refrained from mentioning who had saved her from the menacing Lindigan sisters although Jame had no doubt Jyac knew the whole story. Emoran scouts traveled faster than the wind.

"She's offering a patrol of warriors to ensure my safety." Jame lifted sad eyes to Tigh. "She's having problems keeping Argis from rushing here to my rescue."

She put an elbow on the table and rubbed her chin with her knuckles. All she needed was a quick remedy that could satisfy Jyac and Argis at once.

"That's it." She went to the small writing table in the corner of the room and gathered a pen, ink jar, and several sheets of paper and brought them back to the larger table.

Tigh piled the dishes away from the space in front of Jame, who gifted her with a dazzling smile of thanks.

Silence, except for the scrape of the metal nib against the paper, descended on the chamber. Ink flowed on several sheets of paper for a good quarter sandmark. Jame finally released herself from her own spell and lifted her head from her task.

"That ought to take care of it." She arranged the sheets in order. "I explained what really happened here. Then I told her I want to be an arbiter for a while." She took Tigh's hand and gazed into her eyes. "Then I told her I can't be joined to Argis because I'm in love with you. I wrote a formal petition to allow me to be joined with someone who's not an Emoran."

Tigh squeezed Jame's hand. "And how's she going to take all that?"

Jame emitted a rueful laugh. "Not well. But given time I think she'll understand."

"What if you're not allowed an Emoran joining?" Tigh asked.

"I hear Ingoran joinings are interesting." Jame smiled at Tigh's startled expression. "We're going to be joined no matter what. It'd be nice if we were accepted by the Elders Council but there isn't any law against an Emoran being joined according to the customs of another society."

"But what impact will that have on you becoming queen?" Tigh asked.

"I'd have to do a lot worse than fall in love with an outsider to prevent me from becoming queen," Jame said. "Besides, it doesn't matter. I want us to be joined. I want to spend my life with you."

Tigh pressed Jame's hands to her lips. "It would be my honor to be joined with you and to spend the rest of my life by your side. You're a miracle in my life."

Overcome by the heartfelt words, Jame released Tigh's hands and wrapped her arms around her neck. "No matter what happens, we go through it together and come out of it together."

"Together." Tigh found Jame's lips with her own.

Jame reluctantly broke off the kiss. "I guess I should seal this and get it on its way." She went to the small writing table and applied hot wax and her seal to the scroll.

Tigh picked up the platter of dishes, placed it in the corridor, and waited for Jame before she closed the door.

Jame tried not to think about how Jyac was going to receive her message and put the packet in the mail basket outside the door. She'd have to do it sooner or later. Maybe by the time she had her medallion, Jyac and the Council would accept her decisions.

"That's that," Jame said as she closed the door.

Tigh ran a hand through her hair and dropped cross-legged onto the small rug in front of the fireplace.

Jame saw the familiar defense mechanism in Tigh's mind fold in on itself, creating a maze that no one could penetrate if she let it go too long.

Jame knelt in front of Tigh and resisted trying to make eye contact until Tigh was ready. After two years of working with Guards, she knew a lot more about them than Tigh probably suspected. She had heard her share of stories on what the Guards did to satisfy their physical desires. Love, or affection, was never involved. They believed love ruined a Guard's battle lust. Sex had been nothing more than a selfish sport between them.

"We slept in the same bed last night," Jame said.

"I was unconscious at the time," Tigh said to the floor.

"We don't have to sleep." Jame watched as the battle Tigh waged within herself surfaced in a twitch around the lips.

"My memories are . . . like all the memories I have from that time." Tigh's voice reflected the haunted look in her eyes.

"There's a difference between sex and making love." Jame brushed Tigh's cheek with her knuckles. "I don't want to have sex." Tigh looked at her. "I want to make love."

Tigh shook her head. "I've never—"

"Of course, you have." Jame smiled and enveloped Tigh's cheeks with her hands. "You made love to me all this evening with your eyes. They caressed me gently and tenderly through our meal and they devoured me when we talked about our joining."

Tigh swallowed hard and gazed at Jame.

Jame pressed a kiss on Tigh's forehead. "You make sweet gentle love every time you kiss me. I dream about how your lips softly caress mine." She brushed the objects in question with her finger. "I can't even find the words to describe the giddy, wonderful, sensuous, magical sensation."

Her own lips descended upon Tigh's with each descriptive word until they were wrapped around each other, savoring many more sensations for which words had not yet been invented.

Jame finally broke from the stunned Tigh and stood up and held out her hand.

Tigh took the hand and scooped a startled Jame into her arms and stumbled to the bed on weakened knees.

Much to Jame's wondrous delight, the smiles and tender touches lasted long into the night.

INGEL COULD ONLY imagine how nervous Jame was at the thought of facing the Council of Glaus and convincing them that Tigh the Terrible was not a threat. She knew the Military Tribunal of Ynit wanted Tigh free from their responsibility—although they were cautious about it, not wanting their decision to come back and haunt them. But the situation at Glaus was quite different. Glaus had no reason to want Tigh in their city and had every reason to have her removed.

Ingel rapped on the door of the Sword and Bow and realized this would be her first glimpse into the world Jame grew up in. A tall woman opened the door and beckoned her inside.

"My name is Ingel. I'm an arbiter from Ynit. I'm here to see Jamelin Ketlas," Ingel said, as the Emoran looked her over.

"I'm Balwen, proprietor. This way." She led Ingel into the common room where guests lingered over their morning meals. "They're over there." She nodded to the back of the chamber where Jame and Tigh consumed their meal.

Ingel noted the warrior theme of the decor from the painted depictions of famous battles and heroes to the artful display of weapons hanging on the walls.

"Good morning," she said as she approached their table.

"Ingel. Good morning, have a seat," Jame said.

She raised an eyebrow at Jame's buoyant mood and sat in the offered chair. "I just stopped by in case you had any questions or concerns about the hearing."

"I do have one question," Jame said. "Will it be only before the city council, or will there be a crowd of people there?"

"Unfortunately, being a public hearing, the Council can't keep the people out," Ingel said. "But they promised they won't let any more in after all the seats are filled."

"Sounds reasonable," Jame said.

"This isn't going to be like arguing in front of the Military Tribunal with only friends and family and members of the compound community in the audience." Ingel looked at Tigh, who was munching a mouthful of greens. "As dramatic as it was, I'm not quite sure the Ketlas interpretation of Bailikon's procedure will work in this situation."

Jame glanced at the discreetly listening Emorans at the tables around them. "I don't think I'll need Bailikon's procedure or anything else so dramatic."

Ingel eyed Jame with curiosity. "I hope you're right. The hearing will be right after the midday meal. That means you'll have to stay in here for one more morning."

"Oh, that's all right," Jame said. "I'm enjoying the company."

Ingel looked from Jame to Tigh, noting the light blush coloring both their cheeks. The rumors were rampant about them, but she honored their privacy and refrained from asking.

She caught the faces at a nearby table. The women were glaring at Tigh. She remembered the incident at the safe house in Ynit. The Emorans were less than happy with how close Tigh was to Jame. Much like the Ingorans' unhappiness with Jame representing Tigh.

"How do you feel about the argument Jame has prepared?" Ingel asked Tigh.

"It's the best argument for this circumstance," Tigh said. "Whether she succeeds or not, she'll have given it her best shot and that's good enough for me."

Ingel flashed a glance at the nearby table and noted the glares turned to puzzled frowns. "That's all any of us can ask for." No matter the outcome, she knew Jame would make the hearing worth talking about for a long time.

SARK STRODE THROUGH the scouts' camp in the meadows above the city of Emor. She always spent the sandmark after the midday meal away from the more sedentary duties as Jyac's Right Hand. Staying in mental touch with her former occupation as a scout helped her to keep perspective on the governing of her country.

The young scouts in training were practicing their stealth skills by navigating a course filled with metal odds and ends that clanked with every wrong move. Sark smiled in remembrance of the many long moons she practiced on that course until she could walk through it as soundless as a cat.

Above the clattering and crashing from the course, Sark heard rapid footfalls behind her. She turned and was surprised to see Eiget running toward her.

"Sorry to interrupt your walk, Sark." The palace guard slid to a stop on the slick grass. "The queen would like to see you."

"Thank you, Eiget." Sark fell in step next to the guard. "Any idea what this is about?"

"A message came from the princess. Jyac wasn't very pleased with it." Eiget was famous for her droll understatements.

The walk to the palace was too short for Sark, and she could feel Jyac's displeasure the moment she walked into the chamber.

"This came by overnight courier from Glaus." Jyac held up a handful of papers. Eiget closed the door behind Sark.

Sark approached the table and accepted the letter. She roamed the oversized chamber and read Jame's words. "Not quite what we expected."

"She wants to be joined with that woman," Jyac said. "Argis shouldn't have ever gone to Ynit."

"You think she's just angry at Argis?" Sark remembered how different Jame had acted with Argis during her last visit.

Jyac stood, wandered over to the clear quartz window, and stared outside. "I want to hope she's angry with Argis. She was so uncertain about her feelings all the time she was here. Then Argis rushed off to Ynit following her stubborn pride rather than her brain."

"You know, it's possible Jame no longer loves Argis," Sark said.

"It's possible." Jyac ran a hand through her hair. "But she thinks she's in love with that Guard, an outsider with a ruthless past. A warrior known for her compelling personality who's probably using Jame's skills to help her through her rehabilitation."

"Then Jame will return to us brokenhearted but wiser for the experience," Sark said. "Sometimes that's the best thing that can happen."

"And how do you propose we keep Argis from charging off to Ynit, once again, and challenging the former Supreme Commander of the Southern Territories?" Jyac asked.

"Argis has already struck her, and she didn't even try to fight back. What kind of warrior is that?" Sark tossed Jame's letter onto the table. "If Argis kills her, we'll lose Jame for sure."

Jyac sighed. "We need to send a delegation to Ynit to get a firsthand look at the situation."

"Maybe we won't have to do anything." Sark shifted the sheets of paper on the table and put her finger on a passage. "She says she's going to argue Tigh's right to walk the streets of Glaus as a free citizen. Jame's good but this sounds impossible even for her."

"So, you think the situation will naturally sort itself out if she loses this case?"

"If Tigh is using her, it will," Sark said. "Maybe we'll have Jame back with us sooner than we think."

"Not a word of this until we hear from Glaus." Jyac straightened. "Then Argis can go after Jame with our whole army at her back if need be."

TIGH WAS CONVINCED Jame's voice must have been touched with magic from the moment she was born. How else could the fifty-five members of the Council of Glaus and the near thousand spectators stop their whispers and mumbles as soon as Jame spoke. And all she said was "good afternoon."

Jame looked puzzled at the immediate silence. "First off, I'd like to thank the city of Glaus for giving a deserving woman the chance to prove that not only can she return to society without consequence but will most certainly become a distinguished citizen of the Southern Territories."

Murmurs and whispers rose up from the hall. The Keeper of the Bench rapped a hollow pipe several times.

"Please proceed, Arbiter Jamelin." Yanders Loften, the mayor of Glaus, motioned to Jame.

"Thank you, Mayor Yanders." Jame flashed him a gracious smile.

Tigh almost laughed at the mayor's reaction to a full out assault of Jame's charm. Magic. Nothing less.

"The Guard rehabilitation program has been completely successful," Jame said. "To date, over seven hundred Guards from the regular regiments and eighteen former members of the Elite Guards have been rehabilitated. Now I ask. Has there even been a hint of a problem from any of them?"

"Eighteen Elite Guards?" Yanders asked in amazement.

Jame nodded. "Eighteen. Including Nark the Notorious, Silar, Rewn the Rough, Ienor Quet, and Patch Lachlan." Each name brought a louder gasp from the spectators. "They're all pursuing quiet productive lives."

"Patch Lachlan?" Yanders asked.

"Patch Lachlan." Jame drew the name out as she turned to the still, rapt spectators. "Now many consider Patch Lachlan to have been as ruthless as Tigh the Terrible and maybe would have been much more vicious if the Wars had continued. Would the Council agree to this?"

Yanders looked behind him at the arched benches filled with Council members and all signaled agreement. "Patch Lachlan was the Elite Guard in charge of the siege engines for the taking of Operal. Our trees were chosen because of their size and strength. Many of us here were involved in moving the timber to the borderlands where Patch's army was preparing for the attack on Operal. Both Tigh the Terrible and Patch Lachlan were there and many of us agreed that, while Tigh was cold and ruthless, she exuded a strong intelligence and control. But Patch." He grimaced. "That woman was wild and cruel. Both women were terrifying to witness."

Sometimes, Tigh mused, luck came to those who dug in the right places and knew how to use the small, unexpected treasures found buried there. All it took was a mention of her name before stories of Patch Lachlan spilled out of the good people of Glaus. And all it took was her knowledge of where all the former Guards resided—gleaned from reading everything she could during her short time in the archives.

"Patch Lachlan has been a free member of our society for a year and a half," Jame said. "She goes by her given name rather than her Guard name and has quickly established herself as a learned and respected member of the community in which she lives. Known for her wise and thoughtful personality, Patch has had no trouble fitting back into society. I think if she were still wild and cruel, we would have heard about it by now, don't you?"

The Council members shifted.

"Maybe she's been able to hide her violent tendencies," Yanders said. "Some communities are more tolerant of that kind of behavior than others."

"That's true." Jame nodded then lifted mischievous eyes to the Council. "But not true in this case. So, do you think a former Elite Guard who was wild and cruel and by all accounts destined to be more ruthless than Tigh the Terrible could live in a city such as Glaus as a peaceful law-abiding citizen?"

"Of course not." Yanders straightened then scanned the Council members for any other opinions on the subject. "We witnessed Patch Lachlan as an Elite Guard. It just isn't possible a person like that could act in a civilized manner."

Tigh knew Jame could bring her own passive presence into the argument and question them on whether she was the same woman they had witnessed on the borderlands before the siege of Operal. But that was the most logical next move and most likely expected. A move that could open up arguments based on opinions rather than logic and fact.

"If I were to show evidence that disputes your conviction Patch Lachlan could not live as a respected citizen in a place like Glaus, would you agree the Guard rehabilitation program is successful and Tigh is of no threat to this community?" Jame asked.

The Council took some time to confer on this. Their smug expressions told Jame they didn't believe she could prove her case to them.

Yanders faced Jame and Tigh. "We'll agree to your terms."

"Thank you, Mayor." Jame raised her eyes to the Council members. "I would like to call Patch Lachlan before the Council as evidence of the success of the Guard rehabilitation program."

The stunned spectators gasped and twisted around, expecting the notorious Guard to enter the back of the chamber. When no one appeared, they settled into a tense, expectant silence.

A woman wrapped in the robe of an acolyte to Bal rose from a Council bench. The shocked silence wove a profound and satisfying feeling within Tigh.

Chapter 15

JAME WOKE FROM the kind of dream that only came from the warmth and security of being wrapped in strong loving arms. She peered up in the gray light of the predawn and was surprised to see Tigh awake, just holding her. She shifted and captured Tigh's attention.

"Why aren't you asleep?" Jame tightened her hold around Tigh.

"I was thinking." Tigh brushed her fingertips over Jame's arm.

"Thinking?" Jame asked.

Tigh sighed. "About Patch."

Jame looked up amused. "You know, it's not nice to be thinking of another woman while you're sharing a bed with me."

Tigh swooped down for a kiss and gifted Jame with an affectionate look. "I was just thinking about what she has to do to satisfy the need to fight."

Jame nodded against Tigh's shoulder. "She's lucky there are several other Guards in Glaus she can spar with."

"But fighting contradicts her personality and her profession as an acolyte to Bal," Tigh said. "Her life is dedicated to nonviolence and helping the needy in the community and yet she has to fight to maintain her sanity."

Jame lifted her head. "What about you?"

Tigh frowned. "I don't understand why. But I don't have the need to fight, only the want. To Patch, it's like an addiction that has to be fed or she starts taking it out on everyone around her. I miss fighting and want to feel a sword in my hands again. I miss pulling my mind and body together into a single purpose of engaging an opponent. But I don't have to fight."

"That's good," Jame said. "You'll make a perfect peace warrior."

Tigh gazed down at Jame. "I just wish I could help her."

"Maybe they'll learn what went right with your cleansing and be able to help the others," Jame said.

"Maybe." Tigh wiped a few golden strands from Jame's face. "Are you going to be noted in the legal interpretations again?"

Jame laughed and buried her head in Tigh's shoulder. "I wish Ingel would quit telling me how amazed she is at my arguments. I'm just doing what she taught us. Finding the best argument for the case."

"But most arbiters don't have the Emoran tracking instinct to know how and where to find the best argument," Tigh said. "Your warrior training is much more a part of you than you might think."

"I know," Jame said. "It's ironic my warrior knowledge helps me in a peaceful profession, but Patch can't channel it to help her."

"That's because you were born a warrior and raised around warriors," Tigh said. "You've seen warrior skills and knowledge applied to all aspects of life."

"I don't regret coming from a warrior society," Jame said. "I don't even regret my warrior training. I just sometimes regret I was born a princess."

Tigh pulled Jame up and captured her lips with loving devotion. "That's because you're young and want to live the life of your choosing. But that princess is very much inside you, in everything you do. Without you knowing it, you've been able to incorporate it into your life as much as the warrior skills."

"I don't mind that part." Jame returned the kiss. "I just wish everyone in Emoria would leave me alone until I'm ready to return home."

"Maybe winning the case yesterday will send the message that it would be a waste for you not to be an arbiter for a while." Tigh settled them back onto the bed.

"I hope so," Jame murmured. Lost in thought, she watched the sun rise as Tigh drifted off to sleep.

GINDOR WAS NOT the kind of woman who took lightly what she perceived to be irresponsible behavior. She bent her white head over the letter that Jame had sent from Glaus, noting that it was several days old.

The remaining eleven members of the Council settled into their places at the half moon table in the Council chamber. Jyac and Sark sat midway down the long straight edge of the half moon, watching Gindor's face shift through reactions, each hardening into greater anger and dismay.

Gindor lifted blue-gray eyes surrounded by smooth skin and took the time to study Jyac. "Why are you just showing this to us?"

"We thought the problem would sort itself out," Jyac said.

Gindor raised an eyebrow. "And how was the problem supposed to do that?"

"We determined that Tigh the Terrible is just using Jame and will turn on her when her rehabilitation is complete," Jyac said. "When she wrote that letter, she was going to argue that Tigh was harmless to the people of Glaus. We were positive she wouldn't be able to win. Once she lost, Tigh would have nothing more to do with her."

"So why are we looking at this letter now?" Gindor asked.

"Jame won the case," Jyac said.

The Council murmured both surprise and admiration for their young princess.

Gindor frowned. "You mean she was able to convince the city council of Glaus that Tigh the Terrible was just another citizen visiting their town?"

Jyac nodded. "Yes. According to Balwen, who witnessed it, Jame did it in under a quarter sandmark."

Gindor shook her head. "So that means we still have a problem."

Jyac sighed. "Yes. Jame has grown extremely attached to that Guard. And now she thinks she's in love with her and wants to be joined. We were thinking of sending a delegation to get a better understanding of the situation."

"A delegation?" Gindor pressed Jyac back with her penetrating eyes. "We need to get Jame out of there. She's obviously in serious danger."

"We also thought, once she finds out the truth behind Tigh's association with her, she'll return to us heartbroken but a little wiser with her emotions," Jyac said. "If we try to force her out now, she may completely rebel. Sometimes it's best to make a mistake and learn from it."

"Do you think Tigh the Terrible will let her walk away with just a broken heart?" Gindor asked. "The woman is ruthless and cruel."

"Supposedly she's not like that anymore." Jyac frowned. "Argis punched her in the mouth, and she made no move to fight back. Guards can't help but fight back, it's a part of their enhancements."

"Of course, she didn't fight back." Gindor shook her head in exasperation. "She wasn't going to jeopardize her relationship with Jame. I'm sure the cleansing took away only the impulse to fight. The ability is still very much within her."

"Maybe," Jyac said. "But that doesn't change the fact that Jame is headstrong enough to hold it against us if we storm in there and forcibly bring her home."

Gindor stared at Jyac. "So, you're willing to risk her getting hurt, maybe killed, when that woman turns on her?"

"Of course not," Jyac said. "We're going to have several warriors stationed at the Ynit safe house. The moment Jame wins that woman's rehabilitation, they'll be ready to act."

Gindor glared at Jyac for several heartbeats then relaxed and glanced at the Council members on either side of her. "Argis included?"

Jyac sucked in her breath. "We want to be unobtrusive."

"We won't be able to keep Argis away," Gindor said. "She obviously doesn't know of this new development because she hasn't taken off for Ynit."

"We were hoping you could convince her that she'd better serve the mission if she was here to receive Jame upon her return," Jyac said.

"Would you agree to that if you were in her position?" Gindor asked.

"I think Jame was having second thoughts about Argis before she met Tigh the Terrible," Jyac said.

"Then she should have let Argis know."

Jyac arched an eyebrow. "Have you ever been able to tell Argis something she doesn't want to hear?"

"Then let Argis go on her own to talk some sense into Jame," Gindor said.

"The last time she did that, Jame got angry with her and sent her home," Jyac said. "Jame's not going to be reasonable until she has that arbiter's medallion."

Gindor crossed her arms. "Which should be before Tigh is rehabilitated. Right?"

Silence shrouded the chamber.

"Yes," Jyac said. "Maybe once she reaches her goal, she'll lose interest in defending that woman."

"Maybe Argis will be able to help her change her mind," Gindor said.

Jyac nodded. "I think we should make extra tributes to Laur in support of Argis's mission."

CONTENTMENT. THE IDEA was so foreign to Tigh it took several days for her to put a name to the warm relaxed feeling that had enveloped her since they returned from Glaus. Just sitting across from Jame in the crowded mess hall eating a midday meal was enough to bring peace to her inner world.

"Why do you think Ingel wants to see both of us?" Jame frowned at the note a young student arbiter had delivered to her.

"We haven't gotten into trouble lately," Tigh said.

"Unless she has a problem with my late-night visits to your cell," Jame said. "She'd have said something before now."

"If it was serious, she'd want to see us right away," Tigh said.

Jame nodded as she scooped a forkful of greens into her mouth. "We do seem to get into trouble, don't we?"

Tigh gave her an impish grin. "I've never gotten into any kind of trouble until I met you."

Jame looked down at her food. "Uh, I wish I could say the same." She glanced up and caught Tigh's affectionate gaze.

AS THEY WALKED across the compound, Jame couldn't help but wonder at how the reactions to seeing them together had changed in the span of a season. At first the reactions had been puzzlement and fear. Then they had shifted to respect and curiosity. People even nodded to them in greeting. She couldn't help but smile at the irony as they strolled across the cloud darkened plaza. A sporadic rumbling foretold an afternoon storm.

Daneran ran down the steps of the arbiters' school as Tigh and Jame approached.

"Ingel wants to see you," Daneran said.

"We know," Jame said as Daneran nodded and hurried away.

They walked across the empty common room to the office and found Ingel relaxing in her back parlor. The remnants of her midday meal sat on the low table in front of her.

"Come in," she said as Jame and Tigh hesitated at the door. "Please sit."

She waved a thin hand at the long couch on the other side of the table.

"I've got something here that I think is yours." Ingel lifted the lid off a wooden box on the table and pulled out a small silver box. "Take it."

Jame took possession of the box, noting the elaborate arbiter seal engraved on the top. She pulled off the lid and stared at the brilliant silver medallion. "I thought . . ."

She looked at Tigh who smiled with pride and then at Ingel.

"You've more than proven your skills as an arbiter," Ingel said.

"The judging part of the job is fine, but what about when I'm arguing for one side or the other? I can't argue cases if I know the client is guilty," Jame said.

"How you choose to practice is up to you," Ingel said. "Under normal circumstances, I'd envision your quest to defend only the innocent to be impossible."

Jame cocked her head. "What do you mean, under normal circumstances?"

"What are Tigh's plans, once she's rehabilitated?" Ingel asked.

Jame turned to Tigh. "We haven't mentioned it because we didn't want to do anything to jeopardize her case. She wants to be a peace warrior. My peace warrior."

Ingel nodded. "I thought so. You want to be an arbiter-at-large and I assumed that you wanted Tigh to be with you. Since she can perceive whether a person is telling the truth or not, you won't ever have to worry about the veracity of your client. It'll also make judging cases easier."

Jame couldn't believe how a random skill from Tigh could be the perfect solution to the one problem that had gnawed at her since she began her studies. Their beliefs and skills meshed together, and she knew without a doubt they were destined to work in tandem. She pulled Tigh into a joyous hug.

"I took the liberty of putting your name in for a residence here in the compound," Ingel said. "Most arbiters-at-large use Ynit as a home base until they find somewhere else to settle. I was able to secure a two-room place in the arbiters' corner."

"Two rooms?" Jame asked.

"I assured the housing committee you're to be joined," Ingel said. "Was that assumption incorrect?"

"No, no," Jame said. "We're going to be joined as soon as possible after Tigh's last hearing."

"Congratulations to both of you," Ingel said. "I have the feeling you'll have an interesting life."

ONE OF THE advantages of having a close personal acquaintance with a warrior was having someone strong enough to move cumbersome belongings. Not only that, Tigh got the last of Jame's possessions into her new quarters before the clouds exploded with heavy rain.

Jame looked around at the two big rooms and her scant belongings piled in a corner and was thankful the place was furnished with a table and benches and a bed. But it would still feel empty, even after Tigh moved in her few belongings. They'd fill it up together. The idea washed over her. For the first time in her life, she felt centered and truly happy.

Warmed by this idea, she cast affectionate eyes at Tigh's efforts to coax a flame from the few bits of wood she found in the tinderbox near the fireplace that dominated a corner of the main room. She had taken one last trip before the rains and returned with a large wooden box, now resting on the table.

The blaze finally sputtered to life, and Tigh turned her attention to the mysterious box. She pulled off the lid, removed several parchment bags, and spread them out on the table. Then she took out piece after piece of Ingoran cooking pots and skillets, delicate serving and eating dishes and intricately carved utensils.

"Where did you get these?" Jame ran her fingers over the smooth dishes with the House of Tigis seal enameled into them.

"From under my cot," Tigh said. "They're the only things I brought with me from Ingor. I kept them under the cot for safekeeping. I got the food from the kitchens on my way back." She nodded at the parchment bags.

"The first meal in our home," Jame said.

Tigh leaned forward and kissed Jame. "This is only a housewarming meal. The full Ingoran feast will be for when I'm moved in."

"When you're no longer the ward of the state." Jame nodded, not looking forward to two long weeks alone in the house.

"We can spend the time getting more furniture and other stuff in here," Tigh said.

Jame grinned at the idea of wandering around Ynit scouring the shops for things to make the empty rooms feel like home. "I have some money saved up." She moved her fingers and calculated how much they'd need to make the place comfortable. Now that she was a full arbiter she was no longer on the compound payroll.

"I have a pension," Tigh said. "Between us we ought to be able to fix this place up."

Jame stepped around the table and wrapped Tigh in her arms. "It's funny. All winter I both dreaded and looked forward to finishing my studies. I was confused about how I felt about home and about everyone's expectations of me. Everything was so uncertain once I got my medallion." She looked up at the tender eyes gazing down at her. "Then I met you, and I suddenly knew my destiny. I'll not let anything split us apart. If we don't meet the expectations of others, we'll create our own world to inhabit."

She looked around the chamber, cozy, even with the rain pounding against the roof and spreading an unrelenting curtain of water outside the large front window.

"This place will be a nice start."

"HOW DO PEOPLE live in Bal be cursed cities?" Argis stared down the same lane for the fourth time. "What is Jame doing with her own quarters, anyway?" She ignored the startled looks from several healers walking past her. Giving in to the heat of the day, she left her cloak at the safe house and wandered around the military compound in just her Emoran leathers.

"You," Argis barked at a tall gangly girl. "What's your name?"

The girl looked around and then stared wide-eyed at Argis. "Goodemer."

"Do you know where Jame lives?" Argis asked.

Goodemer nodded. "Yes."

Argis gentled her tone. "Could you show me?"

"Yes. It's just this way." Goodemer led Argis down several awkward turns into a half-hidden lane. "This is it." She pointed to a small adobe structure nestled against the back of a taller building and surrounded by equally small residences.

Argis stared at the cheerful place Jame called home. She turned to the girl. "Thank you, Goodemer."

"You're welcome." Goodemer flashed a good-natured smile at Argis and then rushed back down the lane.

The window shutters were closed, but the door was open, and Argis stepped onto the threshold. Before her was a bright whitewashed room molded out of adobe. Jame stood with her back to the door, putting dishes on a set of shelves that lined the back wall next to the fireplace.

"Jame."

Jame spun around. "Argis. What are you doing here?"

"What am I doing here?" Argis strode into the room. "What are you doing here? You said you'd come home after you got your medallion."

"I sent you a letter explaining everything," Jame said. "Why can't you just accept my feelings have changed?"

Argis shook her head in frustration. "How can you not see she's using you?"

Jame crossed her arms. "You seem to be so good at knowing people without ever meeting them. How can you not see she's not using me?"

Completely lost in any battle involving words, Argis struggled to rein in her anger and frustration. "All we want you to do is not take any chances with her and come home and let someone else defend her."

"Are you questioning my judgment?" Jame asked. "You don't think I have the ability to know when I'm being used or not?"

"That woman is notorious for bending people to her will," Argis said.

"If that's so, wouldn't it have been easier for her to bend you to her will when she had the chance?" Jame asked. "You'd certainly be an impediment to her evil plans. The best strategy would have been to snare you in or make sure you couldn't interfere."

Argis straightened. "I'd like to see her try."

"Are you saying you can withstand her compelling personality but I can't?"

Argis frowned. *Why was Jame making it so confusing? Couldn't she see what was going on?* "That's not what I'm saying. It's just that . . ." She ran a hand through her wavy hair. "Can't you just forget about this and come home?"

"In a word, no," Jame said.

Argis found Jame's forceful confidence foreign and unsettling. She wasn't quite sure she liked Jame sounding so grown up.

"I'm not going to turn my back on something I've made a commitment to, simply because you, my aunt, or the Council are experiencing fears about it. And I'm not going to give up what I want to do with the part of my life that is truly mine before I take over my duties as queen." Jame captured Argis's astonished eyes with her own. "I've discovered my feelings for you have changed. I felt it during my last visit home, but I allowed Jyac to convince me it was just the pressures of finishing my studies and growing up. In retrospect, I realized I shouldn't have given in so easy, and I did you a great disservice by not saying anything."

"But . . ." Argis choked. "But the challenge. The festival."

"They were things I let happen because Jyac assured me my feelings for you would blossom again," Jame said. "I gave you several chances to step away from our relationship. The fact I completely forgot about the festival two years ago would have been enough reason for you. Even then I'd grown apart from you. I was hoping you'd find someone else."

"There will never be anyone else." Argis couldn't believe Jame's words.

"Would you really want me, feeling as I do?" Jame asked.

"I know I could make you happy," Argis said.

"You wouldn't even agree to do the one thing that would make me happy," Jame said. "When I asked if you would give up your life in Emoria and support my wish to be an arbiter for a while, you couldn't even find words to respond."

"I can't give up my position," Argis said. "I've worked too hard to get to where I am."

"So have I. I've worked hard for this medallion." Jame wrapped her hand around the silver piece at the base of her neck.

"What about her?" Argis asked.

"We'd be having this conversation if I had met Tigh or not," Jame said. "If Jyac believes Tigh is using me, I invite a delegation to witness Tigh's hearing and to monitor what happens afterward. But I expect to be allowed to live my life as I choose if my aunt's fears turn out to be unfounded."

"They'll never agree to you being joined with that woman," Argis said.

"That won't change how I feel about her," Jame said. "I'm sorry, Argis. It hurts me to see you hurt. But if I returned to Emoria with you, we'd both be miserable. You have to believe me. Please go home and tell Jyac that Tigh's hearing is a week from today. If she wishes to send witnesses, tell her I welcome it."

Argis straightened, knowing she couldn't win this argument with Jame, and she couldn't force her to come with her. She had tried. Jyac was right. Her place was in Emoria to comfort a heartbroken Jame when she finally returned home.

Chapter 16

"THEY'VE BEEN HERE for two days, and they haven't even made an effort to get to know you." Jame hung her head as she and Tigh walked out of the archives.

"Maybe they want to stay impartial observers," Tigh said.

"They just don't want to know the truth," Jame said.

"Are you sure it's wise to eat at the safe house tonight?" Tigh asked.

"Yes," Jame said. "I want them to see you as you truly are, not as this monster they hold in their minds."

"I was just thinking, it might be uncomfortable for you," Tigh said. "Remember how the Emorans acted in Glaus."

"I'll be all right." Jame smiled at Tigh's thoughtfulness. "And maybe their eyes will be opened a bit more."

A cool wind whipped around them as they entered the small alley that led to the safe house door.

"Summer is passing," Jame said. "It's just as well we're getting settled here in Ynit."

Tigh nodded. "The shutters need to be fixed before the cold sets in."

Otlar opened the door, and Jame saw the disapproval in her eyes.

"Good evening, Otlar," Jame said. "We're here for the evening meal."

"As you wish, my princess." Otlar bowed her head and led them into the common room. Jame exchanged glances with Tigh at Otlar's coolness.

Still rather early in the evening, the chamber was only half full of women. Otlar led them to a corner table where they could sit adjacent to each other.

"Tea or ale?" Otlar asked with a sigh.

"Tea and Ingoran food for both of us," Jame said.

Shaking her head, Otlar walked away, hands flicking signals to the different servers.

A tense silence interrupted the noisy chatter and clatter around them. Jame didn't have to look up from her plate of greens to know the delegation from Emoria just walked in. Sark led Tas and Poag to the table closest to them. The three arranged the chairs so they faced the corner table, bowed solemnly to Jame, and sat down.

Jame noticed they didn't look at Tigh, who had stopped in mid-chew to observe the strange ritual. Now the delegation watched them as if they were the evening's entertainment. Determined not to let them ruin her meal, she poured more tea into Tigh's mug and explained the Emoran social structure in a low conversational voice as they ate their meal.

"I think we've entertained my country women enough," Jame said when only the bowl of sliced fruit and empty cups were left. "Just one more thing. Come on."

Jame approached the delegation's table and captured each woman's eyes. "I'd like you to meet my friend, Tigh." She turned and smiled at Tigh, who stepped forward and stood next to her. "Tigh, this is Sark, Jyac's Right Hand. Next to her is Tas, a childhood friend, and next to her is Poag, a member of the Elders Council."

Tigh straightened. "Well met, Sark, Tas, and Poag."

The delegation looked stunned as they stood up.

"Well met, Tigh," each said.

Jame smiled. "Thank you for coming to witness my first case as an arbiter."

TIGH SMOOTHED DOWN the white tunic and realized this would be the last time she had to wear it. She looked at the packed trunk next to the door and experienced an ache of sadness. This had been her home since her fifteenth year, and she felt more comfortable in the small cell than she ever had in her parents' home.

No matter what happened that day, she would be moving on to somewhere else. If not James' new quarters, then wherever the Tribunal sent her. She prayed that fate wouldn't play a cruel trick on her by luring her into a false hope of happiness and then snapping it away. She quickly shook away those thoughts. The Tribunal had no reason not to grant her freedom.

Familiar footfalls echoed in the corridor. Tigh always grinned at the thought of seeing Jame. She couldn't control it and decided it wasn't worth the effort to try. She turned her head just as Jame, wearing a matching grin, appeared outside the door.

"Good morning," Jame said.

"Hey," Tigh said as she tried to settle her nerves.

"We have a little time." Jame glanced around the cleaned and swept cell. "In a few sandmarks, we'll be celebrating."

"Before we go." Tigh fumbled with her belt pouch and pulled out a bundle of soft cloth. With trembling hands she held it out to Jame.

Jame peeled away the cloth to reveal a bracelet made of delicate spun metals attached to a silver plate engraved with the Emoran crest of the crossed sword and bow.

"It's wonderful." Jame's voice choked with tears.

"In celebration of your first case as an arbiter."

Jame found the inscription inside the silver plate and gazed at Tigh with eyes glistening with love. "It's the most wonderful thing anyone has ever given to me." She wiped her tears with the cloth that had held the bracelet.

Tigh captured her lips in a sweet kiss.

"I hope I can make those words come true," she said.

Jame held up the bracelet so both could see the engraved words. "'To my arbiter, from your warrior with love forever.' You'll always be my warrior in my heart. But, after today, you'll be my warrior in every way. We can't lose. I won't let it happen."

Tigh beamed at Jame's determination. Jame pulled off miracles as an everyday thing and this would be just one more ordinary miracle for her.

She took the bracelet, clasped it around Jame's wrist, and captured her hand. "It's time."

Jame nodded and looked down at their intertwined hands. "It's time."

JAME WAS SURPRISED to see as many people in the chamber as during the first hearing. Friends and family of a Guard at a hearing was unusual enough and it was almost unheard of for anyone outside the compound to be at a hearing to see an arbiter. But Tigh's case was anything but ordinary.

They took their place in the defendants' box and exchanged uncertain glances at the occupants of the front row. Mixing like oil and water, Tigh's misguided, but loyal parents and the delegation from Emoria sat next to each other.

"Bal help us if they try to talk," Jame muttered.

Tigh hid an amused grin.

The inhabitants of the first row seemed to be only interested in Tigh. Both parties watched her for the barest sign of the woman they thought she was, and they looked confused and frustrated when all they saw was the Tigh they had been observing all along.

Tigh discreetly found Jame's hand and squeezed it. Jame gave her a smile that risked permanent creases to her face. She saw in Tigh all the confidence and reassurance she needed dressed in a dazzling blue.

The side door creaked opened and the seven Tribunes filed in. Jame held her breath as she waited to see who sat in the middle chair. Onderal. She let her breath flow out in a disappointed stream. The pressure on her hand brought her attention to Tigh.

"Remember Glaus," Tigh whispered.

Jame nodded as she pulled together her faltering confidence. She had stood up against an unfriendly city and won. Onderal could make the hearing difficult but he couldn't break her, unless she allowed him to. *Never*, her mind growled with resolve. She straightened and turned her attention to the Tribunal.

"The fourth case for today is the hearing for Paldar Tigis to determine her successful completion of the Guard rehabilitation program. She'll be represented by arbiter, Jamelin Ketlas," Onderal said in an even voice. "You may take the floor, Arbiter."

Jame released Tigh's hand and stood up. She grounded herself by clasping her hands behind her back and looking around the chamber. "Thank you, Tribune Onderal. And thanks to all of our friends who have taken time out from the busy day to attend this hearing."

Jame was pleased to see the spectators react with supportive smiles. She knew of the rumors that had picked up on every step of Tigh's struggle with her family, and her own clashes with her people. Their plight had captured the sympathy of the close community.

"I could stand up here and relate the evidence of Tigh's rehabilitation all day," Jame said. "But it's not my evidence that will win her freedom. Her freedom will only come when all of your fears and uncertainties are completely put to rest."

"How do you plan to do that?" Onderal asked.

Jame spread out her hands. "It's up to you. If you have any lingering fears or uncertainties, voice them and I'll alleviate them for you."

"You're a confident one, aren't you?" Onderal looked Jame over with a dour expression. "There's one issue that could compel us to deny your client's freedom forever. The one failing in our rehabilitation. Former Guards have to regularly give in to the impulse to fight or they start to lose their humanity."

Jame glanced at the three Emorans, who exchanged startled glances. She knew that could be a strong excuse to separate her from Tigh.

"And when does this impulse begin to overtake a cleansed Guard?" Jame asked.

"Shortly after their cleansing," Onderal said.

"And what is done to alleviate this impulse while a Guard goes through rehabilitation?"

"You should know. You've spent enough time with your client." Onderal almost sneered.

Jame shrugged. "I've never witnessed the impulse or the remedy all the time I've known Tigh. This impulse must not come very often, if I haven't seen it."

The seven members of the Tribunal stared tensely at Jame.

"According to the healers, the impulse is always present and must be indulged every three days. If the Guard can't give in to this impulse, it begins to affect their personality," Onderal said, although most of the spectators knew the details. "The healers control it by meeting with the Guard every other day and administering an antidote."

"I'd like to call Pendon Larke, the healer in charge of Tigh's rehabilitation, before the Tribunal," Jame said.

The Tribunes exchanged puzzled glances as a grinning Pendon approached the bench.

"Thank you for coming today, Healer Larke," Jame said. "Could you relate to the Tribunal your experiences with controlling Tigh's impulse to fight."

"I'm unable to speak on that subject." Pendon let the silent shock hang for a dramatic moment. "I've never had to administer an antidote to Tigh for that particular problem."

The Keeper of the Bench sounded the pipe several times to bring the ensuing noise down to a stunned mutter.

"What have you been doing to control her impulse?" Onderal asked.

"Tigh has never manifested that problem," Pendon said. "As has been stated before in this chamber, Tigh's cleansing has been the most successful one we've ever attempted. She's been freely wandering this compound all summer and, unlike the other Guards undergoing rehabilitation, there have been no reports of problems or incidents instigated by her. In contrast, the fourteen other Guards being rehabilitated during the same period have been involved in thirty-one angry disputes, sixteen incidents with patients in the injury ward, and twenty-three physical fights. And before you drag out the incident at the Emoran safe house, Tigh didn't instigate that incident and didn't fight back. She doesn't have the impulse to fight."

"How do you know it won't suddenly emerge at some point?" Onderal asked.

"How can we predict that about any of us?" Pendon asked. "Has anyone witnessed even a passing anger from her? You, on the other hand, Tribune Onderal, have been sporting an angry scowl ever since you entered this chamber."

Onderal looked outraged, then, as if realizing he had just verified Pendon's words, relaxed his expression. "Are you willing to stake your reputation on your testimony that Tigh is completely free from violent impulse."

"Yes. Except under one circumstance," Pendon said, with a twinkle in his eyes. "I have no doubt Tigh would do anything to protect the person who has captured her heart." He turned to a shocked Jame. "In other words, she possesses the most natural impulses in the world."

Onderal scowled at the sentiment and glanced at the Tribunes on either side of him. "Is that all you wish to say, Healer Larke?"

"That's all I need to say," Pendon said before returning to his seat in the chamber.

"Is that the only uncertainty and fear that you have concerning Tigh's rehabilitation?" Jame asked, calming her growing anticipation of bringing this long ordeal to a close.

The Tribunes murmured to each other for several heartbeats.

"We are ready to deliberate the case," Onderal said.

The Keeper of the Bench sounded the pipe, and the Tribunal shuffled to their deliberation chamber.

Jame sank down onto the bench, and Tigh wrapped her hand around hers.

"EVERYONE AROUND HERE seems to think they're a couple," Poag muttered, as the three Emorans leaned forward in their seats and huddled their heads together.

"That doesn't mean she's not using Jame," Sark muttered back.

"But what if we're wrong?" Tas asked, flicking furtive glances at Jame and Tigh in the defendants' box.

"If we're wrong we report it back to the queen," Sark said. "If we're right, we do everything we can to get Jame away from that woman."

THE SIDE DOOR scraped opened and the seven Tribunes, wearing inscrutable expressions, entered the chamber.

A grim-faced Onderal cast impatient eyes about the chamber as the spectators returned to their seats and waited in tense silence. "Will the defendant stand."

Tigh and Jame stood. Tigh couldn't keep the nervous flutters away and resisted the need to take Jame's hand.

"The case of Paldar Tigis has been a unique one from the beginning of her recruitment into the Guards." Onderal's voice was laced with reluctant resignation. "But she had always been a model soldier and she led the victorious campaigns that ended the Wars. She has also been a model patient in the rehabilitation program. But we still have the issue of outside perception to deal with. The situation that happened in Glaus will be a common occurrence until the world gets used to a cleansed Tigh the Terrible. We also know that reversals can occur, despite our diligence in the cleansing process. We're releasing Paldar Tigis from service to the Southern Territories under the following conditions."

He paused to let the mumbled reaction subside.

"Paldar Tigis must report to the healers every two fortnights for a year as a precaution. If at any time during her life she shows any reversal in the cleansing process, she is to be taken back into the custody of the state. Are these conditions understood?"

Tigh clasped her shaking hands behind her back. "Yes, Tribune."

"Do you agree to these conditions?"

"Yes, Tribune," Tigh said.

"Then we release you from your service to the state," Onderal said. "Come forward and receive your sword."

A startled Tigh blinked at Onderal. No one had told her they got their swords back. Jame stepped out of the defendants' box and guided Tigh to the Keeper of the Bench, who held a scabbard and sword.

The Tribunal stood.

"For your military service to the Southern Territories, we present your sword as a gift," Onderal said.

Tigh stared at the scabbard for several heartbeats and then accepted it from the Keeper of the Bench. The memories of the solid feel of the weapon in her hands and how it had been a part of her body and soul saturated her senses.

She turned to Jame and dropped to one knee. "I pledge my sword to the service of Jamelin Ketlas to be her peace warrior for as long as she'll have me." Her emotion-filled words were for Tribunes' ears, but her eyes were all for Jame.

Jame stared at Tigh with an expression that was both stunned and delighted. "I wouldn't want anyone else as my protector."

The Tribunal engaged in a muttered conference and then returned their attention to Jame and Tigh.

"In that case," Onderal said, "you must report to peace warrior training to gain your medallion and become, once again, a servant of the state."

The solution was so simple, Tigh wondered why none of the people in charge of her rehabilitation had thought of it. She could have her freedom and still be under the authority of the state, making her much easier to control if there was a need.

Tigh grinned and stood. "I'll report first thing in the morning."

"Very, well. Good luck." A relieved looking Onderal and the other Tribunes sat back on the bench. "Next case."

SHOCK WAS TOO mild a word for what Sark felt as the Emoran delegation followed the other spectators out of the chamber into the warm afternoon sun.

"Jyac's not going to be happy," Sark said as they joined the knots of people waiting for Tigh and Jame to finish their paperwork.

Tas shook her shaggy head. "Argis is going to be livid."

"Gindor is never going to understand." Poag stared at the adobe brick ground.

"If she doesn't feel ready to come home, we just have to give in to her wishes," a woman said.

The Emorans looked up as Paldon and Joul Tigis walk by.

"She just needs to settle her life down a bit," Joul said.

Paldon stopped walking. "She could learn a lot from being the companion to an arbiter."

"This could turn into a treasured gift for the House of Tigis," Joul said.

Sark was so intrigued by Tigh's parents' foreign attitude she didn't notice Jame until she was next to her.

"My princess," Sark said as she watched Tigh follow after her parents.

"Thank you for attending my first case as an arbiter." Jame had an ironic twinkle in her eyes. "We're having a little celebration in our home a sandmark from now. I'd love for you to be there."

Sark turned to Tas and Poag. Their expressions went from outrage to puzzlement to curiosity. It'd be an opportunity to observe Tigh, now that she no longer needed Jame's arbiter skills. The pledge of her sword may have been a ruse. At least, that was what they were supposed to think given their queen's and the Council's conviction Tigh was using Jame. Sark didn't dare to admit it out loud, but she'd be surprised if Tigh was anything but sincere in her pledge.

"We'll be there," Sark said.

"Thank you. That means a lot to me." Jame's sincerity made Sark feel a little guilty about their mission. Everything had been so clear and so certain back in Emoria.

TIGH SHUFFLED HER soft boots against the ground as she listened to her mother's speech about how proud they were of her, and that they understood her need to rediscover her life before returning to Ingor and taking her place in the House of Tigis. She knew her destiny was wherever Jame led her, but she didn't want to disappoint her parents. They had suffered enough because of her.

"Thank you for understanding," Tigh said. "I'll be sharing Jame's quarters with her. She's moved into regular housing. We're having a little celebration. I'd like for you to attend."

"We'd be delighted," Paldon said. "It'll give us a chance to thank everyone for the excellent job they did in restoring our daughter to us."

TIGH FINALLY MADE it past the well wishes of their friends and found Jame. She was surprised at how many lives both of them had touched during her rehabilitation.

"I think we're going to have a full house," Jame said as they ducked down the side lane to their new quarters.

Tigh nodded. The numbness that had accompanied the realization that her ordeal was over had worn off and the reality that she was free hit her with full force. For the first time, she was free to make her own choices for her life, and she had given that privilege to Jame. She had never experienced such a wonderful feeling.

Tigh glanced around and tugged Jame into an alley. Before Jame had a chance to say anything, Tigh enveloped her in her arms and gently assaulted her lips.

"Thank you," Tigh said as she soaked up Jame's closeness.

Jame snuggled closer. "Thank you for allowing me into your life."

Tigh smiled. "I had no choice. You bewitched me with your voice. Now I'm yours forever."

Jame looked up with eyes full of wonder. "Forever. Sounds fine to me."

Chapter 17

TIGH GRINNED AT the inscrutable expressions on her parents' faces as a glowing Bede described how she was a natural for treating sick and injured children. This also helped raise her spirits as she dealt with too many people in a small space. The sooner her parents realized she hadn't changed in the way they had hoped she would, the better. Her sisters were much more suited to the family business.

As she wove around the clusters of friends, Tigh noticed she was being trailed by a group of children, and she escaped out the back door.

SARK WAS NOT a happy soul. She looked around the tidy enclosed back yard at the freshly dug holes waiting for a fall planting and realized Jame was serious about making this place her home. She watched as Jame and her mentor discussed what to plant as they hovered over a cascade of pots in the corner of the tiny lot. She found it disconcerting to see her princess so comfortable around these people from all over the Southern Territories. No one in Emoria had even considered that Jame had become a part of this strange but close community at the military compound.

"What do you think?" Tas asked as she juggled a plate of food and a mug of spiced ale.

Sark sighed. "She seems to be well respected."

"They both seem to be well respected," Tas said.

They watched three children crawl all over a patient Tigh while she received genial congratulations from several healers and counselors.

"Even if we were wrong about Tigh, she still isn't a suitable consort for our princess," Sark said. "Surely Jame sees that."

A bemused laughter bubbled up from the people as Tigh lifted one child to straddle her neck and cradled the other two youngsters in each arm.

"I told you she was strong enough," the girl clinging to Tigh's head said.

Pendon laughed. "The back of an ox."

A grinning Tigh lowered the children in her arms to the ground and swung the delighted girl from her neck and over her head. She held her there for several heartbeats and then her lowered her to the ground.

Sark saw Jame. "Keep mingling."

Tas swallowed a mouthful. "With pleasure."

Sark strode to Jame.

"She's so good with children," Jame said.

"She appears to be," Sark said. "May I have a private word with you?"

Jame nodded and led Sark through the house into the quiet bedroom and shut the door.

Sark looked around the neat, oversized room with a cozy sitting area near the fireplace, the chests that contained their clothes and other possessions, the large bed, the black bladed sword in its scabbard hanging on the wall . . .

"We just moved in Tigh's things," Jame said. "She had to stay in her own quarters until she was released from the state."

"So, she hasn't been living here with you yet?" Sark asked.

"Not yet," Jame said.

"Rehabilitated or not, the queen and the Council are not going to accept her as a suitable life companion for you," Sark said. "You have to realize, deep down, that a union with that woman will never work."

"Why do you think Tigh and I won't be happy together?" Jame asked.

"It's obvious. Look at her family. You come from completely different backgrounds. You have nothing in common."

The last thing Sark expected was Jame's laughter. "I'm sorry. I didn't mean to laugh, but I have more in common with Tigh than anyone I've ever met."

"You're as different as night and day," Sark said.

"Argis and I are as different as night and day," Jame said. "Tigh and I understand each other so well it's almost as if we share the same skin. Before you say that I'm blinded by love, you should know we would have been companions even if we were just friends."

"How can you know that?"

"Because she's my best friend." Jame smiled at the simple answer. "There's no judgment or expectations, just supportive acceptance between us. I can be myself around her and she shows her true self to me."

"Argis was your best friend," Sark said.

"Argis is a close friend, but our friendship has always been based on a kind of role-playing," Jame said. "She plays the role of the warrior worthy of being the consort to her princess. She only sees me in terms of what everyone expects me to be and not who I truly am. I asked her if she'd be willing to be my companion as I pursued being an arbiter for a while and the idea was so foreign to her she couldn't see my need to be an arbiter was the same as her need to be a warrior."

Sark gazed at Jame, startled by her mature observation. "Argis only acts that way because it's how she was raised to act. It doesn't diminish how much she loves you."

"She loves an image of me that doesn't exist," Jame said. "I've been able to discover myself here, and I like who I am as an arbiter and as a member of this community. Being an arbiter will help me be a better queen than living under the protective watchful eye of Argis. I know you've always felt my peaceful leaning equals the inability to take care of myself. I can take care of myself very well. But to make you feel better, I've been lucky to have found someone who not only understands my desire to be an arbiter but who is capable of protecting me if need be."

"Jyac would have convinced Argis to be with you while you practiced your trade," Sark said.

"Jyac knows my feelings for Argis have changed," Jame said. "She knew it during my last visit to Emoria. I don't love Argis, and even if I had never met Tigh, I'd have broken off my relations with her. I told this to Argis a scant week ago. I truly believe she's only in love with the person I was before I came here. I'm not that same person, and I don't regret who I've become. Argis and I would be miserable together."

Sark had observed Jame's reserve toward Argis in Emoria and now understood the reason behind it. Maybe they had all been a little too certain about what turned out to be just another adolescent romance.

"If you've broken off your relations with Argis, that's between the two of you." Sark tried to pull together the most diplomatic words possible. "All we ask is you don't rush into anything with Tigh. You've only known each other a season. Not long enough to undertake something as serious as a joining."

"If Tigh were an Emoran you wouldn't be saying that," Jame said.

"All the more reason to take it slowly," Sark said. "She comes from a different culture, and she's been subjected to all sorts of mental and physical alterations. You can understand why we're apprehensive about your association with her."

"I understand." Jame nodded. "That's why I invited a delegation to witness her hearing and to observe her behavior. That's why I've asked for permission to bring her to Emoria so everyone can see what a perfect companion she is for me."

"I'll fairly report what we've observed here," Sark said. "But I can't guarantee Jyac or the Council will believe me."

"All that's needed is for Tigh to come to Emoria with me," Jame said. "That's all I ask. Just give her a chance to prove she's a worthy life companion for me."

Sark studied Jame, knowing, under normal circumstances, she made a reasonable request. But the specter of Tigh the Terrible loomed too darkly in their minds. "I'll make sure Jyac understands how important that request is to you."

"Thank you." Jame smiled. "I know Jyac will want to see Tigh when she knows how happy I am with her."

JAME WANDERED THROUGH her new quarters, taking in the interesting mixes of people. Tas was flirting with Pakar, the assistant healer at the injury ward. Sark was talking with a pair of soldiers. Daneran and Jadic were teaching a young girl how to juggle fruit. She hoped they remember to clean up any resulting mess. Tigh and her father exchanged quiet words in the small front yard. Poag and Paldon Tigis were having an animated conversation near one of the food tables.

Jame stopped and stared at the two older women. She approached the food table, acting as if she were looking for a particular morsel to eat. Within earshot, she almost dropped the pastry she had picked up.

"It doesn't matter how much greater the distribution, we'd still be paying you a part of our current profit." Poag's voice was edged with the joy of battle, a sentiment reflected in the eyes of Paldon Tigis.

"If we take care of everything but the production, you can concentrate on making the best swords and knives possible," Paldon said.

"We already make the best swords and knives." Poag's eyes glistened with a knowing humor. "You wouldn't be discussing them with me if we didn't."

Paldon graciously nodded. "You got me there, my friend. The House of Tigis has a nose for finding the best of everything."

Jame sighed and decided she needed some air. It would be the greatest of ironies if the House of Tigis became the distributor for the single moneymaking industry Emoria had to boast.

She took one step out of the front door, stopped, and stared at the strange spectacle in front of her. Tigh and her father were doubled over with laughter. She had never witnessed such demonstrative behavior from either of them. Tigh, without a doubt, had inherited her quiet personality from her father. The tension Tigh had worn like a second skin was gone.

Tigh saw Jame and held out an inviting arm to her.

Jame accepted the invitation and wrapped her arms around Tigh. "You two seem to be enjoying yourselves." She smiled at Joul.

"My father was just telling me about my younger sister's joining," Tigh said. "Everything that could have gone wrong, did. And then some."

She caught her father's eyes, and both shook with laughter.

Jame grinned. "You'll have to tell me the story sometime."

"Let's just say Pandon is more like her mother than Tigh is," Joul said with quiet humor dancing in his eyes. "Patlin is going to be joined within the year, we think. I know she'd like for her big sister to be there. You were always her favorite."

Tigh nodded. "Just send word but it'll depend on Jame's job."

Joul smiled at Jame. "And what about your own joining?"

Jame exchanged a long look with Tigh.

"Jame has petitioned for an Emoran joining," Tigh said.

Joul frowned. "Petitioned?"

"Emorans must have special permission to be joined with an outsider," Jame said.

"Ah. We have no such restrictions in Ingor." Joul raised meaningful eyes to Tigh.

"We'll remember that." Tigh tightened her hold around Jame's shoulder.

Several boisterous women burst through the door onto the front yard. Tas, trailed by a bemused Pakar, faced off with a young lean soldier. They drew their swords, and the clash of metal echoed in the quiet lanes of the arbiters' corner.

Jame dramatically covered her face with her hands. "Warriors."

Tigh laughed. "I guess Rodel didn't take kindly to Tas flirting with Pakar."

"That's the story of Tas's life," Jame said. "If there's trouble, she'll find it."

"I thought that was the story of your life?" Tigh ducked a good-natured slap from Jame.

Joul grinned. "I find your people rather refreshing."

"I know one thing," Jame said. "This little celebration is going to be memorable."

"YOU LOOK REALLY good in blue." Jame was stretched out on the bed, watching Tigh pull on the blue dyed leathers worn by peace warriors in training.

Tigh grinned at Jame. She was still adjusting to the incredible feeling of taking the first steps of their life together. She had just one small barrier to pass through, and she hoped the answer would be there when she was face to face with the question.

"I'm afraid you're going to have some observers today." Jame rolled off the bed to help Tigh tighten her bracers.

Tigh released the laces into Jame's capable hands. "They're just doing what they were sent here to do."

"I can't believe they still think you'll turn into a monster once you have a weapon in your hands," Jame said in frustration. "You walked around the compound yesterday holding your sword." She looked up as Tigh went still. "You can't possibly believe you'll suddenly become Tigh the Terrible if you start fighting again."

"That's not it," Tigh mumbled as her fears tumbled forward in her mind.

Jame frowned. "What then?"

"I don't know if I'll be able to fight at all," Tigh said. "I have the want to fight, but I don't know if I have it in me to actually raise a hand against another person."

Jame frowned. "What would you do if someone burst in here with a sword and came straight for me with it?"

Tigh stared at Jame. "I would have fought the Lindigan sisters, if they had given me the chance."

"Right." Jame smiled in relief. "Remember what Pendon said at the hearing? You have the natural impulse to defend who you love."

"But how do I find the impulse to raise my blade against a sparring partner?" Tigh asked. "I can't explain how I feel. It's as if I'd rather be injured myself than risk hurting someone else."

Jame captured Tigh's eyes. "You were going into training with this uncertainty hanging over you?"

"To be with you and to be the one to protect you, I'd do anything," Tigh said. "I'll find a way."

"And how many bruises and gashes would you come home with before you found that way?" Jame asked. "You're not going to do me much good if you're always injured."

Tigh wove this new idea into her complex psyche. "I must learn to keep both of us safe from injury."

"You're a skilled warrior, you can fight without doing injury to yourself or a sparring partner," Jame said. "Look at this training as a way of honing that skill."

Tigh enveloped Jame in her arms. Once again, Jame's simple logic had liberated her from a constricting barrier. "I love you."

"How can I not help but love you?" Jame asked as Tigh released her. "You're the only person I know who can leave me speechless. Not to mention turn my insides onto a quivering ball of mush."

"And you're the only person who can heal the wounds within my soul." Tigh grasped Jame's hand in hers. "I thank all the deities who oversee my destiny for sending you to me."

"I always thought the deities sent you to me." Jame brushed her lips against Tigh's. "Either way, I'll be thanking them forever."

Tigh happily wrapped her arms around this walking miracle in her life. She now had something to fight for.

CALLING THE OPEN sandy yards behind the main fortress building a sparring field had always been a joke amongst the Guards. All the long practice they endured in the desert heat was against inanimate or imaginary opponents. The Guards would have killed each other if they had sparred together.

Kartlin, a leathery-skinned woman in her middle years, strode across the sand, the wind picking up the puffs of dust produced by her determined boots. She stopped in front of Tigh and crossed her arms.

"We know you know how to fight," Kartlin said. "We know you have the temperament for the job." Tigh raised an eyebrow. "The proper temperament is the most important qualification for a peace warrior. It's been a while since you've handled a weapon. You can work with that lot over there."

Tigh looked at a half-dozen competent fighters practicing their formations. "I've never sparred with anyone before."

Kartlin nodded. "I'll get you warmed up."

Tigh took in Kartlin's desert-stung features, surrounding world hardened green eyes and nodded. "I don't know how I'll react."

"Do any of us really have so much control over ourselves we don't experience a heartbeat of eagerness, fear, anticipation, uncertainty, and every other emotion in between when someone raises a weapon against us?" Kartlin asked.

Tigh followed Kartlin to a worn patch of ground. The students across the field stopped their practice to watch.

Tigh saw the three Emorans skirt the sparring pits until they stood along the edge of the area where she and Kartlin selected staffs from a long rack of weapons.

Tigh flipped and maneuvered the staff, reacquainting her mind and her body with its feel. It felt . . . liberating. She raised steady eyes to Kartlin, who watched her while twirling her own staff.

Kartlin lunged forward, caught Tigh on the calf, and landed her on the ground in a cloud of dust.

All noise around them ceased. Tigh climbed to her feet, oblivious to everything except she had let Kartlin hit her. She had to focus on fighting back yet couldn't find the impulse to raise the staff against the waiting Kartlin. Her panicked mind tried to reach out for Jame's words. *Fight without doing harm.*

Kartlin sprung forward, and Tigh got her staff in place to stop the blow. Kartlin stepped back and allowed Tigh to get used to the sensation of weapon against weapon.

"Now come at me," Kartlin said.

Tigh swallowed. The wood in her hands felt foreign and clumsy. She gave her head a rapid shake. "I can't."

Kartlin looked around at the spectators and lunged at the unarmed Poag, who stood apart from the others. Tigh sidestepped in front of Poag, whipped around her staff, and knocked Kartlin's weapon from her hands.

With her sword drawn, Tas rushed to Poag's side and watched Tigh with a wary expression.

Kartlin retrieved her staff. "Now pretend I'm about to attack someone." She swung her staff at Tigh.

Tigh knew what she had to do but her thoughts and her actions were not controlled by logic. She was controlled by whatever happened to her during her cleansing. Her blue leathers, once again, took on another layer of dust as she found the ground much closer to her body than she preferred.

"What's the matter with you?" Everyone turned shocked eyes to Tas who was pointing her sword at Tigh. "How do you expect the queen and the Council to approve of you if you don't have the backbone to defend yourself, much less Jame?"

The words stung, and Tigh whipped her staff so fast Tas found herself sitting swordless on the ground.

"All right." Kartlin drew out the words. "I don't think you have any problems putting off attackers. We just need to work on motivation."

Tigh sighed and put a handout to Tas, who stared at it before warily taking it.

"Sorry about that," Tigh said.

"That's all right." Tas picked up her sword and slipped it into its sheath. "Nice move."

"All right." Kartlin studied the group of advanced students. "Who wants to work with Tigh?"

Much to Tigh's surprise, all of the young fighters stepped forward. She anticipated a long day in front of her.

"I'VE NEVER SEEN so many bruises and scrapes on one person in my life." Jame helped Tigh pull off her shirt and eased her into the low tub filled with steaming water.

Tigh let the warm water finish stinging and start soothing her battered body. "But I learned to fight back."

"It wasn't easy was it?" Jame took a cloth and ran it over Tigh's tight muscles.

"Not at first but I was getting it all worked out toward the end of the day." Tigh closed her eyes at Jame's tender touch. "I really think I can do it."

"I'm glad you dumped Tas on the ground." Jame added a salve to her cloth.

"What?" Tigh twisted around.

"Emorans respect skill with weapons more than skill with words," Jame said. "Tas will spread the word among the warriors that you're a formidable fighter. It doesn't matter how many times you were dumped yourself, Tas felt the sting of your skill in her hands. That's all that counts."

"Do you really think it'll help?" Tigh asked.

Jame scooted around to face Tigh. "How can they not help but accept you? You embody the Emoran spirit."

Tigh grinned at the idea that she could contribute to Jame's appeal for an Emoran joining.

Chapter 18

ARGIS STARED AT the Ynit delegation as they trudged across the square dappled by the late evening sun. Nothing about them suggested any kind of immediate action had to be taken. More baffling, Jame wasn't with them. She followed the trio as they entered the palace.

Sark turned at the sound of Argis's footfalls behind them. "We need to make our report to the queen."

"This concerns me as much as it does her," Argis said as she caught up to them.

"Not anymore," Sark said.

"What do you mean?" Argis sputtered with indignation.

"You forgot to tell us Jame had broken off her relations with you," Sark said.

"She was under the influence of that woman," Argis said. "Where is she?"

Sark sighed. "Perhaps you should come with us."

Panic swept through Argis. "Is she all right? Has she been hurt?" She turned to Tas.

"She's fine, Argis," Tas said. "Just come with us and listen to our report."

Frustrated, Argis followed after the travel weary delegation.

JYAC AND HER consort, Ronalyn, sat in the private royal dining chamber. The smooth-walled room had a circle of leather and cloth cushions with a low-lying wooden bar arcing in front of them. The entrance to the chamber was cleared of both cushions and bar, allowing food to be delivered from the middle of the room to anywhere on the bar. A fire crackled in a small fireplace behind Jyac, warming the natural cool cavern air.

Ronalyn, a gentle dark-haired woman with soft brown eyes, filled Jyac's plate.

"Eat." Ronalyn captured Jyac's attention. "Watching the door won't make them arrive any faster."

Jyac gave Ronalyn a fond look and gazed down at her plate. "Jame's not with them." She picked up a fork and pushed the stew around. "I should have made the effort to listen to what she was trying to tell me."

"You had no way of knowing any of this would happen," Ronalyn said. "I wish I could have been here."

"Me too. But your sister's needs had to be attended to," Jyac said. "I kept thinking of Jame as a bright-eyed child, too idealistic for her own good. I didn't know how to handle that mature young woman, struggling to find her own path to a long and happy life. Why couldn't I just accept the fact she had fallen out of love with Argis? Why couldn't I just accept that she wants to practice being an arbiter? She has a right to her dreams. Maybe if I'd been more reasonable, she'd have never gotten mixed up with that Guard."

"On the other side of the blade, maybe she's really in love." Ronalyn laid a hand on Jyac's arm. "Are we prepared to accept that possibility?"

"I must be convinced with my own eyes." Jyac straightened at the noises in the corridor and tried to relax. "They're here."

Poag, Sark, and Tas filled the doorway.

Jyac beckoned them in with a wave.

"Argis wants to join us," Sark said.

Jyac knew it was better to have Argis where she could see her, no matter the news from Ynit. "Come in, Argis."

The newcomers settled onto the cushions around the table. Ronalyn pushed welcomed mugs of spiced wine and dishes of food in their direction.

"Here is a letter from Jame." Sark pulled a thick packet from her belt pouch and handed it to Jyac.

"No one has ever accused Jame of being short on words." Jyac weighed the document in her hand. "Why don't you give me your side first and then I'll read what Jame has to say."

The three exchanged glances.

"We'll first tell you what we witnessed," Sark said. "Then we'll give you our personal impressions, if you desire to hear them."

"Good strategy." Jyac nodded and then spent the next three sandmarks being introduced to the mature, brilliant young woman her niece had become. She knew she had no choice but to give Jame a chance to prove her desire to pursue her chosen profession and to defend her choice of life companion.

DANERAN AND JADIC bounced out of the door of their former residence almost running into a startled Jame.

"We have our assignments." Daneran pulled Jame into an impromptu dance.

A laughing Jame allowed herself to be passed to Jadic for a turn before the they stood grinning at each other.

"So, what are you going to be doing?" Jame asked, ready to explode from curiosity.

Jadic grinned. "I put in for a position in Ewit, and it turns out old Poark is retiring so I'm bound for Ewit."

"That's wonderful, Jadic. I know you really wanted to practice in your home," Jame said.

"I'm going to Aregan," Daneran said.

"On the northern coast." Jame nodded.

"It's two sandmarks from my mother's farm," Daneran said. "So, you could say, I'm pleased with the assignment."

"Congratulations to both of you for getting what you asked for." Jame tried to keep a touch of apprehension out of her voice. Getting a desired assignment was more luck than design. "I'm on my way to find out where I'll be going."

"Good luck," Jadic said. "At least you don't have anything to worry about. I heard more places put in a request for you than for any of us ordinary souls."

"What?" Jame was stunned.

Daneran laughed. "Come on, Jame. Not only are you the top of our class, you successfully defended Tigh the Terrible before a military and a civil Tribunal. Any place would want you."

Jame sighed. "Any place but my own country."

"I think those Emorans who visited were pretty impressed by you and by Tigh," Daneran said.

"You're right," Jame said with a reassuring smile. "I'm just waiting to hear from my aunt. I hate waiting."

"Don't we all," Jadic said. "So, what are you still doing out here?"

Jame laughed and walked into the building that had been her home for two years. She was surprised at the lack of nostalgia she felt. Her heart had truly moved on.

Jame rapped on Ingel's opened door.

"Jame. Come in." Ingel looked up from her work and waved a beckoning hand. She sorted through a stack of paper and pulled out an official-looking document. "I hear Tigh's training is going well."

Jame settled into the visitor's chair. "She's doing wonderfully. It took a while for her to learn how to defend herself, but now she's a sight to behold. All the other warriors want to spar with her just to study her technique."

Ingel smiled. "You have no idea how pleased everyone is that she's been able to make the adjustment. You're going to make a formidable team."

"I don't know about the formidable part, but I know we make a good team," Jame said.

Ingel studied the document. "You know we got an overwhelming number of requests for you."

"Daneran just told me that."

"When you first came here, we envisioned the opportunity of having a permanent arbiter in Emoria," Ingel said. "Your country has never allowed us to place anyone there."

"If it wasn't for the need of an arbiter when I was young, I'd have never known about them." In her mind, Jame saw an enthusiastic little girl following the poor arbiter everywhere, asking enough questions to try the patience of an acolyte of Laur.

"And we have benefited from that chance encounter," Ingel said. "If you ever decide to settle in Emoria before you become queen, we'll gladly reassign you. For now, you want to be an arbiter-at-large, and we have honored that request. But it's my duty to tell you that many of the places that put in a request for you have offered a considerable wage for your services."

Jame shrugged. "I have no use for money. Whatever Tigh and I make between us will be more than sufficient."

Ingel nodded. "The only at-large assignment we have available at the moment is for the Southern Districts."

"The whole Southern Districts?" Jame asked, astonished.

"Yes." Ingel's eyes twinkled in amusement. "We always need an arbiter with the ability to cover a wide range of jurisdictions. Lots of disputes happen between people in different towns and territories that can't be legally handled by the local arbiters."

"So, we wait in Ynit for these cases?" Jame asked.

"Most arbiters can't afford to do that," Ingel said. "You travel around like the other arbiters-at-large and will only be called in if you're needed to settle a special cross-jurisdiction dispute."

"Sounds like what I had in mind," Jame said.

"Good. Here's your assignment document." Ingel passed the paper to Jame. "You have to sign it in my presence."

Jame put her name to the document.

Ingel signed it, rolled it up, and put it in a small leather pouch.

"We're holding the peace warrior-at-large for the Southern Districts assignment for Tigh," Ingel said. "Your duty will begin as soon as she has completed her training."

Jame took the pouch holding her future. "This is so wonderful. I could have never dreamed any of this but it's still a dream come true. I guess sometimes we don't know what we want until we're face to face with it."

Ingel smiled. "I'm glad it's worked out for both of you."

"Thank you for giving me the chance to defend her," Jame said.

"I consider it the best decision I've ever made," Ingel said.

GINDOR STARED AT Jyac as if she had sprouted another arm. That would have been preferable to what she was hearing from her normally rational queen. She lifted her eyes to the high ceiling of the Council chamber, beseeching Laur for the patience to convince Jyac she was making a tragic mistake.

She leveled her coldest stare at Jyac. "I can't believe you're willing to consider Jame's joining with that woman."

"It wouldn't be the first time an Emoran princess has been joined with an outsider," Jyac said. "The delegation to Ynit saw nothing to suggest they're not sincere in their feelings for each other."

"We're talking about Tigh the Terrible here," Gindor said. "A master of intimidation and manipulation."

"You heard the reports from Sark, Poag, and Tas," Jyac said. "All of that has been cleansed from her. For Laur's sake, Gindor, she pledged her sword to Jame in front of the Military Tribunal. She has to know the people of Emoria are honor bound to hunt her down and kill her if she goes against that pledge."

Gindor stopped her rage to let that thought penetrate. She tapped the table with an impatient fingertip and wove a new plan through her mind. "I'm disturbed by the fact that Jame is sharing a home with this woman. If they were in Emoria, they'd have to be joined at sword point. Fortunately for us, we cannot extend our laws to outside our borders. This means all we have to do is deny Jame's petition to be joined with this woman. That will force her to rethink these foolish romantic ideas she's having."

"And what if she doesn't? What if she's truly in love with this warrior?" Jyac asked.

"I think it's an infatuation at the most," Gindor said. "A reaction to her changing feelings for Argis. I predict a heartbroken Jame will be back in Emoria before the year is out."

"None can predict if a relationship will last," Jyac said. "The question is, are we being fair to Jame by not accepting her conviction that she's found her life companion?"

"On the other side of the arrowhead, what would happen if we allowed them to be joined, and Tigh takes advantage of her standing in Emoran society? Are we willing to risk letting a woman with her leadership skills into our royal family?" Gindor asked. "We're not just considering a joining between an Emoran and an outsider. We're considering a joining between our princess and a brilliant military strategist who was as well known for her ruthlessness as for her leadership ability. A person who has tasted that kind of power isn't going to be satisfied being just a peace warrior to an arbiter."

"You still think she's using Jame?" Jyac asked.

"Yes," Gindor said. "Think of it from her point of view. She's led the greatest army this world has ever seen. And this army will never exist again because of the cleansing. Before the Guards, Emoria boasted the greatest warriors. I think she wants to lead another army, but this time for her own dreams of power. I don't doubt she planned this from the very beginning. She most likely heard there was an Emoran arguing cases for the Guards. Why else would she have rejected all those other arbiters? She wanted Jame to defend her."

Jyac frowned. "Why didn't she just ask for her?"

"That would have been too obvious," Gindor said.

"What if you're wrong?"

"Let's settle on a compromise," Gindor said. "We deny Jame's petition to be joined with that woman. If they're still together, and Jame hasn't returned to us heartbroken by this time next year, we'll reconsider the petition."

Gindor looked at the Council members on either side of her and received slow, thoughtful nods of agreement. She then gazed at Jyac.

"That is acceptable," Jyac said. "I just hope Jame understands our caution."

JAME CONCENTRATED ON raking the sand around the artfully placed stones in the tiny front yard and frowned at a distant distinctive clip clop of hooves on the adobe brick lane. As the sound grew closer, she raised curious eyes just in time to see Tigh, wearing a happy grin, round the corner leading a large ginger-colored horse.

"What's this?" Jame asked, putting down the rake.

Tigh raised an eyebrow. "This is a horse."

"Let me rephrase that." Jame gave her a tolerant look. "What is this all about?"

"This is about a horse," Tigh said. "Our horse."

"Ours?" Jame approached the watching beast.

"This is Gessen." Tigh patted the horse. "She was given to me after the Siege of Operal."

Jame ran her hands through the flaxen mane. "You never mentioned you had a horse."

"I wasn't sure what happened to her," Tigh said. "They took away everything else, so I figured she had a new owner. But it turned out she wouldn't accept any other owner. She's been stabled here all this time."

"Why didn't they let you know she was here?" Jame asked.

Tigh shrugged. "They forgot about her until now. Then they decided to surprise me with her as a gift for receiving my peace warrior medallion."

It took all of two heartbeats for Tigh's words to penetrate. "You have your medallion?"

Tigh pulled the medallion, strung around her neck, from beneath her tunic. "I took all the tests this morning."

Jame wrapped her arms around Tigh and gave her a happy kiss. "Now we can get on with our lives." She looked at the horse. "Gessen's a little big for a house pet."

"She can stay in the common stables when we're in Ynit," Tigh said. "I just brought her by to show her off to you."

"We have to celebrate," Jame said. "It's my turn to treat you to a romantic dinner by the Rih River."

Tigh's eyes sparkled. "Do you think we can get the same table as the last time?" she asked in Jame's ear.

Jame caught her breath as a jolt of desire ran through her. "I'll pay them anything to make sure we get it." The intimate tables of the only Ingoran establishment in Ynit were not only private but overlooked the gentle Rih River and the city gardens. The setting combined with the delectable food had brought out Tigh's romantic side.

Tigh led Gessen to one of the hitching posts that lined the lane and followed Jame into their house. Once inside, she stood in the middle of the room with an uncertain expression on her face.

"What's wrong?" Jame asked.

Tigh took a deep breath and walked into the bedroom followed by a concerned Jame. She knelt in front of her trunk, removed several things, and then paused at a neatly wrapped bundle. She lifted the bundle out of the trunk and took it to the bed.

Jame stood next to Tigh and looked on as she pulled back the soft cloth covering and revealed a pile of black clothing. Tigh ran a hand over the supple leather.

"Your leathers," Jame said.

"Yes," Tigh said. "I've been thinking about them. I liked them."

"And you want to wear them again."

"They're only black leathers," Tigh said. "Just because they were worn by the Guards doesn't make them any different from any other set of leathers."

"If you want to wear them, then wear them." Jame placed a reassuring hand on Tigh's arm. "I think you'd look good in them."

"Really?" Tigh turned to Jame with a quirky grin.

"Yeah," Jame said. "It's not what you wear, it's what's in your heart and mind. Maybe by seeing you in them people will forget about when the Guards wore them."

"Thank you," Tigh said in relief. "I guess it's time to retire the blue leathers."

THE RIH RIVER provided a cool oasis for the city in the desert. Thanks to its spring fed origins in the Phytian Mountains, water flowed year-round to the sea. As would be expected, property along the Rih was scandalously expensive and jealously kept by those fortunate to own a piece of the river's edge. The old building housing The Merchant's Lair had been snatched up by several enterprising Ingorans and the establishment became a southern refuge for travelers from Ingor.

Jame, nestled against a relaxed Tigh on the cushioned benches that faced the river and gardens, was just happy The Merchant's Lair existed. The outer tables were really covered balconies with panels, illustrated with subdued paintings that lined the back of the benches and an intricate iron grill served as a barrier to the outside.

A panel to one side of the balcony slid open and a server entered with an ornately decorated box. Jame watched with fascination as the server pulled stunning silver and black covered dishes from the box and piled them into an elaborate design on the table. He then bowed, backed out of the chamber, and closed the panel.

Tigh sat forward, bringing Jame with her. "This is a meal for celebrating life changing events. We've both gone through so many life changes in the last few months, it's time to celebrate them all."

"Each day I've spent with you has changed my life," Jame said.

Tigh cupped Jame's cheek in her hand and kissed her. "My life would be nothing without you."

Warmed by the jolt of happiness shooting through her, Jame turned her attention to the table. Delicate aromas escaped the covered dishes and pulled her into the feast.

Tigh knew the secret to unraveling the design without causing an avalanche of food. Jame took delight as images of birds, animals, and flowers appeared as they consumed the contents of each dish and placed them back in the box.

Jame stared at the last layer of dishes that sat on the table. She was, at first, puzzled over how the server knew, then she grinned. "You planned this."

Tigh shrugged. "Just a coincidence."

Jame delivered a couple of playful punches to Tigh's arm. "I think it's wonderful."

"In that case," Tigh said, "I planned the whole thing."

A laughing Jame wrapped her arms around Tigh, and they admired the crossed arbiter's mallet and sword artfully rendered with dishes of various sizes and shapes.

"Before we eat this final part of the meal, we must follow tradition and drink a toast to our future." Tigh picked up a thick, round jar from the opposite side of the design. She pulled out the stopper and poured a rich aromatic liquid into a pair of tiny cups.

Jame took one of the cups and followed Tigh's lead as they moved them in a ritual offering to the moon and the sun. They then sipped the heady liquid from each other's cup.

Still spellbound by the ritual and as the warmth of the potent liquid hit Jame's senses, she became lost in the need to taste the wine on Tigh's lips. She felt as if their hearts and souls were pulled together by forces beyond their understanding and knew that nothing would ever be strong enough to force them apart.

Tigh uncovered the first dish in the design, revealing a sweet candied fruit. "A meal of celebration must end sweetly."

"What about the evening after the meal?" Jame was lost in the sensual world that Tigh had enveloped her in.

"That is even sweeter than the richest confection," Tigh breathed against Jame's cheek.

"Then I look forward to celebrating our life together every day and every night." Jame smiled and the earthly sweets were forgotten.

Chapter 19

JAME REREAD THE words on the note. Sark and Poag were back in Ynit. Waiting at the Emoran safe house to speak to her. She mentally slammed her fist against the wall. Good news always arrived by messenger; bad news was always in person.

She ran a hand through her hair and worked on calming the mixture of anger and uncertainty crashing through her mind. *Maybe it's just a minor setback of some kind.* She forced herself to be soothed by this thought.

She walked to the small desk in the corner of the bedroom, put the stopper back on the ink jar, and wiped clean her quill. The morning had been perfect for catching up on her journal. Quiet, with just a hint of autumn touching the air. Tigh had taken Gessen out onto the sandy plains south of the city to reestablish their bond.

The walk to the Emoran safe house was not long enough for Jame's unsettled mind, and she stopped for several heartbeats outside the door to pull together the resolve to face whatever Sark and Poag had for her.

A somber Otlar opened the door.

"Good morning, Otlar," Jame said. "I'm here to see Sark and Poag."

"They told me to expect you, my princess," Otlar said. "They're in the eagle room on the second floor."

"Thank you." Jame crossed the quiet common room to the back stairs.

The eagle room. The same one Argis had stayed in. Out of the way from the rest of the rooms. She sighed and strode to the door in question. After studying the artistic rendering of the noble bird, she knocked.

Sark, looking as if she'd been caught in an unpleasant situation, opened the door. Jame walked in and glanced around. Poag was looking out the window. Poag's body language spoke of embarrassment and defeat.

Instead of making her more unsettled, Poag's behavior lifted Jame's confidence. Whatever the news was, it wasn't a popular decision.

"Let's sit." Sark indicated several chairs in front of the small fireplace. The aroma of spiced tea, in a kettle on a warming shelf, filled the air.

Jame sat, and Sark poured out a mug of the tea for each of them.

"There's only one thing that requires a face-to-face meeting rather than a written message," Jame said, taking pity on the messengers. If she were in

Emoria, Jyac and Gindor would be having this talk with her rather than their Right Hands.

"We gave a favorable report," Sark said. "Jyac was willing to give you a chance to prove you really want to pursue this profession and that Tigh is a suitable life companion for you."

Jame sighed. "So, it's Gindor? What could she have possibly said to change Jyac's mind?"

Poag's chin dropped, and she shook her head at the window.

"Gindor thinks Tigh is using you," Sark said.

"Using me," Jame said. "You mean to get me to successfully free her from the rehabilitation program? If that were true, she'd be long gone."

Sark shook her head. "Gindor thinks Tigh deliberately chose you as her arbiter and entered into a romantic relationship with you to get inside Emoria so she could form another powerful army to continue her ruthless campaigns. This time to feed her own need for power."

Jame stared at her in disbelief. "Gindor sees the world from Emoria outward. But the truth is, Emoria barely exists for the rest of the world. We may have once boasted the greatest warriors but to those outside of Emoria today, they live only in legends. If Tigh wanted to form an army to pursue mad dreams of power, she had the opportunity during the two years she was in hiding before her cleansing. While she was still Tigh the Terrible."

"You must understand, Jyac has to take the safety of Emoria into consideration," Sark said. "They're having problems accepting that a victorious military leader would be willing to become a passive follower of a peace arbiter."

"Under normal circumstances even I'd have problems with the idea." Jame captured Sark's sympathetic eyes. "But we all know that anything concerning the Guards is beyond usual logic. Will they let me bring Tigh to Emoria so they can see the truth for themselves?"

Sark stared at the dying fire. "Gindor has convinced Jyac that Tigh must be considered a risk to Emoria."

"So, they won't see her?" Jame swallowed on a dry throat as a devastating disappointment washed over her. "They won't even grant that simple request?" She turned her head away to wipe an unwanted tear from her cheek. The denial was like a sting of betrayal from her people.

"Jyac defended you," Sark said. "But she also understands Gindor's caution. They came to a compromise."

Jame gave Sark a puzzled look. "Compromise?"

"If you and Tigh are still together as peace arbiter and warrior and still wish to be joined a year from now, they'll reconsider your petition," Sark said.

"We want to be joined now," Jame said. "If we were in Emoria, we'd be having the ceremony at the point of a sword."

"Gindor isn't comfortable with the fact that you're sharing a home with Tigh, but Emoran law doesn't extend outside our borders," Sark said. "She thinks the safety of Emoria is more important than the indiscretion of an Emoran princess."

"It sounds like too many made up excuses to me." Jame let her simmering anger surface. "They have the word of the Military Tribunal for the Southern Territories that Tigh is not dangerous. If they aren't willing to accept my judgment on the matter, then that, at least, should mean something to them. A year isn't going to make any difference."

"They just don't want you to rush into this," Sark said.

Jame, not in the mood to be reasonable, stood. This wasn't just a matter of the acceptance of a life companion, this was a reflection of Jyac's attitude toward her. Turning away from becoming a warrior didn't make her weak and defenseless, but that was the underlying sentiment she felt from everyone in Emoria. If they wanted proof she could make sound decisions about her life and who she wanted to spend that life with, she'd give it to them. On her own terms.

"Please inform the queen and the Elders Council that I don't accept their reasons for denying my petition to be joined and I don't accept the terms of the compromise." Jame straightened.

Sark stood to face her.

"I've made the decision to be an arbiter and to have Tigh as my life companion. They have a choice to accept my decision or not. It won't change how I'll live my own life. If they feel this is not acceptable behavior for the queen's heir, then I suggest they find another heir."

A wide-eyed Sark stood frozen. Poag turned from the window with an expression as stunned as Sark's.

"Stay well, Sark, Poag. I hope we meet again someday." Not wanting to hear their responses, Jame turned and strode out of the room.

THE FREEDOM WAS like nothing Tigh had ever felt before. More invigorating and satisfying than rushing into battle. Horse and rider were of one mind as Gessen galloped across the desert scrub in joyous abandonment.

Tigh steered Gessen along the upper cut of the deepening canyon formed by the Rih River as it flowed nearer to the sea. Except for the occasional farm, the land was untouched by the cultivating hand of humans. Tigh wondered why she had never noticed the majestic and stark beauty of the land, with its subtle colors and striking formations caused by erosion, during her field training when she had been a Guard.

Jame would be able to find the words to describe the way the canyon walls rose up from the rapid river. Tigh smiled at the idea and glanced up at the cloudless sky, noting the position of the sun. Jame would be expecting her for the midday meal.

JAME LEANED AGAINST the wall on the opposite side of the gate from the sentry hut as she watched Tigh ride Gessen across the desert toward her.

She pushed off the wall as a concerned-looking Tigh stopped in front of her. "Sark and Poag are back." She was surprised at how despondent her voice sounded.

Tigh scooted back on the light saddle and held out a hand to Jame.

She grabbed the hand, and Tigh lifted her onto Gessen. An amazing relief shuddered through her as she leaned back against Tigh's solid body. Tigh snaked a strong, yet gentle arm around her waist. All her unsettled thoughts from just moments before vanished with the warmth and security she felt in Tigh's arms.

Tigh guided Gessen away from the wall until they sauntered along the meandering Rih.

Jame allowed the landscape to take over her senses and watched with fascination as the river dropped further and further into a widening crevice until they overlooked a calm blue inlet of the sea.

The soft lap of the water against the narrow rocky beaches and the plaintive calls of the gulls spread a soothing balm over her. The alien mix of salt and fish floating on the breeze hit her senses, causing her to wrinkle her nose.

"I never realized there were so many ships docked down here," Jame said as a good size ship creep into the busy harbor bordered by large rambling adobe warehouses.

"It's the best way to get supplies to Ynit," Tigh said. "We used this harbor to move troops during the Wars."

"That doesn't look like a cargo ship." Jame squinted at a smaller white vessel.

"That's one of the ferries," Tigh said. "They go to Artocia and Ingor."

"Ingor," Jame said. "They denied my petition. They won't even allow you to visit Emoria. Gindor has convinced my aunt you're a threat. They came to a compromise though. If we're still together after a year, they'll reconsider the petition."

"Then there's hope," Tigh said.

"There's more to it than that," Jame said. "I've a choice of meekly giving in to their terms or to show them I'm capable of taking care of myself and making the right decisions for my life."

"You didn't accept their terms," Tigh said.

"Remember how your parents thought you wouldn't jeopardize your inheritance?" Jame asked. "That's what everyone in Emoria thinks about me.

They can't fathom me doing something that would jeopardize my title and my destiny." She twisted around and captured Tigh's bewildered eyes. "The decision is now up to them because there isn't any way I'll give up having you in my life."

Tigh tightened her arm around Jame. "I should be arguing for you not to turn away from your country and your people. But I don't want to give up the chance to spend my life with you."

Jame brushed tears of relief from her cheeks. She gazed at the white ship. "How often does the ferry run?"

"Every three days," Tigh said. "Are you thinking of taking a trip?"

"I hear Ingor is beautiful in autumn." Jame caught the soft amusement sparkling in Tigh's eyes.

"It is," Tigh said. "Especially in Miterie Park on the highest hill in the city. There's a temple to Bal that overlooks the Sea that's very popular for joining ceremonies."

"Really?" Jame grinned. "What does one have to do to have a joining ceremony there?"

Tigh bent close to Jame's ear. "Accept the proposal of a poor lovesick Ingoran whose life won't be complete until she's joined forever with the woman she loves."

Jame twisted around so fast she caught Tigh off guard, and they tumbled off of a disinterested Gessen. Tigh's reflexes pulled her around so she landed on Tigh instead of the soft drift of sand.

"That particular response is not covered in the Ingoran joining manual," Tigh said as Jame recovered from her sudden change in location.

"We'll have to suggest an amendment." Jame lowered her head and gave Tigh a more appropriate response.

"You'll have to put up with my family," Tigh said as Jame relaxed against her.

Jame grinned. "They can't be any worse than a country full of Emorans."

"Someday, we'll get the chance to compare," Tigh said.

Jame nodded against Tigh's shoulder. "Someday."

SARK STARED IN disbelief at the note in her hand. "Jyac's going to kill us."

"Now what?" Poag looked up from her perusal of a scroll on Ynitian culture and customs.

"Jame's going to Ingor. To be joined," Sark said. "We have to stop her. Give us a chance to get word back to the queen."

"I'll prepare the message and get it to the courier before she leaves this morning." Poag stood up. "You go talk some sense into our princess."

Sark grimaced. How could she possibly talk sense to the person who had successfully defended Tigh the Terrible? "I'll do my best."

Poag looked up. "You have to do better than your best. Jame mustn't be allowed to enter into a foreign joining before Jyac has the opportunity to make a response."

"I'll think of something." Sark opened the door. "As you said, I have to stop her."

The early morning coolness was tolerable enough. But Sark couldn't understand how the inhabitants of Ynit could stand the afternoon pounding of sun. The heat didn't improve her disposition, and she reached the warren of crooked lanes Jame currently called home, more agitated than reasonable. She was more than a little angry at Jyac and Gindor for thinking Jame would realize how foolishly she was acting and quietly come home. Jame was not a child who had lost her way. She was a young woman who knew how she wanted to live her life.

Sark rounded the last corner into the quirky snippet of a lane where Jame lived and slowed her step at the sight of a large horse grazing in the yard. A saddle and several saddlebags were lined up nearby.

She paused outside the open door and listened to the voices inside—discussing what needed to be packed and what to add to the list of things for friends to keep an eye on while they were gone. She also heard words of endearment and joy at this first step in their journey together.

Sark forgot she was listening to her princess. All she heard was a young woman filled with the joy of love. Talk sense into her? Jame wasn't the one who needed to listen to sense. She resolved it was better to endure the wrath of her queen than to prolong this attempt to ruin Jame's life. She'd rather have Jame return to Emoria as a strong and independent woman than one who had given in to the arbitrary demands of Queen and Council. Jame had shown her true Emoran heritage in not giving in to a compromise. A shiver of pride scuttled down her spine.

She turned to walk away as Jame, carrying a pack, hurried through the door.

"Sark," Jame said. "Did you come to see us off?"

Sark was caught off guard by the joy that almost caused the air around Jame to sparkle. "Yes, my princess. I wish you happiness."

Jame put down the pack and laid a comforting hand on Sark's arm. "You can tell Jyac you tried to talk me out of this. She'll be angry enough with me. You don't need to let that anger spill over to you."

Sark straightened at Jame's insight and thoughtfulness. "No, my princess. I'll tell her the truth. We'll never be able to resolve this mess if we further the delusion."

Jame held Sark's determined eyes for several heartbeats and nodded. "Tell my aunt the trust the people have in a queen begins the moment a queen is born. I want to prove to my people they can trust my judgment, and what better example to use than my trust of a woman the rest of the world sees as a monster."

A riveted Sark stared at Jame and felt a tiny thrill at the idea that this young woman was going to be a formidable ruler of Emoria. "I'll tell her."

"Thank you." Jame relaxed and pulled Sark into a heartfelt hug.

"Stay well, my princess," Sark said with unconcealed respect.

"Stay well, Sark." Jame smiled as Sark stepped away. "Give my regards to my aunt."

"I will." Sark turned and quickly strode away. She had to stop Poag from posting the message. They would take word back themselves. Their mission to Ynit was finished.

JAME HADN'T BEEN quite sure how she'd react to being on a ship when she first stepped foot on the vessel. But once she got used to the rhythmic movement and the wonderful sense of freedom as they scuttled around the southwestern coast of the continent, she loved everything about being on the water.

Tigh, on the other hand, maintained a queasy stomach throughout the whole two-day trip.

"How are your parents going to react to us just showing up like this?" Jame asked as they sat on a small bench near the prow of the ship and watched the elegant cascading architecture of Ingor drift closer and closer. The dramatic rise of the hills up from the small harbor was a stunning sight as the city glistened in the afternoon sun.

Tigh took a swallow from a small skin filled with a special herb mixture she always kept with her while on the water. "My father will have convinced my mother our joining is a good idea."

Jame cocked her head at Tigh. "You're more like your father than your mother."

Tigh nodded. "Much to my mother's continual disappointment. Fortunately, my sisters take after her."

"So, you've always gotten along with your father better than your mother?" Jame watched a pair of gulls dart around each other.

"He may not have always understood me, but he's always supported me," Tigh said.

"One of the hardest things I had to get used to when I left Emoria was being around males," Jame said. "Most Emorans may see only a handful of males in their entire lifetimes."

Tigh shifted and looked a bit uncomfortable. "Uh, what about, uh . . . ?"

Jame frowned at her for a heartbeat before realizing what she was trying to ask. "Laur gives us the gift of children. When a couple decides to have children, they go to Laur's Temple and ask for the gift. They spend the night in a special chamber in the Temple where they participate in a ceremony during which Laur presents them with the seed for a girl child."

"So, you had two mothers," Tigh said.

"My birth mother was Jyac's sister, and her partner was a scout." Jame stared at the myriad of boats floating in the harbor. "They were both killed barely a moon after I was born. They were in a hunting party gathering supplies before winter set in. They got caught in an avalanche on the slopes of Jacalore Mountain. Jyac and Ronalyn took me in and raised me as if I was their own child."

"Do you, uh . . ." Tigh took a deep breath. "Do you have to be an Emoran to take part in this ceremony?"

Jame turned and stared at Tigh. "You want to have children?"

Tigh looked down at her hands. "I don't want to jeopardize your chance of producing an heir."

Jame took Tigh's hand and pulled it to her heart. "All that is needed for Laur's gift is the complete love and devotion the parents have to each other. But it doesn't matter because when I'm ready to give my people an heir, you'll be a citizen of Emoria. I have faith that Jyac and the Council will eventually accept you. They're narrow in their thinking because their world is narrow. But having me in Ynit has expanded their world a bit. They just need a little time to adjust."

Tigh lifted Jame's hand to her lips. "It would be an honor sharing a child with you."

ACTIVITY FROM THE deck hands diverted Tigh's attention from Jame. A long wide pier reached out to greet them. They stood and slung their packs onto their backs and joined the other passengers in an open cabin as the ship lurched next to the pier.

Shouts from the deck hands were followed by ropes thrown to uniformed men and woman waiting on the pier. Before the plank was dropped for the exiting passengers, a woman in bright Ingoran colors strode up the pier and took her place by the ship.

Tigh nudged Jame. "Have your papers ready?"

"Right here." Jame pulled her new arbiter document and her well-worn Emoran papers from her pouch.

Most of the passengers were Ingoran merchants, and they moved down the plank and flashed their papers at the pier master. A foreigner spent a longer time as the pier master made a show of inspecting the man's papers. Tigh kept from rolling her eyes at the woman's expression when she saw Jame coming down the plank.

Jame's plain but well-cut brown leathers, the travel bag adorned with Emoran braid, and the light blond hair all but shouted foreigner to the pier master, and she put on her best superior expression as she held out her hand for Jame's papers.

Tigh tried hard to keep from smirking at the woman's reaction. A peace arbiter and an Emoran princess never walked off a ship in Ingor before.

"Let's see your arbiter's medallion," the pier master said.

Jame pulled the medallion from beneath her tunic and held it so the pier master could read the name inscribed on it. "Do you want to see my Emoran braid?"

"Is there anyone who can verify these papers?" The pier master ignored the question.

"I can." Tigh stepped next to Jame and handed her papers over.

The pier master looked up at Tigh and then at her papers. "You're a peace warrior and a member of the House of Tigis?"

"That's right." Tigh raised an eyebrow. "Since when did Ingor question arbiters-at-large?"

"We've been careful with all foreigners since the end of the Wars," the pier master said. "If you were truly Ingoran you would know that."

"This is the first time I've been here since I was recruited to serve in the Wars seven years ago." Tigh pulled her discharge papers from her pouch.

The woman read through the papers. She looked up at Tigh, and her expression lost much of its arrogance. She handed the papers back to both of them. "You may pass."

Jame waited until they were halfway down the pier to vent her anger. "How dare she even question an arbiter's papers."

"It looks as if the Wars have changed Ingor." Tigh steered Jame to where several young girls and boys held the horses that had been liberated from the ship's hold.

Gessen stamped an impatient greeting as Tigh murmured an apology and a promise of some nice big apples.

"I'm not used to being treated with suspicion," Jame said as Tigh led the way off the pier and up a jagged street.

"The Wars have made people more suspicious, less open than they were before," Tigh said. "Perhaps that will fade with time."

"It's the Emoran papers," Jame said. "Will our joining make me an Ingoran citizen?"

Tigh stopped walking and turned to Jame. "Yes."

"Good," Jame said. "It's only fair, after all. When we're joined in Emoria, you'll become an Emoran citizen."

"It'll be good for Ingor to have to call an Emoran a citizen," Tigh said.

Jame grinned and grabbed Tigh's arm as they continued their journey through the crooked streets of Ingor.

Chapter 20

TIGH DIDN'T WANT to leave Gessen in the lower stables her family maintained so she led the way past neat small residences splashed with whites and yellows. The wide road switched back up the hill until only a few residences lined each segment of the road.

"The main business establishments for the most successful merchants are down there." She pointed to a flat area with wide boulevards and sprawling buildings. "They're easily accessible from the harbor and the overland roads."

Jame nodded. "The success of a merchant has a lot to do with where their business is."

Tigh grinned. "But they first have to be successful to build a business there. The residences for all those merchants are at the tops of these hills. At the bottom of the hills the houses are quite small, and they get larger as they go up, depending on the success of the merchants who own them."

Jame, used to the climbing the Phytian Mountains, thought nothing of rambling up the hill. She gawked at the high stone walls broken by an occasional iron fence, allowing a glimpse of homes that looked as if they cascaded down the steep incline of the hill.

"What's that?" She frowned as they passed a gully lined with precisely placed stones. Long thick ropes ran down the middle of the trench like a waterfall of hemp.

"That's the lane for the pulley trolley," Tigh said.

"Pulley trolley?" Jame looked up and down the stone bed, noting that the ropes were wrapped around a series of wheels at the top of the hill. The bottom of the gully was too far away for her to get more than a glimpse of what appeared to be a blue painted wooden box.

Tigh shrugged. "That's how the residents go up and down the hills."

Jame looked around them in puzzlement. "This is a perfectly good road."

"Ingorans aren't raised to engage in strenuous physical activity," Tigh said.

"They think this little walk is strenuous?" Jame frowned.

They continued around another curve that switched them back to a flattened out narrow lane, signifying they were at the top of the hill.

"They should try getting around Emor."

Tigh turned and smiled at Jame. "Steep?"

"Emor is in a canyon with towering walls of stone," Jame said. "The shops and taverns are on the canyon floor, but the homes are above them all the way up to the meadows. We get around on narrow paths cut into the walls."

"If Emor had been settled by Ingorans, they would have figured out a way of getting around without having to exert themselves," Tigh said.

They rounded a soft curve and a gate the width of the lane stood in their way. The entire design of the iron was a giant H and T, leaving little doubt they had arrived at the House of Tigis.

Jame stared through the gate at the large stone buildings surrounded by a neat green lawn and small gardens bursting with cheerful colors and sculpted figures.

Tigh stepped to the side of the gate and pulled on a heavy rope. A bell, housed in a small turret perched on the stone wall, sounded.

"This is where you grew up?" Jame couldn't reconcile the unpretentious Tigh with the strong statements of wealth and high social standing coming from the estate.

"Yes," Tigh said.

A young man in the blue and purple colors of the House of Tigis stepped out of a small stone building twenty paces inside the gate. Wearing the self-important smirk of an employee of Tigis, he made a show of sauntering to what appeared to be visitors of no importance.

Jame furrowed her brow at this behavior but kept quiet after seeing the not so amused expression on Tigh's face.

"You've made a wrong turn." The young man waved a bored hand when several paces from the gate. "You can't get through this way."

"We haven't made a wrong turn," Tigh said.

He squinted at them. "What do you want?"

Tigh raised an eyebrow. "We want in. We're here for the joining of Paldar Tigis and Jamelin Ketlas, princess of Emoria."

Jame just barely kept from grinning. She loved this playful side of Tigh.

"Paldar Tigis?" The young man's expression got caught between a sneer of disdain, a flicker of fright, and a look of uncertainty. "She's not here and we haven't heard of any joining."

"She's not there because she's here." Tigh captured the young man's eyes with her own. "Once she's there she'll make sure everyone knows about the joining."

The young man swallowed, and his eyes widened with the realization of who Tigh was.

He ran to the side of the gate and tugged on a wooden lever that, through an iron mechanism suspended over the gate, pulled the two halves apart and outward.

"Thank you," Tigh said over her shoulder as she led Gessen onto the grounds with Jame at her side.

Jame turned to Tigh. "I can see why you wanted to leave."

Tigh laughed. She laid an arm across Jame's shoulders and pulled her close. "Come on. Let's go scare some more high and mighty employees of the House of Tigis."

EVER SINCE JYAC made the official announcement from the palace balcony earlier that day, she had expected any number of responses to trickle back to her, but silence hadn't been one of them.

She stepped into the square of the quiet city. No hammering from the smithy, no chattering wafting down from various parts of the bluffs . . . only the Temple bells clanging together in the slight breeze. A quick glance around the top perimeter of the city assured her the sentries were still at their stations. She knew where her people had gone. The same place she'd have gone if she had heard news that was difficult to accept. For some reason, Jame's popularity always took her by surprise.

Jyac fetched Ronalyn from her daily study of the ancient scrolls in the archives, and they walked up one of the paths leading to the meadow above the city.

Before them, the women of Emor were gathered in a solemn silent prayer for their wayward princess. The Elders Council stood with heads bowed in the middle of the ceremonial circle. It looked to be a spontaneous gathering, as if everyone needed to seek solace in each other.

"They think Jame has turned her back on them." Jyac pulled a scroll from her belt pouch and studied it for a heartbeat.

"I think that will help them understand," Ronalyn said.

Jyac nodded.

They passed between a series of intricately carved posts that marked the traditional entryway into the ceremonial circle. They walked past the Elders' tight ring in the center of the circle to the raised platform on the opposite outer rim.

The Elders broke their circle of meditation and rearranged themselves into a half circle facing their queen.

Gindor leveled steely eyes at Jyac. "Have you finally come to pray for Laur to give your niece and heir the guidance she needs to find her way home?"

"No." Jyac held up the scroll. "I've come to let Jame tell her people in her own words why she's taken this other path before she returns to Emoria."

A low murmur rippled through the attentive women.

"As you wish, my queen." Gindor bowed. "And I accept that we're divided on this issue."

"You're gathered here to entreat Laur to give Jame guidance to bring her home to Emoria," Jyac began.

From where she stood in the ceremonial circle her words could be easily heard throughout the meadow. The Emorans accepted the phenomenon as a gift from Laur.

"I ask that you pray for a safe journey for Jame as she pursues her life outside our borders."

"How can you ask us to give her our blessing?" Argis asked in an anguished voice. With a face distorted in anger, she strode into the circle and stood before Jyac. "She's chosen to wander all over the place with that woman as a companion. She's going to be joined to that woman in a foreign ceremony."

"We had a choice." Jyac straightened and swept her eyes over the gathered women. "We had a choice to bring Jame home against her will or let her decide what she wants to do with her life. Bringing her home against her will would risk breaking her down emotionally or cause her to rebel and leave us forever. Jame is destined to be Queen of Emoria, we must learn to trust her decisions and she must learn from her mistakes so she can grow strong and wise. We've not had any indication that Jame and that former Guard are not sincere in their feelings for each other and for the life they've chosen to follow. Argis, I know it hurts, but you must remember, even if she did return to Emoria, she wouldn't have been joined with you."

Argis clenched her fists. "I stand in defiance to the queen on this issue. I could eventually learn to live with the knowledge that Jame no longer loved me, but I can't live with the knowledge that she has willingly chosen to share her life with that Guard."

"Your defiance on this issue is accepted, Argis," Jyac said. "But let me give you a friendly warning. If you take it upon yourself to do something about that Guard, Jame may choose never to set foot in Emoria again. Which means you'd better not set foot in Emoria again if you drove your future queen away from her place among us."

"I understand, my queen." Argis straightened, slipped her sword from its scabbard, and whipped it into a salute.

"Thank you, Argis." Jyac accepted the salute with relief. "Now open your ears and your hearts and hear what your princess has to say."

Jyac read Jame's impassioned letter—of her need to prove that her people could trust her judgment and her need to pursue being an arbiter so she could learn to be a wise and just queen. Jame spoke of her love for Emoria, and how she was hurt by the idea her people thought she'd bring harm to them. Because of that she would only return when they accepted her life companion as a citizen and royal consort.

The rest of the day was spent in thoughtful discussion and, much to Jyac's relief, ended with all her people bowing heads in prayer for Jame's happiness and safety in whatever path she chose to take.

JAME HAD ENVISIONED Tigh's sisters to look like her. She certainly hadn't expected identical twins with the coloring of Joul and the personality of Paldon.

A dark-haired young man with weak brown eyes and a mild demeanor trailed Pandon, the oldest twin. They had just recently been joined, and Jame caught Pandon glancing with affection at the young man. Patlin, the younger twin, held hands with a confident-looking red-haired girl and was engaged in an animated discussion with Tigh.

"I hope to get to the Phytian Mountains some time," Juon said. At eighteen, he was a male version of his oldest sister, tall and muscular with soft blue eyes and black hair.

"They're the most beautiful in the spring when the flowers are in bloom," Jame said. "Although Ingor is a wonderful looking city."

"You must get Tigh to take you to the Arcade down on Merchant's Square," Juon said. "It's the largest shopping arcade in the Southern Territories."

"I'll be sure we see it on our next visit to Ingor," Jame said. "We won't have time this trip. We'll be leaving right after the joining tomorrow."

"Leaving so soon?" Juon sounded genuinely disappointed. "I thought you'd stay around a while. Tigh has been away a long time."

Jame smiled at how easily the younger generation got into the habit of using Tigh's Guard name. "We'll be back for Patlin's joining, but we have a job to do."

Pandon and Patlin and their respective companions waved across the room at Jame and Juon and then pushed through one of the doors leading to the endless terraces that surrounded the main house.

Tigh joined Jame and pulled her close. "You're not going to the concert?" she asked Juon.

Juon shrugged. "I'm meeting some friends at Bushra's Hideaway."

"Do the parents know?" Tigh lowered her voice to a conspiratorial whisper.

"Uh, no," Juon said. "You won't tell them will you?"

Tigh laughed. "Of course not. Enjoy yourself."

"You're the best, Tigh." Juon laughed and trotted out of the chamber into the main hall of the house.

"Which leaves just the two of us." Jame wrapped her arms around Tigh.

"My parents won't be back until late." Tigh looked around the airy garden room. "The Guild meetings are usually long and tedious."

"So, will you finally show me your room?" Jame asked.

It had been a point of discussion ever since they boarded the ship to Ingor. Tigh refused to describe the personal sanctuary where she grew up.

"Come on." Tigh pulled Jame along.

"I like your family," Jame said as Tigh guided her into the main hall with its high octagonal ceiling and stone staircases that swept up to the other floors.

"Most Ingorans are good people," Tigh said. "If you get past the merchant mentality."

They wandered down a gallery punctuated by small sitting rooms, went through another large garden room, and out a side door. Before them were several small cottages circling a shallow fishpond.

Tigh paused and stared at the golden fish sparkling in the water, illuminated by sheltered night torches. "I spent a lot of time dreaming of studying in Artocia while watching those fish go about their watery lives." She squeezed Jame's hand. "Now I have a new dream."

"It's funny how things turn out," Jame said.

"This way," Tigh said as they skirted around the pond to the first cottage. She opened the door. The fireplace and several lamps had been lit and their belongings were piled next to the bed.

Jame stepped into the chamber and took in the small wing made up as a sitting area and another wing with walls of shelves full of scrolls and a worktable and chair. A washing chamber was through an opening in the back, next to the bed.

"It doesn't look too much different from my room back in Emor," she said, noting the subdued colors and high quality of the materials and furniture.

"Really?" Tigh asked.

"I mean, my chamber is a part of a cave, but everything else is much the same," Jame said. "Of course, Jyac or the Council would never ever let us stay there together until we were joined."

"Fortunately for us we're in Ingor." Tigh grinned, lifted a startled Jame, and carried her to the bed. "In fact, it's considered good luck if the happy couple are too exhausted to remember the words of their joining ceremony."

"Hmmm." Jame pulled Tigh onto the bed. "We can't go against Ingoran tradition can we?"

TIGH ROLLED HER eyes at her family's idea of casual. She'd never imagined casual joining ceremonies had become a stylish trend in Ingor since the end of the Wars. Or that there was a line of casual clothing created for those attending the joinings. Never mind all that control contradicted the concept of casual.

Tigh and Jame had on the same clothing they wore during the Solstice. A decision that had more to do with how they liked the way the leathers looked on each other than any sort of concern over proper casual joining apparel.

Jame looked panicked as the brightly painted trolley box they were in lurched and plummeted downward. "These are much more interesting to look at than to travel in."

Tigh wrapped reassuring arms around her. "At least we didn't indulge in the traditional joining wine."

She glanced at her family who were watching the neighbors' estates fly by. Ingorans were always in search of new landscape and architectural ideas.

Jame grimaced. "I would have surely embarrassed myself. Ingorans ride these things all the time?"

"Since practically the day we're born," Tigh said.

"And a little spicy food upsets your stomach?" Jame arched an eyebrow at Tigh.

The trolley scraped to a stop.

With Tigh's help, a relieved Jame climbed out of the apparatus, then watched with widening eyes as the Paldar clan climbed onto another trolley.

"That one's going up." Tigh led Jame to the roomier carrier. "It goes right to Miterie Park."

Tigh grinned as the trolley crept up and around the hill, revealing whitewashed panoramas of Ingor and the boat-filled Nirlion Sea glistening in the morning sun.

"It's beautiful," Jame said.

"We're very proud of our city." Paldon stared at the harmonious meeting of city and sea. "There's Miterie Park. A wonderful choice for a joining."

"It seemed right, somehow," Tigh said.

The trolley rolled to a stop on the harbor side of the park. Jame climbed out and looked around. The Temple to Bal was a small ornamental building with all sides open to the hilltop breezes. Terraces where people lounged and enjoyed the stunning view cascaded down from the Temple. The rest of the knob was neatly trimmed expanses of grass accentuated by the occasional statue or small plot of flowers. She could just make out a Glak field with narrow stone spectator stands on the far edge of the green.

The aura of peacefulness enveloped Jame as she walked into the airy Temple. She thought this change in atmosphere strange, since the Temple didn't have any walls and they were still outside. An acolyte wrapped in the pale robes of Bal stepped through an opening on the widest pillar holding up the roof of the Temple. Jame noticed the pillar covered a set of steps that led downward to beneath the stone floor.

"Our daughter wants to be joined," Paldon said.

"Such a beautiful morning for a joining," the acolyte murmured. "Come and gather around the altar."

Tigh took Jame's hand and gave it a squeeze and Jame smiled up at her. The acolyte made them stand in front of a pedestal that supported a shallow ceramic bowl flanked by two silver cups. The Tigis clan stood in a circle around the pedestal.

The acolyte took her place on the other side of the pedestal. She dipped the end of her sleeve into the sweet fragrant water in the bowl and wiped it across Tigh and Jame's foreheads.

"Hold your hands over the bowl, palms down," the acolyte said. She cupped her palms together and dipped them into the bowl and trickled the liquid over Tigh and Jame's hands. "Turn your palms up." She repeated the ritual cleansing of their hands. She then guided Jame behind one of the silver cups and Tigh behind the other cup so they faced each other with the pedestal in between. Their eyes met as the acolyte directed them to hold hands over the bowl.

"Bal smiles on you and gives you the good fortune of his blessing," the acolyte intoned. "All he asks in return is that you continue to love and honor each other for as long as you walk this earth and as you journey through eternity." She turned to Jame. "Will you honor and love for as long as your souls exist?"

"I will." Jame's voice was husky from the emotion swelling inside her.

The acolyte turned to Tigh. "And will you honor and love for as long as your souls exist?"

"I will," Tigh whispered.

Tigh swayed, and Jame released her hands as she crumpled to the polished Temple floor. Having a proficient knowledge of Tigh's body language, she saw it coming before Tigh uttered the words.

A grinning Juon stepped forward and patted Tigh's cheek. Her eyes popped opened, and she stared at him in profound puzzlement.

"Come on, sis." Juon helped her to her feet.

The rest of the family smiled at Tigh's obvious depth of feeling for Jame.

"Sorry." Tigh's expression was sheepish and, to Jame, endearing.

"I'll take it as a compliment," Jame said, and they clasped hands once more.

The acolyte pulled a long strip of cloth from her sleeve. "In the eyes of Bal and the city-state of Ingor you are joined." She wrapped the cloth around the closest set of hands. She then lifted a jar from the bottom of the pedestal and removed the glass cork, releasing the aroma of the joining wine. After pouring a bit into each silver cup, she made the sign of Bal's blessing over the liquid offering. "Take your cups and offer the wine to your life companion as a toast to many long lifetimes of happiness together."

Tigh lifted the cup with a trembling hand as Jame, surprised that her own hand shook a bit, did the same. Their eyes fixed on each other as they guided the cups to waiting lips and drank the warm vibrant liquid.

The air around Jame crackled with magic as everything fell away from her senses, leaving just the two of them to share their souls at the altar of Bal.

Somehow the cups were lowered back to the pedestal, and the acolyte removed the cloth from their bound hands. Jame snapped out of the momentary dance in the realm of Bal, and Tigh looked equally dazed.

The acolyte smiled. "You may affirm your joining with a kiss." Tigh stepped around the pedestal and gathered Jame in her arms. The sounds of her laughing and cheering family faded as she captured Jame's lips with her own.

As her family indulged in a glass of the joining wine, Tigh led Jame to the top of the terrace overlooking the harbor.

"Will I ever be able to live down fainting at our joining?" Tigh asked, as they wandered hand in hand along the wide expanse of stone that comprised the first terrace.

Jame pretended to ponder the question. "I'll make you a deal. I'll never mention it, if you promise not to faint at our joining in Emoria."

Tigh stopped walking and turned to Jame. "Does the ceremony involve sweetly fragrant water and talk of honor and love through eternity?"

Jame worked to keep a solemn expression. "It involves a sword and the ceremonial spilling of blood."

"In that case, I promise I won't faint," Tigh said.

Their laughter echoed across the park as they walked hand in hand into their dreams of the future.

T.J. Mindancer may be a figment of someone's imagination or just someone who likes to imagine she's a figment while she creates worlds for her characters to inhabit. She has spent her life working with books as an academic librarian and as an editor for two publishing companies and has had some of her scribbled words published under a couple of pen names—at least one, not a figment. Her work includes the *Tales of Emoria* series of books and shorter tales set in the Emoria world. She also likes to make up places in the real world and write about them. She lives in her Tiny House of the Dragons in Northern California.

www.ingramcontent.com/pod-product-compliance
Lightning Source LLC
Chambersburg PA
CBHW022155260626
47155CB00018B/1936